COLD KILL

Recent titles by Rennie Airth

John Madden

RIVER OF DARKNESS
THE BLOOD-DIMMED TIDE
THE DEAD OF WINTER
THE RECKONING
THE DEATH OF KINGS
THE DECENT INN OF DEATH

Novels

COLD KILL *

* *available from Severn House*

COLD KILL

Rennie Airth

This first world edition published 2020
in Great Britain and the USA by
SEVERN HOUSE PUBLISHERS LTD of
Eardley House, 4 Uxbridge Street, London W8 7SY.
Trade paperback edition first published
in Great Britain and the USA 2020 by
SEVERN HOUSE PUBLISHERS LTD.

British Library Cataloguing in Publication Data
A CIP catalogue record for this title is available from the British Library.

ISBN-13: 978-0-7278-9029-0 (cased)
ISBN-13: 978-1-78029-677-7 (trade paper)
ISBN-13: 978-1-4483-0381-6 (e-book)

This is a work of fiction. Names, characters, places and incidents
are either the product of the author's imagination or are used fictitiously.
Except where actual historical events and characters are being described
for the storyline of this novel, all situations in this publication are
fictitious and any resemblance to actual persons, living or dead,
business establishments, events or locales is purely coincidental.

All Severn House titles are printed on acid-free paper.

Severn House Publishers support the Forest Stewardship Council™ [FSC™],
the leading international forest certification organisation.
All our titles that are printed on FSC certified paper carry the FSC logo.

Typeset by Palimpsest Book Production Ltd.,
Falkirk, Stirlingshire, Scotland.
Printed and bound in Great Britain by
TJ International, Padstow, Cornwall.

Night, once again
While I wait for you
Cold wind turns into rain

Masaoka Shiki (1867–1902)

ONE

He had been watching the three workmen for an hour, though he wasn't sure why.

Habit, probably, plus a natural aversion to haste, plus something else – something to do with labels and packages and the connections, if any, between them.

Whatever it was, it all came under the heading of *patience* – patience with a capital *P* – which Charon just happened to believe was the secret to a long and stress-free life.

Oh, it was fine to be brave and strong and clever – add a pinch of good looks and nine out of ten would think they had hit the number – but when it came to the long haul, if you really wanted to outlast the other guy, then patience was what was called for. Patience, and still more patience . . .

Even when it was wasted?

Especially when it was wasted, dummy, that was the point. The time to take care was when everything looked normal. The fact that it probably *was* normal didn't change a thing.

These three workmen, for instance. They had been there on the job when he arrived, fenced in by bollards that formed an island in the middle of the road, and because they were strangers, new to the street, not part of its daily comings and goings, he had sat in his car watching while they went about their work.

What they were doing was repairing the surface of the road, lifting the old cobbles and levelling out the ground underneath before replacing them again. Tedious work, even at the best of times, and given the prevailing conditions – a raw December afternoon in Paris with a light rain falling – they certainly showed uncommon devotion to their craft.

Which was just as well, since anything else would have started all sorts of bells ringing.

Anything out of the ordinary – the way they stood, or the

way they moved, the direction of their glances, any small thing
– and that meant waiting . . . waiting until you were sure,
because sooner or later people gave themselves away, even
the best.

Step forward patience.

Take a bow.

Charon yawned. He had seen enough. He was ready to
move. Just a few more minutes, a few more cobbles . . .
Imagine it, a lifetime of cobble-lifting. It really made you
think. What did they have to look forward to, this trio of
hunchbacked worthies? Aching limbs, dulled senses and at the
end of the day a houseful of squalling brats and a wife with
more wear on her than a *route nationale*. How they must
dream! Of lottery wins and fast cars and girls – girls in all
shapes and sizes: blondes, brunettes, redheads, and each one
as young and fresh and dazzlingly lovely as the one who
had suddenly appeared on the sidewalk up ahead – yes, that
one there!

Charon blinked. Now where had she come from?

He watched as the young woman paused, glancing left and
right to check the traffic before hurrying across the street to
a *tabac* on the other side. Blonde and loose-limbed, she was
wearing a pair of form-fitting jeans topped by a yellow silk
blouse and, just for a moment, the grey afternoon seemed
brighter. In a few moments she reappeared clutching what
looked like a pack of cigarettes, and having recrossed the road
quickly vanished through the doorway of an apartment house.

Charon sat and stared. Minutes passed.

Finally he shook his head. He couldn't help it: he just had
to laugh.

It was all so predictable. Take a pretty girl, any pretty girl,
walk her past a bunch of workmen on a city street and what
did you have? Urban comedy, that's what. The girl walked
by and the men whistled at her. It was inevitable; inescap-
able; dammit, it was probably a commandment handed down
by *you-know-who* round about the time the first pyramids
went up. Instruction to all pyramid workers: *Thou shalt
whistle at pretty girls.*

And it was true, you had to laugh, because no matter how

many times you had seen it, like a man slipping on a banana skin it was always funny-funny-funny. And what was even funnier this time was the reaction of Charon's three workmen.

They hadn't even looked up.

Explanation?

Well, a couple came to mind, and the first was that all three were gay: a possibility, to be sure, but in the realms of likelihood about as remote as the rings of Saturn.

Which left the other, and really it was the only one that made any sense.

They hadn't looked up in case they caught her eye – it was as simple as that – which meant they knew her and she knew them and they were all there by appointment.

Not for the first time, Charon marvelled at his instinct. No disrespect to patience, but in the end it came down to something deeper than that, something that went back to the very dawn of Homo sapiens, dwelling for all he knew in what remained of his reptile brain that had warned him all was not as it seemed.

He had sensed it from the first, and now he knew.

The workmen weren't workmen.

And they hadn't come to mend the road.

Well, now!

Breathing a little faster from the sudden exertion, Charon stepped over the body and paused at the head of the stairway.

Just as he'd thought: three in the street, one up here and the girl downstairs in the apartment below. Why had they brought her? Probably to field calls, pass on instructions, send for the ambulance later. Stuff like that.

He'd been lucky with the girl, first spotting her in the street and now, not five minutes ago, hearing her open the door of the apartment one floor below and call out softly, 'Misha . . . Misha?'

And Misha-whoever-he-was, who'd been up here all day waiting for him – and what fun *that* must have been – had gone downstairs for a minute, no more, but a minute was all the time Charon had needed to slip out of the box room and pick his spot deep in the shadows of the darkened landing.

Lucky, too, that he knew this apartment house from top to bottom, had long ago scouted the empty box room and the skylight that opened on to the roof. From there it was little more than a stroll across neighbouring roofs to another skylight in a small hotel not a hundred paces away at the end of the street. Except it wasn't luck, it was foresight.

Too bad about Misha, though. Charon had been hoping for few minutes' conversation, but one glance at the heavy pair of shoulders ascending the stairs had banished any thought of a tête-à-tête. As Misha came out of the light into the shadows Charon had hit him twice in the throat – savage chopping blows shattering the thyroid cartilage (along with the hyoid bone for good measure) – after which it was doubtful if Misha would ever speak again. Or breathe, come to think of it.

Which left the girl, and Charon truly regretted that. He loved beauty in all its forms – beautiful clothes, beautiful objects, beautiful women – everything in fact that money could buy.

He walked down the stairs to the next landing and knocked on the door.

Footsteps, the rattle of a chain, a soft voice.

'Who is it?'

Charon understood the question, if not the words, which were in Russian.

'Misha.'

She opened the door.

There were times, no question, when Charon felt he was just a little weird.

By rights he ought to be tearing his hair, climbing the wall, breaking crockery. Wasn't that what people did when they saw their world fall to pieces? As in shattered, shredded, pulverized, powdered and scattered to the four winds? (And that was the good news.)

Yet here he was laughing at it all, and the reason was simple. Right at the heart of everything, buried under the rubble of hopes and dreams, the ingenious schemes so lovingly pieced together was – would you believe it? – a joke! Irony, pure irony.

My God, it was true what they said – you couldn't trust anyone.

What now?

He went to the window and looked down at the empty street. There was no sign of the workmen – yellow flashing lights marked the enclosure in the middle of the road where they had laboured all day – but it wasn't hard to guess where they'd gone. Try that café a couple of doors down from the *tabac*. No matter to him, he would leave the way he had come.

And go where?

Zurich? London?

London was a must. If he had to guess, it was where he would find her. It was also probably the last place he should go. They had been waiting for him here – why not there?

He had always been a gambler – within limits. Risk was in the very air he breathed. But he was used to having control, a measure of it anyway, enough to tip the odds in his favour. And now?

Charon shrugged. No point in trying to read the future, not without a crystal ball, and there was a distinct lack of those in the vicinity. At least he was alive when by rights he ought to be dead – an unpleasant surprise for quite a number of people, and for one in particular, something a good deal worse than that.

Time to go.

He turned from the window and went to the sofa where the body of the girl lay stretched out in front of the fire. He had placed a red silk cushion beneath her head. It was an object of some significance to him – and particularly now – bringing back memories as it did. Earlier he had held it on his lap, tracing the design with one finger while they talked. Picked out in paler colours, it showed an Ottoman lady, from the sultan's harem no doubt, seated with folded legs, gazing down into a limpid pool. 'She's thinking of her lover.' He remembered the words just as he remembered the souk through which they had wandered together. 'And I'll bet it isn't the sultan.' He had bought the cushion then, aware that the gesture must have seemed a sentimental one, and amused by the thought that he had never come close to experiencing that particular emotion and wondered at others who did. He had kept the pillow resting on his lap while

they talked, the girl and him, and when the moment came it
had served its purpose.

Looking down at her now, he saw that her features were
composed in death and drew some satisfaction from the knowledge. He was glad he hadn't had to hurt her. He took no
pleasure in causing pain. Death was another matter – the all-
encompassing answer to the last great question – and those
with a mind to see things that way (a mind such as his, for
example, if such a thing existed) might acknowledge him
as Death's faithful servant: Charon the Ferryman. One day
they would meet, he and his master, swap stories, but not
today – oh, no.

She had told him what she knew, which was little enough,
but what did details matter set alongside the one overwhelming
truth. Listening to her, Charon had felt a cold hand tighten
about his heart. He gave nothing away. They had sat together
by the fire chatting like lovebirds while a nerve twitched in
her pale cheek and her blue eyes pleaded with him. And he
had wanted to let her live, truly he had, but by then it was
too late. He knew what she knew, and once *they* knew that,
well, it would give them an edge, and an edge, even the
smallest, was all they would need.

On an impulse he bent down and kissed her smooth forehead. Homage to beauty. Let the men who had sent her find
her here. Let them contemplate their handiwork – and his.

And lest there be any mistake, he took a coin from his
pocket – a silvery one-euro piece – and slid it gently between
her lips.

TWO

The hunk was headed her way.

From her window seat near the back of the plane Addy watched him walking down the aisle, checking the seat numbers against his boarding pass. She had spotted him first in the terminal. Tall, fortyish, with a touch of grey at the temples, he reminded her of one of the stars of those old movies Rose loved – Cary Grant in *To Catch a Thief,* say. He'd been right behind her in the check-in line, and for a wild moment Addy had thought of stepping on his toes – by accident, of course – or dropping her purse, or just plain fainting; anything to strike up a conversation.

It was the kind of crazy thing she often thought of doing but seldom did. Seizing the moment, grabbing it by the collar and saying, *Stop! Hold it right there!* Because suddenly then there'd be a new situation, possibilities, and who could say where they might lead?

It had nothing to do with men *per se,* though when it came to men, Addy sometimes wondered if a little grabbing and seizing might not be the answer. Neglect – a girl could die of it, just wither away, and while Addy knew lots of men (really they were boys) her own age – twenty or thereabouts – actors for the most part, nice kids, even loyal friends, somehow when it came it . . . no, let's be honest . . . there were one or two who might do very well as lovers if things ever headed in that direction, which plainly they didn't.

Yet all around her, kids were hooking up. Why not her? Could it be that she scared men?

The question was one Addy had examined more than once (try a hundred times), usually when looking at the mirror. Small, dark-browed, fierce: the adjectives had been applied to her by the drama critic of the *Fairfield News* when she had played in a summer stock production of *Much Ado About Nothing* a few months back.

'Small, dark-browed and fierce, Adelaide Banks made a compelling Beatrice'. She had memorized the words.

What had the citizens of Fairfield made of *Much Ado*? They had made for the woods. The same critic had deeply deplored the lack of audience support for this jewel of a comedy blah-blah-blah and wondered aloud what could be done to draw people back to the theatre? (Addy was for house-to-house arrests and summary executions.)

Still, maybe he had a point. Fierce. 'Ease off, Addy,' her drama coach kept telling her. 'Too much intensity.' And sometimes, '*Pas trop de zele*', because he was that kind of asshole.

Certainly, if it came to keeping score, which was something she would never entertain – my dear, how vulgar – but if you twisted her arm, if you dragged her up to the blackboard and made her do it, chalk 'em up, the results were not encouraging. A grand total of two.

Two!

And one of them hardly counted, Jamie whatever at summer camp when she was sixteen, who'd come on like Secretariat, snorting, practically pawing the ground, and then barely made it past the finishing post.

Which left Brad, Bradford Carlyle, a truly beautiful human being – Addy's heart still did a little tap dance to the memory of him. Benedick to her Beatrice. They'd had a week together, onstage and off, Addy hardly marked the difference – '*Speak low, if you speak love*' – and while it totally blew her mind, what it did to her body was even more spectacular.

She was still trying to put it all together – the wonderful winging feeling when they were onstage tossing the lines at each other, just waiting for the curtain to fall so they could tear off their clothes and really get it on – when it all fell apart. Brad – her beautiful Brad – she still couldn't believe it. She'd come bursting into his room one afternoon, hot and happy, and caught them at it. Actually *doing* it: one on top of the other.

'Think of it this way, Adds,' one of her friends in the company told her later. 'You're the first girl Brad's looked at since the eighth grade, and probably the last.'

And so . . . so let's kick the subject, Addy thought. *What do I care right now?* The hunk had paused three rows away, looked like he'd found his seat. *I'm leaving, I'm actually leaving. It's a miracle!*

No, really, because earlier, when they'd announced the third delay in their departure, Addy had known she was never going to make it. They'd be stuck at Kennedy for days, probably wind up spending Christmas in the terminal, cook a turkey, hand out presents. There was this depression. (She'd seen it on the TV newscast in the bar over her second Perrier-with-a-twist – booze played hell with her complexion and she wanted to look her best, her very best, when she got to London, if she ever did.) A depression sitting over most of Europe. Blizzards, the man had said, with a little smile – New York was bathed in winter sunshine, what did he care – blizzards and icy roads, winds from Siberia, all kinds of shit, and it seemed England was not excluded from this Europe-wide fuck-up. Judging by the map, it was slap-bang in the middle of it.

Addy had never been to London. Never seen Big Ben or the Tower of London or Buckingham Palace or the Queen, and the truth was she didn't give a rat's ass for any of them. (Sorry about that, Your Majesty.)

Just Rose.

And now that the time was approaching when she'd see her again . . .

'Hi,' said a voice, and Addy looked up. He was stashing his bag in the overhead compartment. 'Good morning.' Not Cary Grant, not at all; tougher looking, but the smile was a winner. He sat down on the seat beside hers. *'Buongiorno?'* Eyebrows raised in a query. *'Bonjour? Buenos dias? Guten morgen?'* He shook his head. 'Look, you don't have to explain – I understand – first rule of air travel. Never speak to your fellow passengers. I went to Mexico City last month and there was this guy – he had a McDonald's franchise in Paramus – told me all about hamburgers. Everything. I couldn't stop him, he just kept plugging away. What really and truly went into a Big Mac, and how the quarter-pounder had seen its best days, and finally I said to him, "Look, you don't understand, it's not that I don't care – it's that *I truly do not want to know.*

This is knowledge I can live without, this is excess baggage," and the guy couldn't believe it. He said, "Do you feel that way about Chicken McNuggets?" So what I'm saying is I understand, and I promise, from here on in – not another word.'

And Addy, who'd been waiting her chance, said, 'Do you mind if I say something?' and they both broke up, Addy laughing so hard she got a pain. The man held his hand out.

'Mike Ryker. And don't say I didn't warn you.'

He had brown eyes and a small scar on his left temple. She'd already taken note of his thickly muscled shoulders as well as the three-piece suit he had on, which looked like the sort of thing a banker might wear.

'Addy Banks.' She smiled.

'Addy?'

'Adelaide.'

'After the city?'

'No, after my grandmother. It's kind of a family name.'

His hands, as he fixed his safety belt, were quick and sure. Addy made a habit of studying people closely. It was part of learning to be an actor.

'What do you do, Addy?'

She took a deep breath – here we go . . . because usually when you told people you were an actor, the first thing they asked was, 'What have you done?', and when the answer, like in her case, was approximately zero, they'd give you this look. An actor . . . sure . . . and there were times when small, dark-browed Addy Banks felt an overwhelming urge to . . . but what the hell?

'I'm an actor,' she said.

'Great.' His face lit up. 'That's a real break. Now we won't have to talk about *my* job which is commodity broking, and if you ask me what that is exactly, I'll tell you, but I promise you'll regret it.'

Addy opened her eyes wide. She was starting to enjoy this. 'But that's something I've always wanted to know about.' Addy the actor – for a moment she had him going, he just stared at her in disbelief. But she couldn't hold it, she started laughing and he nodded as though to say, OK, point to you, and Addy felt a warm glow start to spread all over her body, top to toe.

The day had fallen on its feet. She felt great.

Great, grown-up, in control of her destiny – and flying to London to see Rose.

THREE

Picture a mountain, snow-tipped, the lower slopes carpeted with pine trees.

Picture a lake. White, green, glittering blue.

Picture a fishing boat, just one. See the fisherman cast his net. Look how it hangs in the air printing its criss-cross pattern on the calm, reflecting surface.

See the crane standing motionless at the water's edge.

Picture them all: the mountain, the lake, the man, the bird . . .

Kimura stirred. The image he sought to capture and hold in his mind was only a dream, but it was one they had shared and he clung to it still.

> *Night, and once again*
> *While I wait for you, cold*
> *Wind turns into rain*

Although he knew she would never come to him now, not in this life, he murmured the words of the haiku they had both loved, and in the calm that followed he found the strength to drag himself back to the present.

He was cold and hungry, but what of it? Let his body suffer while his mind stayed clear. What troubled him more was the air he breathed. Unusually sensitive to smells, Kimura found the sharp, pungent odour of unwashed human bodies a torment, and now he had worse to contend with.

Sometime during the night, one of them had been sick.

He had heard nothing – not surprising given the constant throb of the engine, the drumming of the tires, the rattle and creak of the metal shell that encased them – but as the first light of dawn threaded its way through the air vents, his twitching nostrils had detected the sour reek of regurgitated food.

Presently he was able to see them – four dim figures huddled at the end of the narrow compartment: a family of dark-skinned North Africans. (Libyans? Tunisians? Whatever they were, it meant nothing to Kimura.) They were jammed together, the parents sitting propped against the side walls while the two children lay curled at their feet. Inches away a puddle of vomit spread in a widening circle over the metal flooring.

Crowded though the compartment was, there was room to spare. Between the two ends lay several feet of empty space where any one of the party might have stretched out at greater ease. But they had kept their distance from Kimura. It was as if they were reluctant to draw too close to him, though there was little in his appearance to alarm. A slight figure, he had sat throughout the journey cross-legged and composed, all but motionless. Once, the previous afternoon, the father had crawled the length of the compartment and humbly offered him a piece of bread. But whatever it was he saw in the other man's eyes had sent him scuttling back, and since then there had been no intercourse between them.

Two hours after dawn the steady pulse of the engine diminished and the vehicle they were in drew to a halt. Voices could be heard outside, the banging of doors. A strong wind beat against the metal sides and there was a tang of salt in the air: a rich, reviving fragrance.

Soon they moved forward again, but slowly, and only for a short distance. The faint light from the air vents dimmed and they came to rest.

Time passed.

Then movement again, but a different kind of motion – slow and smooth at first, then increasingly bumpy. Soon they were pitching up and down and tossing from side to side, and Kimura had to brace himself against the metal backrest to preserve his balance.

The woman began to moan. Her husband leaned over to comfort her, but then, as though jerked by an invisible cord, he twisted away from her abruptly and retched into the pool of vomit beside them.

Kimura shut his eyes.

One day he would build a house by a lake in the shadow

of a snow-tipped mountain. He would cast his net into the blue reflecting water and the air would be filled with the scent of pine trees.

Where he would build such a house was uncertain. It seemed unlikely, no impossible now, that he would ever return to his own country. But there were other lands, other mountains, and he would seek them out.

But first he must find the woman. Wherever *she* was, the man he sought would not be far away.

FOUR

A ddy looked over.
Mike was asleep, or seemed to be, eyes shut, chair tilted back. Asleep or faking.

Poor guy, he probably needed a break. They had shared a bottle of wine over dinner – so what if her complexion didn't like it, let it suffer for once – and Addy had hardly drawn breath; the life and times of Adelaide Banks. Orphaned at four (her parents had been killed in an automobile crash, and yes, it was sad, but in reality she barely remembered them), she'd been raised by her grandparents. They were also dead now, a year ago, within a month of each other, and of course she missed them, missed them like hell, but the truth was right from her earliest childhood, mixed in with all her memories, easing every pain, sweetening every pleasure, there had always been Rose.

'That's some aunt you have there,' Mike had said, when he managed to get a word in.

If he only knew.

Addy took out the typewritten letter she'd received a week before. It was so like Rose not to send her invitation by email; old-fashioned Rose who loved nineteenth-century novels and wrote letters – typewritten and also handwritten *letters* on actual *paper* – to the people she cared for; who kept an old copy of Palgrave's *Golden Treasury* on her bedside table and told Addy that social media was for the brain dead, a dictum Addy had adopted for herself to the wonder of her friends and peers who believed quite seriously that you couldn't live without it.

> *My darling Addy,*
> *United is holding a ticket for you. All you need do is check in, and I'm not going to call you because I know exactly what you'll say. 'Oh, but you mustn't, Rose . . .'*

And don't bother to try calling me. I've just lost my phone again. Yes, I know, I'm always doing that but I'm off to Paris for a few days and I'm darned if I'll buy another one until I get back and have a chance to look for the one I lost. Anyway, I'll be busy in Paris – tell you all about that when we meet – and I'll be back by the 18th December at the latest, the day you arrive.

Honey bear, we must be crazy. You there, me here. For goodness' sake, it's Christmas. Just get your sweet self over here. Please.

Addy, I need you.

The letter took up half the page. The rest was filled with Rose's signature, a sprawling R which Addy loved because it was just like Rose herself: warm and open and embracing.

But the letter bothered her.

Addy, I need you.

It wasn't like Rose to say that. Oh, not that it wasn't true: of course Rose needed her, needed someone. Ever since Uncle Matt had died she'd been one of the walking wounded. It had broken Addy's heart to see her the last time she came over to New York – when was it, six months ago? – with her friend Lady Molly Kingsmill, who was some kind of grand English dame, a blonde looker (Addy had to admit it) but still no better than *numero due* in the loveliness stakes when compared with Rose: dark-haired, dark-eyed Rose.

The trip had been a mistake. Addy had sensed it from the first. New York held too many memories for Rose. It was the city where she'd fallen in love, and even though it was more than a year since Uncle Matt's plane had gone down, the pain was still there.

Addy had wanted to help so badly. If she could just have Rose to herself for a while, if they could talk – if *Rose* could talk, get it all out. But somehow the chance never came – Molly had seen to that: Molly and her plans for Rose.

'I'm going to be blunt.' She had taken Addy out to lunch the day after they got in, just the two of them. 'We've got to find Rose a man.' And it was all Addy could do not to haul her off and bust her one right there in the restaurant. Who did this English bimbo think she was, talking that way about Rose – *her* Rose?

'I'm counting on you to help.'

Big deal. It turned out Molly didn't need any help. She knew everyone. They'd hardly touched down before she was on the phone, setting things up: dinners, parties, weekends out of town. It seemed there were any number of people just dying to see her, and oh, by the way, do you mind if I bring my friend Rose, you'll love her?

Addy had to laugh. It was the men, a whole string of them, popping up like rabbits plucked from a hat – Molly working the phone like a pro – and most of them were single, and all of them were available and some of them might even have been straight (New York! New York!), only nobody got around to checking them out.

Least of all Rose.

Addy had watched them fall for her. They'd sit across the table or wherever, staring at this unbelievably beautiful woman (that was how Addy saw her, anyway), trying to figure out a way to pierce – well, it wasn't her reserve, because Rose wasn't like that, not now, not ever; she was warm and friendly, and if she didn't talk much about herself, she was always ready to listen. So what was it – this thing around her, this invisible shield?

Addy knew. The answer was simple. Rose wasn't there, not the part of her that mattered. She could look at them, the men Molly produced, look *through* them, and see another face . . . another time.

And it was wrong, it was wrong, Addy knew it. You had to move on. Molly was right (and fuck her for being right). What Rose needed was a man. Never mind the feminists, Rose had lived her life, the best part of it, through Uncle Matt, and now he was dead. But she was trapped back there in the past, and somehow they had to get her unstuck so she could open her eyes, take a fresh look at life, see there were all kinds of wild and wonderful things that could happen to a person. Hey, a person could even fall in love. Again.

The last night, Addy had finally got her aunt to herself. Molly was off at some 'do' – it was one of Molly Kingsmill's

words, one of quite a number that set Addy's teeth on edge
– and Rose had taken her out to dinner at The Tavern on the
Green.

'I know – strictly for tourists, but I've always loved it.'

Spoken with a wry smile, or was it bitter? Addy knew the
story well. They had met in the Metropolitan Museum, Rose
and Uncle Matt. It was a chance encounter, she browsing,
he filling in time between business appointments, when they
just happened to meet in front of Renoir's *Young Girl Bathing*,
and just happened to fall into conversation, and just who did
they think they were kidding? Addy knew very well what had
happened. Uncle Matt had taken one look at Rose and made
pretty damn sure they fell into conversation. And as for his
so-called appointments, they couldn't have been that important
since before you could say 'Abstract Impressionism' he'd
asked her to join him for lunch.

Guess where?

Still, the choice of restaurant was fine with Addy since it
would give her a chance to get Rose talking about Uncle
Matt, and even now, six months later, she still wasn't sure
how she'd managed to blow it.

They had talked all right. Correction. Addy had talked
– about herself. It just seemed to happen, or maybe Rose
made it happen, because they had hardly sat down when
she started in on Addy. Money. That was Rose's problem, or
rather it was Addy's, anyone could see that, and why did she
have such a hang-up about it?

'Why won't you let me help?'

'Rose, we've been through this before.'

'Waiting tables – now that's what I call mind-expanding.'

'Not to mention soul-destroying. Poor me.'

'Bear, I'm talking about a small allowance.'

Which was bullshit, because Rose was already paying for
her acting classes. That was their deal. Rose would meet the
fees, and one day Addy would pay her back – one day when
she was rich and famous and the toast of Broadway.

'Working all day at class, waiting tables at night – it's crazy.
What kind of life do you have?'

And so Addy had told her. In brief, to begin with, since

there wasn't that much to say about acting school, then in more detail because it turned out there was really quite a lot once Rose got started with her third-degree stuff. Soon Addy was telling her about the production of *Macbeth* the group was working on, and how they'd given her the lead, and how tough it was to get inside the head of someone like Lady Macbeth.

'I mean she's evil, Rose, really evil, at least that's the way it reads, and you have to try and figure out why.'

'Maybe she had a lousy upbringing.'

'Or maybe she's just bad through and through. I guess there are people like that.' Addy paused, and then, 'Did I say something?'

Because Rose had given her the strangest look, it really threw Addy.

'I mean . . . I mean, she doesn't give a shit. Anyone gets in the way, off with his head.'

Rose smiled. The look, whatever it was, had gone. 'I bet she didn't take handouts either.'

'Aw, Rose. Give me a break.'

And so one way or another they never got to talk about Uncle Matt over dinner, and by the time they got back to the hotel where Rose and Molly were staying, the chance had slipped away. Rose was beat.

'Too many late nights for your old aunt.'

Too much Molly, more like it.

Addy went up with her to her room and waited while Rose got ready for bed. The room was full of memories, Rose's things, and the perfume Addy remembered from her childhood: *Chanson d'Amour*. It was just like Rose never to have switched.

There was the silk robe with the flower pattern, Chinese or something, that Rose had brought back with her from the East, the tortoiseshell hairbrush and comb, and the old copy of Palgrave that had belonged to Grandpa, Rose's father.

And on the bedside table, two silver-framed photographs. One of Rose and Addy that summer on the Cape: Addy small and scowling, mad about something, while Rose stood behind her, arms crossed protectively over Addy's shoulders, smiling at whoever was taking the picture, Uncle Matt most likely. He was in the other photo, staring out and away, not really focused on anything. Good-looking sonofabitch. Addy hadn't known what jealousy was until Uncle Matt showed up. Rose stood beside him, her face turned to his: then, now, always.

Rose's things: they were all there, everything she cared about, everything she wanted with her.

Everything?

Addy felt a small hole open in the pit of her stomach.

Rose came out of the bathroom in her nightdress. She glanced at Addy, who was sitting there on the bed trying hard to look casual. What did she care? It was just a piece of junk, nothing to make a scene over. Anyway, it must be filthy by now, falling to bits, and probably covered with fleas. All the same, you would have thought—

'Hey!' Something hit the back of her head. 'What—?'

Before Addy knew it, Rose had grabbed her from behind, wrestling her down, and there was something between them on the bed, something round and soft and hairy. Rose was laughing.

'Go on. Admit it. You thought I'd dumped him.'

'I did not. I never . . .'

'Little bear, little bear . . . Little bear of little brain.'

And then Addy was laughing with her and they were hugging each other and it was like time had made this great leap backward and nothing had changed.

'You were just waiting, weren't you? It was a set-up.' Addy looked at the shaggy brown body on the bed. 'Poor old Grumble. He could use a bath.'

'Are you kidding? He'd fall to pieces. He keeps shedding hair as it is. Pretty soon I'll have a bald bear.'

'An ugly bald bear.'

'Who says he's ugly?'

Addy laughed, remembering. It was when she was living with Grandma and Grandpa up in Connecticut and Rose used to come out from the city at weekends to see them. Saturday nights Rose would give Addy her supper and then put her to bed and the two of them would read Winnie the Pooh stories together. Rose took to calling her Bear. Addy loved it.

So much so that when Rose had a birthday coming up Addy got Grandpa to take her to the nearest Walmart, and with a bagful of dimes and quarters, carefully hoarded, and with a little help from Gramps, she had purchased Rose's birthday present. 'Well, it is certainly a bear, you could say that for it,' Grandpa had muttered, though that wasn't saying much. He called it a clunker, a word Addy hadn't heard before but liked the sound of. The bear had rough brown hair and black button eyes and a permanent scowl that came from having its mouth sewn on wrong. At least, that was Grandpa's opinion, though Addy thought it gave the bear just the right look – serious, even menacing. Try messing with me . . .

Grandma said, 'Oh my lord, what is that?'

'It's the most beautiful bear I've ever seen,' Rose said when Addy gave her present to her. 'What's his name?'

'Grumble,' said Addy.

'That's his *name*?' Grandma said.

'Grumble,' said Rose. She took the bear in her arms. 'I'm going to keep him for ever,' she told Addy. 'Do you hear me? That's a promise. Where I go, he goes.' And Addy had never felt so happy in her life.

Nothing had changed. She put her arms around Rose and hugged her again.

'Rose,' she began – maybe this was the right moment. Her aunt moved away and stood up. She looked down at Addy.

'Rose, I don't know how to say this, but—'

Rose put a finger to Addy's lips. She shook her head. 'You mustn't mind me,' she said, which was dumb, really dumb, because what else could Addy do but mind? 'Your aunt's not herself.' She took the photo from the bedside table, the one of her and Uncle Matt, and gazed at it for what seemed like the longest time. Addy held her breath. 'Desolate and sick,' Rose said.

'What . . . what did you say?'

'Like the fella in the poem, that's me.' She went on staring at the photo. 'Desolate and sick of an old passion.'

Then she looked at Addy and her eyes were filled with tears.

Addy had checked it out later, found the lines in a dictionary of quotations and then run down the poem on Google. '*Non sum qualis eram bonae sub regno Cynarae*'. Didn't exactly ring a bell. Ernest Dowson, 1867–1900. She had memorized the lines.

'. . . and I am desolate and sick of an old passion,
Yea, hungry for the lips of my desire . . .'
'Come again?'
Addy started, turned. Mike was awake now, smiling at her. 'You were saying?'
'Nothing.' She shook her head. 'Nothing . . .'

FIVE

It was a little after four when they came to a halt for the last time, though Kimura did not know it was their final destination until he heard noises beneath them and saw a section of the metal floor being loosened. It fell away and a voice from below called out to them.

He waited while the family clambered out. Apart from a plastic bag that bore the remains of their food, they carried no baggage – not now. When they had boarded the truck on the outskirts of Frankfurt the previous day, the parents had each lugged a bulging suitcase bound with straps, but the driver and his companion had made it clear that these would have to be left behind. Why? Kimura had seen no obvious reason for this prohibition, but since it did not concern him he had stood to one side and watched as the men, impatient with the woman's incessant high-pitched pleadings, had settled the matter by heaving the cases over the fence of the lay-by into a ditch beyond. Kimura himself had only the clothes he stood in, which was perhaps fortunate for all concerned.

He followed the family through the trap door and found himself crouching beneath the truck, ankle-deep in snow. Nearby he could hear voices raised in anger, one man shouting above the others. He crawled out from under the truck.

There were three of them: the driver and his companion, and a third man. They stood in a menacing circle about the father while the woman sat slumped on the ground close by. She looked dazed, exhausted, equally oblivious to the snow and the two children, a boy and a girl, who clung to her arms and stared up at their father with wide, frightened eyes.

Kimura took in the scene at a glance, and then examined his surroundings. The truck was parked in what looked like a scrapyard. The rusting chassis of motorcars stood stacked in lines alongside piles of twisted metal. Brick walls enclosed the area, one of them divided by a pair of iron gates. At the back of the yard was a wooden hut that served as a makeshift office.

The driver was doing the talking. A big man, unshaven, he had all the marks of a bully, thrusting his body up close to the father, jabbing at his shoulder with a finger, bearing down on him, battering him with a stream of words.

Kimura had only a limited knowledge of English, and he found it hard to follow what the driver was saying. His accent was strange, at least to Kimura's ears, and the words followed each other so quickly that he had difficulty separating them. But presently he understood. The man was demanding money: more money. Kimura himself had paid the equivalent of one thousand pounds for his passage and he assumed that the price his fellow travellers were charged was of a similar order.

Well, that was their misfortune. Time was short. He started towards the gates, and as he did so, the driver, catching sight of him, called out something.

Kimura turned and saw the hulking figure coming towards him, striding across the snow, red-faced and angry, shouting as before, but this time uttering a single word.

'Mate!'

Mate? Kimura knew what it meant but was under the impression it was a term applied to animals, generally those in the wild. Still he took no offence. Why should he? He could see that the man hurrying towards him, brandishing his fists and mouthing other, incomprehensible words was a fool: a fool as well as a bully.

Because only a fool would approach another as he did, heedless of danger, blind to whatever he might be facing. Kimura himself would never have taken such a risk. Study your opponent. Watch how he moves. Attend to his bearing. Does he carry himself like one accustomed to combat? Above all, look at his hands. The hands tell all.

If this fool blundering across the snow had taken the time to study Kimura's hands he might have noticed that running along the edge of each, from wrist to fingertip, was a calloused ridge; though whether that would have changed anything was open to question. A fool was a fool.

As the driver came up to him, Kimura took a step back,

feigning fear, and then struck, hitting him with the hardened edge of his hand at a precise spot under the nose, and as the bone broke and the blood spurted, the man stumbled and fell to the ground, shrieking in pain. His companion, struck dumb by the sight, barely had time to raise his fists before Kimura was on him. Spinning on one foot, he drove his heel into the man's unprotected kneecap, cracking the patella like a walnut, and then there were two of them down in the snow, screaming like animals in the wild, and the third man was running for his life towards the office and Kimura let him go because time was pressing and he had much to do.

Walking quickly to the gates, he went out into the street. Left or right? He had no idea which way to turn, but away to his right, at least three blocks distant, he saw the lights of a line of traffic crossing at an intersection and set off in that direction.

He had walked perhaps half the distance when a black saloon car, parked a little way down the street from the entrance to the yard, pulled away from the kerb and set off behind him. It moved at a steady speed, gradually shrinking the gap between them.

SIX

Hauling her bags through the jostling crowd, fighting every inch of the way – what was the big attraction anyway, the whole carriage emptying, everyone getting off? – Addy came out of the Underground at Knightsbridge and wow!

There it was, right in front of her, strung with lights and glittering like a fairy tale castle – Harrods!

She stood and gaped, remembering what Rose had told her: how they would stroll down there in the morning for their hot croissants and coffee. You could buy anything in Harrods, Rose said, from a bread roll to a diamond necklace, and looking at it now Addy thought it wasn't just the department store, it was the whole scene: the lights and the dazzling store windows and the snow – snow on the streets and sidewalks, snow falling out of the pitch-dark sky. This was Christmas. How it was meant to be. The only thing missing was Santa and his reindeer, and too bad they didn't go jingling by just then because she could have hitched a ride. There wasn't an empty cab to be seen, just traffic crawling along the slushy street. Time to make like a Sherpa; she took a fresh grip on her bags and set off.

Using the instructions Rose had given her when she was over in New York, Addy had come in on the Tube from Heathrow. She and Mike had said goodbye in the terminal. He was travelling light – all he had with him was hand luggage – while Addy had one of her bags in the hold, and it had made no sense for him to wait. All the same she wished he had. But he'd promised to call her in a day or two, which was something.

'Let's get together,' he had told her. 'And I want to meet this aunt of yours.'

Addy just bet he did, after the way she'd gone on about Rose. Why did she do these things to herself? He had looked every bit as good by daylight as he had the night before – tall and alert, up for anything. For a while when they were talking he had seemed almost to come on to her, holding her gaze with his, looking deep into her eyes – it had given Addy goose bumps – and she wished now she'd asked him more about himself: her and her big mouth. All she knew was that he had two ex-wives (some recommendation, that), one daughter, and did a lot of travelling in his job. Here and there, but mainly to London where he kept a change of clothes at an old roommate's flat where he'd be staying. He had waved to her as he left the baggage area and Addy had felt her heart skip a beat.

From the Tube exit she crossed the wide street in front of the store – that would be the Brompton Road, she had it all memorized from the map Rose had drawn for her – walked up Montpellier Street (pretty name), turned left, then right, then left again, and each time she made a turn the road got narrower and the snow got deeper, but just as Addy was wondering whether she'd lost her way, she saw it on one of the pair of pillars framing an arched entrance: *Rutland Mews North*. She had made it! Glory be, as Grandma used to say.

Addy paused at the entrance to the narrow cul-de-sac to take it in. So this was where Rose lived. It gave her a warm feeling to think that horses had once been stabled here. She pictured them being led out of their stalls, stamping and snorting, filling the air with good horsey smells.

Feeling a little like a pack-pony herself – she could swear she was starting to steam – she trudged down the mews looking for Rose's house, which was number six. Lights were showing in all the houses except one. Even before she reached it Addy was getting a bad vibe. It couldn't be, could it? She stood in front of the darkened house which had a 6 clearly painted on the white door and thought, *What in the name of Sarah Bernhardt and all the saints am I going to do?*

Ring the doorbell? She did that, and heard the answering peal from inside. There was no response.

What now? She couldn't just stand here in the snow. Should she look for a pub or a café to wait in?

'I say, hullo, good evening . . .'

Addy turned and saw there was a woman standing in the doorway of the house opposite.

'Are you Addy, by any chance?' she asked.

'Yeah – yes, that's me. I'm Addy.' Glory be! A saviour!

'Rose told us you were coming. I've been expecting her all day, but it's all right, I've got a key to her house. Come in, please, you'll catch your death out there.'

Addy walked across the mews and the woman said, 'I'm Sarah Hudson. Rose has told me so much about you.' She shook Addy's hand and then picked up the bag she had put down and took it into the hallway of her house. Addy followed on her heels.

'Look, I'm sorry to bother you—' she began, but the woman cut her off.

'Don't say that. It's so nice to meet you, and we'd do anything for Rose. We all love her so.' She was fiftyish and plump, with rosy cheeks and bright blue eyes. 'I'm so concerned about her. This weather – can you believe it? She was sure she'd be back by today, but I heard on the radio they've stopped all flights from Paris.'

Damn! Addy swallowed her disappointment. 'You said you had a key, Mrs Hudson?'

'Sarah, please. Yes, I've got it here.' She opened a drawer and took out a key. 'You can hang on to it until Rose gets back. But please, won't you stay here with us tonight?'

Addy saw that she meant it, but she'd been waiting for more than a year for a chance to visit Rose, to see where she lived. The house was just a few steps across the way and she knew she couldn't wait a moment longer.

'That's very kind of you, Mrs . . . Sarah, but if you don't mind, I'd really like to get settled.'

'Are you sure?' She handed Addy the key. 'I wish you'd change your mind.' She sounded wistful. 'We're going away ourselves, my husband and I, the day after tomorrow, weather permitting. Our daughter and her husband live in Italy and we're going to spend Christmas with them. But you'd be welcome to stay with us till we leave.'

Addy smiled, shook her head, no way. 'When did Rose go to Paris?' she asked.

'Let me see . . . it was more than a week ago.'

'That long? Did she say what she was doing there?'

Sarah Hudson shook her head. 'I didn't actually speak to her. She must have left early. She slipped a note through the door telling me she planned to be back by the time you arrived, but if she was late could I let you in.'

Hmm . . . intriguing. What was it Rose had said in her letter about the Paris trip? 'I'll tell you all about that when we meet.' Addy couldn't wait.

'I think I'll go over now,' she said. 'I want to unpack and take a shower.'

'Let me come over with you—' Mrs Hudson began, but Addy cut her off.

'No, please.' She hoped she didn't sound rude. 'It's just . . . well, I've been dying to see where Rose lives and I'd love to explore.'

The woman looked crushed for a moment and Addy felt a brute. But then her face brightened. 'There's probably nothing to eat in the house. At least come over and have dinner with us. My husband will be home soon. We usually eat around eight, but come over any time.' She gave Addy's hand a squeeze.

'Thank you, I'd really like that.' And she would too. Sarah Hudson was a doll and Addy had a feeling that her hubby would turn out to be the same. Rose's friends. She took hold of her bags and walked across the mews. Sarah stood watching as she unlocked the door of number six and went into the darkened house.

SEVEN

Kimura sat in the workmen's café warming his hands on his third cup of tea. At least that was the name given to the muddy liquid, though if someone had told him it was buffalo's urine he would not have been astonished. But it was hot and wet and, together with a cheese sandwich of dubious origin, had served to take the edge off his hunger.

He had just completed a lengthy, difficult but ultimately satisfactory conversation with an old woman in a black coat and a woollen muffler who had seated herself at his table. Without invitation, to be sure, but since that seemed to be the custom of the place, Kimura had raised no objection.

For a while she had watched as he studied the guidebook – *London A–Z*, it was called – which he had purchased at a bookseller's in Frankfurt. Kimura knew where he wanted to go – he had found the address on the map – but he didn't know where he was, and consequently had no idea how to get there. A taxi was the obvious solution, but he had seen none passing and had no intention of going outside into the snowy street to look for one: not so long as the black car remained parked on the other side of the road.

He had been aware of it following him some way before he reached the intersection, but had given no sign, and on reaching the main road had crossed it without pausing and gone straight into the café without a backward glance. Here he was safe, for the moment at least, as long as they believed he had not seen them. Because if they bided their time they would certainly find a better place to take him than in a crowded café, surrounded by witnesses.

There were four of them in the car – impossible odds, given that Kimura knew who they were. Not their names, of course, or even their faces, but he knew who had sent them, and their purpose.

So he had waited in his temporary haven and studied his map until suddenly, without warning, the old woman spoke.

'Lost, are you, dearie?'

Kimura knew the meaning of *lost*, and since conversation had been broached, he had nodded politely and set out to explain in carefully phrased English sentences precisely what his problem was.

The woman had waited until he had finished and then, speaking very slowly, had explained to him what route he should follow to reach his destination, what train he should catch on the Underground, and where he should change lines. Kimura had listened gratefully, baffled only by the way she kept addressing him as 'love', which was even more puzzling than 'dearie'.

'But first we've got to get you to Kennington station,' she said.

Having weighed the problem, she rose to her feet and went to consult the man behind the counter, the one dispensing the buffalo's urine. A brief exchange followed, after which she turned to a nearby table where a bald-headed man sat drinking a cup of tea and scanning a newspaper. He had looked up when she spoke to him, nodded, and then turned to glance at Kimura.

The old woman returned to the table.

'That bloke's a taxi driver,' she said. 'He'll take you where you want to go. That's provided you've got the dosh . . . money, I should say?'

By way of reply Kimura brought out a handful of bank-notes from his pocket, a mixture of currencies, and laid them on the table between them. Having studied the hoard, the old woman selected a twenty-pound note from the pile.

'That should do it,' she said, and then returned to the other table where the bald-headed man received her offering with a brisk nod. Turning to look at Kimura a second time, he lifted a thumb in the air.

'All set then, love.' The old woman was back. She looked pleased with herself. 'He's ready when you are.'

Kimura gestured at the notes on the table. He looked enquiringly at her, but she shook her head.

'No, love, that's all right. You'd best be on your way.'

Leaving his tea unfinished, he rose, pocketing his money, and having bowed his thanks to her, he followed the taxi driver out. Together they walked to his empty cab which was parked a short distance away. Without so much as a glance at the black car, Kimura climbed into the back.

The driver spoke to him through the connecting window. 'Kennington, is it, guv?'

Kimura stood watching as the passengers entered the carriage and when the doors shut and the train pulled out of Leicester Square station he was satisfied that none of his pursuers was aboard: not in this carriage at any rate.

He had thought of asking the taxi driver to take him all the way to his destination, but knowing that his pursuers would simply follow him in their car he had decided to try and lose them in the Underground and thus far had not spotted them. But the platform at Kennington where he'd stood waiting had been crowded and he couldn't be sure that one or more of the pack hunting him had not boarded the same train he was on.

In spite of the proximity of danger, he felt calm, almost relaxed. The anger that had fuelled his actions for so long, enveloping him in a red cloud of fury, threatening to unhinge him, had settled into an iron resolve. He could feel it inside him now, compressed like a cold lump in the pit of his stomach, and knew it would remain there until his quest had reached its fated end, whatever that might be.

Meanwhile the train was pulling into another station – Green Park, the sign said – and when the doors opened Kimura saw a group of his fellow countrymen boarding at the far end of the carriage. There were seven of them, five men and two women, tourists by the look of them. The two women were talking to each other, while three of the men were busy with their phones. What about the other two? Kimura studied the pair. One wore a black leather coat, while the other had a moustache that curved around his lips, giving him a walrus-like look. Something about their bearing made Kimura uneasy. They didn't look like tourists. They didn't look like businessmen. As the carriage filled up, he lost sight of them in the press of bodies.

When they reached the next station – it was Hyde Park Corner – Kimura kept his place by the door. The crowd in the carriage had thinned a little and he caught sight of the pair again: Walrus and Leather-coat. They weren't looking his way, but that meant nothing. If they were who he thought they were, if they were still on his trail, then matters would be coming quickly to a head. They couldn't risk losing track of him in the crowded Underground. As far as they knew, he remained unaware of them. But once he made his move, the hunt would be on: a hunt to the death.

The train was moving again. Kimura kept his eyes on the pair, and as they approached Knightsbridge and began slowing, the man in the leather coat turned his head and looked down the carriage towards him. In that moment Kimura made his decision: he met the man's glance. And then, because the adrenalin was starting to pump in his veins and there was no point in further subterfuge, he nodded. *Here I am, take me if you can.* The man acknowledged the gesture with a faint smile.

As they drew to a halt, Kimura readied himself and when the doors opened he sprang out, forcing a path through the passengers waiting to board, heading for the *Exit* sign at the end of the platform. First at the escalator, he went bounding up, two steps at a time, pausing only for a moment to look back. Walrus and Leather-coat were at the bottom, just starting to climb the moving stairs. Further back two other men were barging their way through the crowd. Kimura saw a woman knocked off her feet.

The exit was crowded; small queues had formed while people keyed their cards to the machines. Without pausing Kimura ran past them, vaulting over the barrier and continuing along a wide passageway towards some steps he had seen with the shouts of the Underground staff echoing behind him. Racing up the steps he came out on to the snow-covered sidewalk. To his right was a broad thoroughfare clogged with traffic, difficult to cross in a hurry. He turned left and ran down the side street. On the other side of the road was a big department store with brightly lit windows. Without pausing he crossed the street and hurried through a pair of swinging glassed doors.

Better . . . *much* better . . . all around him there were milling crowds of Christmas shoppers. He could lose his pursuers here, leave by another door and be on his way before they realized what had happened. There was no sign of them when he glanced back and he went on without stopping, passing through another set of doors into a room filled with perfume counters. The battery of scents made his head swim; it brought on a sudden attack of fatigue. How long was it since he had slept? But he kept forging ahead and found himself passing through a succession of marble-floored halls where food of all kinds was on display: shelves packed with cheeses, pastries, mousses, an array of cold meats. His head reeled; he was hungry, so hungry.

But he pressed on, changing direction, zigzagging through the seemingly endless store, past counters selling jewellery into another room where silver gleamed in glass-fronted cabinets, and he knew it was taking too long, much too long, but the press of shoppers around him hindered swift movement.

And then he saw it ahead of him: yet another set of swinging doors. An exit.

Kimura burst out on to the street. Which way now? Yes, he remembered – it was to the right. He turned to go that way, and then stopped dead. Coming down the sidewalk from the corner ahead, trotting, and then breaking into a run when they saw him were Leather-coat and another man.

Kimura turned and plunged back into the store. At least there was no sign of Walrus and the fourth man inside, but he knew one or both must be close on his heels and when he spotted an escalator to his right he ran to it and swiftly ascended to the floor above. But just as he reached the top, he glanced back and saw Leather-coat enter the door from outside. The two men's eyes met.

There was a second escalator nearby and Kimura bounded up it, cursing himself. Of course they would seek to cover the building from the outside once they had seen him enter it. He was thinking too slowly. Hunger, fatigue and the accumulated stresses of the past few days were dulling his perceptions, blunting the razor edge of awareness he would surely need if he were to remain alive. He continued to climb, running up a further escalator until he had reached the third floor where he paused for a second, trying to bring some order to his scattered thoughts.

Be calm, he told himself. Consider the options – behind him the moving stairway he had just come up was blocked by a crowd of shoppers – the two from the street must be following him upstairs. What about the others? They would still be on the ground floor, searching for him there. He would make his way to the opposite end of the store, descend to street level and then leave the building by the same door he had entered. What if they had left a man to guard it? In his mind, Kimura shrugged. In that case it would be just too bad – for one of them.

As he glanced over his shoulder his heart gave a lurch. Leather-coat! The man was close behind him. He was forcing a path through the crowd on the escalator, thrusting people aside, and as their eyes met for a third time Kimura knew it would end here. It was likely the man was armed: he was ready to finish things now and take his chances of escaping in the crowd.

There was a doorway in front of him and instinctively he took it, plunging into the department beyond, which was filled wall-to-wall with beds of all sizes. Turning, he saw Leather-coat lunge towards the doorway he had just come through and go sprawling as he tripped over someone's foot. Kimura raced on, passing through the room in only a few seconds, quitting it by another door that led into a room just as large as the first and like it was also filled with beds. But these were of a more elaborate kind, and away in a corner he saw a four-poster hung with drapes and with a pair of painted screens placed on either side of it framing the whole display. A further glance behind told him he was out of his pursuer's sight. Precious moments!

Not wasting a second, he hurried to the corner and without pausing to see whether he was observed he slipped behind the nearest screen and then watched through a narrow gap between the screen and the bed as Leather-coat came running into the room. After only a few steps he stopped and stood still. His gaze swept the room, and with a sudden tightening of his chest, Kimura realized what the man already knew: that there hadn't been enough time for him to have passed through it and escaped. That he must be here, hiding somewhere.

As Leather-coat scanned the room – there were only a handful of shoppers around, together with a single attendant who was busy with a customer – the second man appeared, and after they had conferred briefly he left the way he had come. On his own now, Leather-coat walked to the centre of the room and halted there. Remaining in the same spot he began to turn round and round slowly, like a lighthouse projecting its beam, keeping the whole room under observation.

Kimura understood at once what his enemy's plan was. Leather-coat was waiting until he had a team assembled. Only then would he proceed to search the room. He himself had minutes at most to make up his mind. What should he do – make a run for it? There were only two doorways out of the room, and Leather-coat could reach either of them before he did. Tackle him face to face? All things being equal, that would have been Kimura's choice. But he was sure now that the other man had a gun. What reason would he have not to be armed? The conclusion was obvious, and even as Kimura reached it, Walrus and one of the other two men came hurrying in, and then it was too late for choices. Now it was just a matter of time.

He watched as Leather-coat dispersed his forces – one man to each of the exits – and then began a systematic search of the room, starting along the wall away on the other side, peering behind the beds that were lined up, pulling drapes that hung from the wall aside with his left hand, while his right stayed in the pocket of his coat.

Watching him, Kimura came to a decision. He would wait until Leather-coat's back was turned and then run to the nearest exit where Walrus was posted. He was standing to one side of the door with his hands in his coat pockets, his eyes sweeping the room. Kimura held out little hope for himself. No matter how swift his attack, the man would have time to draw his weapon and shoot, after which there would be screaming and chaos, people running this way and that, while the three of them quietly departed, each one going a different way, and who would be there to stop them? He knew that death was near, but he felt no fear, only shame – shame, and a regret so deep it pierced him to the marrow. He had failed. It was over.

He was readying himself to move when his view of Walrus was blocked by a party of Arab women in black, ankle-length robes who had entered the room a few minutes earlier and were busy now examining a bed a little way away from where Kimura was hidden. They stood in a group, talking quietly among themselves. Kimura waited for them to move: he wanted a clear path to the door. Presently one of them wandered away from the others and came towards him. An anonymous, feature-less figure – the sequinned robe she wore covered her head and her face was hidden behind a veil and a black mask. She stood a few feet away from Kimura, fingering the drape hanging from the four-poster's frame, and then came closer to examine the screen behind which he was hiding. Now she was only inches away from him: through his narrow peephole Kimura saw a faint sprinkling of pockmarks on her pale brow. The scent of patchouli reached him.

It was now or never.

Pulling the screen aside, he put an arm around her neck and yanked her into the corner with him and then quickly used his other hand to pull the screen shut. Too shocked for a moment to cry out, the woman made no sound, and in the seconds he gained by her silence Kimura shifted his grip. Spinning her around, he clapped his left hand over her mouth and then pinned her arms to her sides, holding her body tightly against his. Meanwhile he listened for sounds from outside – shouts, screams – any sign that they had been observed. He heard nothing.

He already knew what he had to do and he felt pity for this woman of the desert. Strong and wiry, she had begun to fight against his grip and he knew that if he altered it for even an instant to search for the nerve in her neck – a few seconds pressure there would render her immobile – her flailing arms might dislodge the screen in front of them. There was nothing for it. Increasing the pressure of his left hand, he dug his fingers into her cheekbones until he had a firm hold on her

jaw. Then, with a sudden wrenching jerk and twist, he broke
her neck.

The woman slumped in his arms. He lowered her gently to
the floor. With deft fingers he stripped the body. Beneath the
black robe was a white shift and under that loose, knee-length
drawers which he left untouched. Undressing to his underpants,
he donned the shift and the black billowing robe. The shift
was tight about his shoulders and chest, but they were much
the same height and the garments reached down to his ankles.

He had trouble with the veil – he had to unpin it, and after
drawing the robe over his head, pin it again on either side, all
the time working only by feel. Last of all he settled the mask
and then ran his hands lightly over his body, checking everything. Shoes! Kimura had on a pair of white, rubber-soled
trainers. He bent down and felt for the woman's feet. She was
wearing light sandals over a pair of thick woollen socks. He
took off his trainers and slipped his feet into the sandals. They
barely fitted – the straps bit into his heels – but they would
have to do.

He peered through the narrow gap he had used before. The
Arab women had noticed the absence of their companion.
They were looking around the room, murmuring to one another.
One of them pointed towards the door where Walrus stood
guard, and after a moment they moved off in that direction
and went out.

Kimura checked the rest of the room. Leather-coat was much
closer now. He had covered more than half the area and was
starting along the wall towards him. Kimura waited until his
back was turned. Then he slipped quickly between the screens
and walked towards the door where Walrus stood guard. With
eyes downcast, he could see only the bottom half of his enemy's
body, but he noted that his hands were still buried in his pockets
and he felt the man's gaze on him. Although his heart was
thudding and every nerve in his body crying out for release
– how he longed to leap at his foe, see terror flare in his eyes
as he struck the death blow – he walked steadily through the
doorway past him, unchecked and unnoticed.

Within minutes, he was outside again and hurrying along
the sidewalk in the still-falling snow.

EIGHT

A ddy hadn't been in the house ten minutes when the bat showed up.

She was busy switching on lights downstairs, checking the heating (it was on), getting a sense of the place – Rose's house was exactly as she'd imagined it, small, tastefully furnished but with the feel of a real home – when the doorbell rang.

Thinking it must be Sarah from across the way, Addy opened the door and went, 'Aargh!' That was how it came out – something between a gasp and a squawk – because standing there on the doorstep was . . . well, if it wasn't a bat it was the next best thing.

The man was tall and wore a long black coat and a black felt hat, but it wasn't that – it was the eyes. They stuck out like a pair of grapes. Protuberant – that was the word. Protuberant eyes, a receding chin and ears that put Addy in mind of a couple of ice-cream scoops. Scared the shit out of her.

'Forgive me.' The bat made a neat bow. (Foreign – no question about it. Addy had an ear for accents. And how about that *r*? It sounded Russian to her.) 'Is Mrs Carmody at home?'

Definitely Russian. A Russian bat.

'No.' Addy shook her head. 'I mean not right now. I'm expecting her soon.'

'This evening perhaps?' The eyes seemed to widen. He kept staring at her. It gave Addy the creeps.

'Erm, no . . . I mean I don't know, tomorrow maybe. It's the weather, you see . . .' Addy waved her hands about as though that might help. The creeps were getting creepier. She didn't know why, but for some reason she was scared. Not shocked, like a moment ago, but scared-scared. And it wasn't because of his eyes or his ears or his long black coat. It was *him*. Something about him.

The bat went on staring at her. Addy got ready to yell. (What was the matter with her? There were people around, Sarah, neighbours, lights in all the houses.) All she knew was if he made one move towards her, just the tiniest motion . . .

'Until tomorrow then.'

He made another bow, then turned and walked away and Addy's breath came out with a whoosh.

'Can I say who called?' Count Dracula?

The bat didn't answer or look round. He gave no sign he'd heard her, just went on walking towards the end of the mews and then he was round the corner, gone.

Addy stepped back and shut the door, locked it, put on the chain. And then took a couple of deep breaths.

What a performance!

Another triumph for Miss Adelaide Banks in her well-known interpretation of *There's Something at the Bottom of my Garden,* otherwise known as *The Overheated Imagination.*

Just wait till she told Rose. The guy was probably a friend of hers, some Russian émigré type, a poet maybe. There were lots of Russian poets. Maybe this one had spent time in a labour camp when he was a boy, which accounted for his peculiar appearance. Haven't you heard – they used to hang them by their heels from the rafters at night? And now he was living in the West and Rose had met him some place, at a concert, say, and . . . and though Addy liked making up stories about people she met, inventing whole fantasy lives for them, she knew, was bullshit.

The guy had scared her, and she didn't know why.

But Rose would – might – and Rose would be here soon, and in the meantime she wasn't going to think about bats and vampires and things that went bump in the night. *For Christ's sake, Addy, you're going to sleep here.* She would get settled, take a shower and then go over the road and have dinner with Sarah and her husband. Yeah, and tell *them* all about it.

First she went into the kitchen and checked the back door – it was locked and bolted – then carried her bags upstairs and unpacked them in the small guest room at the front of the house. Between the guest room and Rose's bedroom at the back was a bathroom – Addy could have found her way around blindfolded, Rose had gone over every inch of the house in her letters – and after she had taken a shower and changed into a fresh pair of jeans and a T-shirt, she opened the door to Rose's room and peeped in.

Not to pry, she told herself, just to take a peek, see everything was in order. Rose's photograph of the two of them was standing on the bedside table where she'd have expected to find it, though the one with Uncle Matt was missing. Perhaps Rose had taken it to Paris with her. The important thing was Grumble had gone too. He wasn't in his usual place sitting on the throne of pillows on Rose's bed kind of surveying things. Addy had never forgotten what her aunt had told her all those years ago.

She went downstairs and checked the time. It was a little after six. Addy decided she would give it an hour and then go over and join Sarah and her husband. She lit the gas fire, hauled out a couple of old photograph albums from the bookcase that had caught her eye earlier and settled down on the white hearth rug in front of the flickering flames.

Memory time.

Addy loved family photos – and particularly the way Rose stuck them in an album, didn't just leave them in her phone or laptop – the ones of them both together and of Grandma and Grandpa back in the old days (even if you were only twenty there were still times that seemed like ancient history), but she had her own copies of most of them and soon she skipped forward, following the tracks of Rose's life with Uncle Matt.

Mexico . . . Bangkok . . . Athens . . . New Delhi. Uncle Matt had worked for a big trading company, General something, and they had spent months, sometimes years, living in all kinds of romantic places. When Addy was a little girl she used to wait for the postcards she knew Rose would send her, longing for the one that would say, *Dearest Bear, looks like we'll be meeting soon* . . . and then Rose would be back, sometimes alone (Addy much preferred that), sometimes with Uncle Matt, and if it was summer they would go to the Cape or Nantucket and Rose and Addy would spend hours on the beach together and Uncle Matt (if he was there) would promise that next year he was going to fly Addy over to wherever they were living and show her the best time. But he never did.

Truth to tell, they had never really hit it off, she and Uncle Matt, and Addy knew it was her fault. She'd been just too damned possessive of Rose, always wanting her attention, wanting her love, but although both had been given in great measure, Addy had never been deceived. You only had to see them together, Rose and Matt, see the way she looked at him, to know where her heart lay.

Spain . . . the end of the line. Addy found a photo in the second album of Rose and Uncle Matt in fancy dress: Rose in a lace mantilla with a comb in her hair, Matt in bullfighter's garb. Matt the matador! Still, you had to hand it to him – anyone else would look like an asshole, but Uncle Matt could play the part. Long and lean, he was facing the camera with that arrogant stare those guys cultivated. *Hey, toro!* Matt the matador. Matt the actor. It took one to know one.

It had all ended a year ago in the mountains, the Sierra Nevada, where Uncle Matt's plane had gone down – a piece of junk he'd rented in some no-account town on the coast because he'd had to get to Madrid to catch a flight to New York. It was something to do with work that wouldn't wait. Rose had been going with him, but changed her mind at the last minute – Addy didn't know why, she'd never dared ask – and Uncle Matt had bought it. And the worst thing was Rose had never forgiven herself. Not because she hadn't stopped him going. Because she hadn't been on the plane with him.

Jesus! Addy shut her eyes. You should leave memories alone, let them lie. Rose had called them from Madrid afterwards. After she'd gone up into the mountains with the police and they had shown her the wreck: after she'd identified Matt's body. Addy had never talked to her about it, never asked her anything, but Rose had told Grandpa that seeing her husband's body was the worst moment of her life.

'I think I went crazy for a while,' she had told him. It wasn't long after that Grandpa and Grandma had died, within weeks of each other, and Rose had been left with only Addy for family.

The album ended with the Spanish photos. There was

nothing more after that. The last pictures had been snapped on somebody's yacht. *Mallorca,* Rose had printed at the top of the page. There were photos of both of them on deck with other people, different groups, and – hey! – Addy bent closer. Wasn't that . . .?

Well, wouldn't you know it! Molly Kingsmill, in the all-too-visible flesh. She was sitting on the rail between Rose and Uncle Matt: Lady M herself. In a white bikini. With boobs out to here.

So that was where they'd met, Rose and Molly. Somehow Addy had always assumed it was London. But now it made more sense, Rose deciding to come and live here. It must have been Molly's idea, her new chum Molly. Addy couldn't help it. She knew she was jealous and possessive and probably a pain in the ass, but she just couldn't see what Rose saw in the woman.

But no doubt she'd have another chance to find out. Molly would be around as soon as Rose got back, count on it. Christ! Maybe they'd have to spend Christmas together, the three of them. All Addy hoped was that Mike came through – called her, like he said he would. It'd be something to dangle under Molly's aristocratic nose, something to stuff up her jumper (if there was any space left). But then a terrible thought occurred to her. She was ready (she hoped) for Mike to take a shine to Rose rather than her. It would be the natural thing, given their age and her age and all that shit. But what if he got the hots for Molly?

Enough! Addy slammed the book shut. Think of something else, *anything* else. She took the albums back to the bookcase and as she put them away her eye lighted on a word, a title, a name!

Olivier.

Magic. Pure magic. She hauled out the book and there he was on the jacket – those eyes, that mouth – white-haired and stricken, and it must be, yes it was . . . Addy had checked the cover. Olivier as Lear.

King Lear. That was a tragedy, and there was another as far as Addy was concerned and it was this: she had been born too late. Oh, not by much. Just a few decades earlier and

she could have hoped that one day they might share the same
stage. Adelaide Banks and Sir Laurence Olivier. (Well, the
other way round, naturally.) True, he would have been old
even then, but Addy was slight and she would have done it
somehow, made herself light, light as thistle-down, and he
would have carried her on to the stage, blinded and howling
out his pain and grief.

Thou'll come no more.

Never, never, never, never, never!

And it was true, it would never happen now, not ever . . .

The doorbell rang again.

Addy checked the time. Just before seven. Must be Sarah
come to fetch her, she thought. She put the book away and
went to the front door and – oh, no, wait a minute – maybe
the bat was back. He'd said tomorrow, but Addy wasn't taking
any chances and she looked first to see that the chain was in
place before she unlocked the door and opened it a few inches.

It wasn't the bat and it wasn't Sarah. It was some Arab
woman wearing a mask and a veil and even as Addy regis-
tered the fact – there wasn't time to be surprised – the woman
launched herself at the door, smashing it open, ripping the
chain attachment out of the frame so that it swung inwards
catching Addy a crack on the forehead that sent her reeling
back, tripping over a stool behind her and landing on the
floor, flat on her ass.

Too amazed, too dumbfounded, too totally blown away to
do anything but sit there gawping.

Next moment the woman was there in the hallway beside
her, and Addy lost it – she plain went berserk, because vampire
bats were one thing, but some scrawny little Arab bitch busting
in! Scrambling to her feet, she hurled herself at the creature,
yelling at the top of her lungs, but the figure she grabbed at
wasn't there and instead something hit her in the pit of the
stomach like a hammer and next thing she knew she was on
the floor again, this time doubled up on her knees with the
breath knocked out of her, gasping and choking.

A hand like a steel claw caught hold of the back of her
neck and she felt her head being lifted. Then it was there,
right in front of her – the veiled face. The woman was looking

at her. The eyes behind the mask were black and unmoving. They seemed to burn into hers. It went on for seconds.

Then the hand on her neck shifted. It took a grip on Addy's dark curls and suddenly she was wrenched upright and dragged towards the stairs, *up* the stairs, on her feet at first, then on her knees, and the woman wouldn't stop, she just kept on hauling, and Addy tried to yell but she hadn't any breath, and when they reached the top the woman went first into Rose's room, pulling Addy behind her, then turned to go to the guest room, and though Addy was swinging at her now, punching her in the back and the ribs, it was like hitting a tree trunk, the woman didn't seem to feel it, and—

And someone was shouting.

It was a man's voice coming from the floor below.

The woman let go of Addy's hair and went to the stairs. Staggering after her, Addy saw a grey-haired man standing in the hallway.

'You . . . you . . .'

He shouted when he saw the Arab woman and tried to grab hold of her when she came down the steps, but the black-cloaked figure easily eluded his waving arms and ran out into the night.

From the top of the stairs, on shaky legs, Addy witnessed it all, and then did something she'd done before at acting school. (She'd tried it this way, she'd tried it that, but whichever way she tried somehow it never seemed natural. This time, though, it was for real.)

She fainted clean away . . .

And came to on the sofa in the sitting room downstairs to find Sarah bending over her asking, 'Addy . . . Addy . . . are you all right?' And although her head was still spinning – she was having trouble trying to recall exactly what had happened – at least she was safe and sound.

For a while anyway, but the feeling didn't last. Soon afterwards the cops arrived and from that moment on things went downhill fast.

An Arab woman? What Arab woman?

There were two of them in plainclothes: a Detective

Inspector MacSomething and a younger guy who wrote down everything Addy said in a notebook. Also some other cops in uniform who wandered in and out of the house – Addy could see the flashing light on their car outside through a chink in the sitting-room curtains.

Did she know any Arab women?

They were polite enough, but in a British kind of way that wasn't really polite. They were just humouring her, and it was clear from the expression on their faces that they thought she was wacko.

How about her aunt then – did *she* know any Arab women? Was Rose by any chance Israeli?

Great guess. Give the man a cigar. You could tell by the name, couldn't you? Carmody. Big Tel Aviv family. Ask anyone. Addy had to bite her tongue to stay civil.

Had anything like this ever happened to her before?

Like every time there was a full moon? Jesus!

The questions kept coming.

Thank God, Sarah was there, she and her husband Bill, who had heard Addy yelling from across the mews and come running over. Bill was the grey-haired man Addy had seen at the bottom of the stairs just before she passed out. And Bill had seen the Arab woman, hadn't he? So they knew she wasn't making that up. But it didn't help. She still felt lousy. Her head throbbed, her stomach ached and her scalp was still burning from the attentions of that hair-pulling bitch.

Not knowing how badly she was hurt, Bill had also called an ambulance, which arrived before the cops, but after a medic had looked her over and found nothing broken, no serious damage et cetera, he'd told her there was no need for them to take her to hospital. (How about the patient's self-esteem? Addy wanted to ask. Care to run a check on that?)

Once he was done, the detectives had gone to work. Addy told them what had happened. Told them a second time. Told them a *third* time. She could see they weren't buying it.

'And you're sure she didn't say anything?' DI MacBirdbrain asked for maybe the five hundredth time. Addy's headache was getting worse. She wondered whether she ought to tell them about the bat, decided no. They'd put her away for sure, probably in a straitjacket.

The younger cop who was taking notes looked up. 'Could it have been a man?' he asked.

Hey! Why hadn't she thought of that herself? Addy nodded eagerly.

'Yeah, I think so. She was too strong, know what I mean?'

She felt better already. It had really been bothering her: the thought that not only had she had the shit kicked out of her, but the perpetrator was some itsy little dame.

'A man dressed as an Arab woman?' MacDumbo frowned. This was getting deep. Better send for Sherlock.

Someone was making a noise outside the front door. Addy heard voices. A woman was speaking. 'Just tell me who's in charge . . .' And then the door opened and in swept . . .

'Addy! Is that you? What on earth's happened? Where's Rose?'

She was wearing a fur coat with her blonde hair piled on top of her head like a golden helmet and, looking up at her, Addy couldn't credit her own reaction. She would have sworn on a Bible – whole stacks of them – that she would never in her life have been pleased to see Molly Kingsmill.

But she was.

'Hi, Molly . . .'

'Addy! Good God! What on earth are you doing here?' She strode over to the sofa, pushing the cops aside. 'Who are you two?' She glared at them.

'Madam, if you don't mind . . .' MacNumbnuts began, but Molly did. Molly minded like hell. Molly wanted to know *exactly* what was going on, *like right now*, and it was left to Addy to simply lie back and watch. There was nothing she had to say, nothing she needed to do. For once she was on the other side of the footlights, part of the audience, taking notes almost, because if you were an actor you had to know everything: how people behaved, all sorts of people, and lying there Addy knew that what she was witnessing now was a master class in what it was like to be rich.

Rich and beautiful and upper class – to be all those things at once and not give a shit about anyone.

NINE

Night, and once again
While I wait for you . . .

Kimura murmured the words through clenched teeth.
But it was no use. The effort it took him to control his
chattering teeth drove the thought from his mind. He
had never been so cold.

In his flight from the mews he had lost both sandals and
had had to run through the snow in socks that had rapidly
become drenched with icy water. The socks were discarded
now and his feet warmly covered, but feeling had still not
returned to his toes and he flexed them repeatedly, striving
to restore the sluggish circulation.

At least he was safe – for the present – but a long night
stretched ahead of him and the sleep his body craved would
not come. He had blundered unpardonably. Breaking into the
house had been the act of a madman, but when the young
woman had opened the door he had caught only a glimpse of
her face, and since most Westerners looked alike to him, he
assumed he had found his quarry.

Fury had overwhelmed him then. Like a dam bursting its
barriers, the red cloud of rage had swept all caution aside and
sent his body hurtling through the doorway. Now whatever
advantage he had started with – the fact that he was still alive,
shocking to those who might have thought otherwise – had
been tossed away. And there were other perils. How long
would it be before Leather-coat and his men picked up his
trail again?

The wrong woman, but the right house. Kimura had seen
the photograph on the bedside table. Where was she now, the
one he sought? And who was the girl? Had he been able to
stay longer, he might have found answers to those questions.
But the arrival of the man downstairs had forced him to flee.

Not that he couldn't have dealt with him – a single blow would have sufficed – but there would have been no point to it. The alarm had been raised and he had to flee; it would have been an act of brutality, nothing more, and Kimura, by his own peculiar lights, was not a brutal man.

He shifted uncomfortably on the hard, wooden surface, drawing the flowing white robes more closely about him. Strange bed . . . stranger bedclothes. The darkness in which he lay was pierced by faint shafts of light coming through elongated windows. Some distance away, at the other end of the building, he could discern the outlines of a long table and the cross that rested upon it. It was the first time he had ever been inside a Christian church.

He had stumbled on it by chance. Running through the dark streets his first thought had been to distance himself from the mews. It was still snowing heavily, and the few pedestrians he encountered had turned to stare as he raced by. In order to free his legs he had hoisted the shift above his knees, and with his masked face and billowing black robe he must have appeared to them, momentarily at least, like some demon conjured from the pit. None had tried to stop him: none had pursued.

He had known he must find shelter for the night, but where? Even a parked car would be better than nothing – but what if it were equipped with an alarm? Hurrying along a deserted street, he had come on the church by chance. The bulky, anonymous structure stood back from the sidewalk, and while Kimura had no idea what purpose it served at first, he had been drawn by the darkened windows and on circling the building had found a door at the back hidden from the street. A few minutes work with an iron post uprooted from a sagging fence had secured his entry . . . and sanctuary.

As luck would have it, he had entered the vestry, and there he had his first stroke of good fortune. Moving stealthily across the floor in the darkened room his foot had struck what proved to be a cardboard packing case filled with clothes of all kinds. Worn and frayed though they were – he was working by touch alone – for the most part they were still serviceable and he had carefully sorted through the case, picking out trousers and shirts and sweaters and all the socks he could find. Able at last to shed the dead woman's clothes, he had tried on various garments until he found a set that roughly fitted him. The problem of shoes remained, however: there were none in the packing case. But after he had dried his frozen feet he put on the socks – three to each foot – and then set about exploring the rest of the building.

Coming out of the vestry, his first sight of the nave with its rows of wooden pews made him think he had entered some public meeting place. But then he saw the cross on the altar and realized where he was. Although he knew little about the Christian religion, the image of the crucified Christ was a familiar one. But he was puzzled by a set of small wooden figures he saw grouped near the altar. Just visible in the pale grey light were a woman and a baby, and near them were some sheep and oxen together with three men, richly dressed and crowned like kings. Kimura knew it was the Christmas season, the time when Christians celebrated the birth of Christ, and he assumed this was a shrine of sorts and hoped there might be offerings left nearby, food in particular, any sort of food: fruits, vegetables, cakes – his hunger, sharpened by the cold, was acute now. But a quick search of the surroundings yielded nothing beyond a few handfuls of hay and presently he returned to the vestry.

During his brief exploration of the room earlier he had discovered a locked cupboard. Using the iron fence post, he prized open the doors and found the space inside divided into two compartments. One of them contained a number of white priest's robes hanging from a rail; the other was fitted with shelves and on one of them he had found two bottles of wine and a square box half filled with thin white discs the size and shape of coins.

Testing them between his fingers, he discovered they had a soft, papery texture and put one in his mouth. It tasted like paper, but had a different substance, dissolving easily as he chewed it. It was food, hardly nourishing, but unquestionably something designed to be eaten, and Kimura had devoured the contents of the box, washing down the bland wafers with mouthfuls of sweet wine. Then he took the robes off their hangers, went back into the nave and made up a bed for himself on one of the pews.

But although his mind and body cried out for sleep, he had lain awake for what seemed like hours, tormented by the thoughts that raced through his mind like clouds driven across a storm-filled sky.

Time and again his gaze returned to the altar and cross. How strange that chance should have brought him to this place. Was it an omen? Although his knowledge of the religion was slight, he knew that the people who came to this place to worship believed in God and the Devil, and while God, if he existed, had never manifested himself to Kimura, the Devil was another matter. He was an old acquaintance and it was said he walked the earth in many forms.

Kimura knew but one: a true devil.

A man who walked through life with a light tread and a laugh on his lips, yet dealt death so swiftly and surely that even Kimura, with all his strength and skill, could not be sure how the final encounter between them would end.

The one who called himself Charon.

TEN

Earth had nothing fairer to show that winter's evening than the view from Westminster Bridge – or so Charon told himself, pleased by the thought that had just occurred to him. The snow was a revelation. It was everywhere – covering the road and sidewalk, blanketing the river, falling in lazy spirals from low-hanging clouds that glowed orange and yellow from the reflected lights of the city. *Turner, thou should'st be living at this hour!* He had spent the latter part of the afternoon at the Tate Gallery and his mind's eye still throbbed with the swirling canvases.

And as though the beauty were not enough, there was another, more practical reason why he welcomed the blizzard: it kept people off the streets. Normally, Charon favoured crowds – one man could pass unnoticed in a throng – but the business of cover worked both ways. The hunter could also be hunted, and since Paris he had not moved a step without being alert to the threat of sudden ambush.

He walked quickly across the bridge, not looking back until he reached the steps leading down to the Albert Embankment, and then paused to admire the view – the golden eye of Big Ben, the snow-blurred outlines of the Houses of Parliament, the white sweep of the river – while at the same time assuring himself that he was not being followed. Satisfied, he went down the steps and set off along the walkway flanking the river.

Soon, like it or not, he was mingling in a crowd, most of them tourists who had gathered around the London Eye, hoping they would be in time to ride on the giant Ferris wheel before it shut down for the night. He had happened to be in London when it had opened at the turn of the century and remembered the sweeping view it gave of the great city. Recalling the sight, he reminded himself that there was something he wanted to see on this visit if he got the time.

For one reason or another, he had never made the pilgrimage before and now might be his last chance. Situated somewhat further down the Thames, it was the reconstruction of the Globe Theatre as it had appeared in Shakespeare's time. People might laugh at him (if they dared) but Charon had always felt a kinship with the bard. They had the same godlike understanding of human nature, he believed, even if his own appreciation of the species' worth was somewhat lower down the scale than the Swan of Avon's.

'What a piece of work was man . . .' How did it go? '. . . How noble in reason, how infinite in faculty?' Charon grinned. He supposed it was possible to think of people that way, though personally he had always found them much the same – at any rate, predictable.

Or, to put it another way, was there any such thing as a man who was truly unique?

Charon made a modest bow in his own direction.

Because it was true – there was no one quite like him. Who else could do as he did now – walk through the city this lovely winter's evening, light of heart, buoyant of mood, full of wonder and delight at the world around him, untroubled by the thought of the perils that lay ahead.

Years ago, he had consulted an analyst. (He had chosen, with care, an aged Viennese practitioner, a survivor, Jewish of course, though it was not that which had drawn Charon to him – it was the shadow of death writ plain to see on the old man's ravaged features. This would be no long-lived memoirist.) He'd not gone to him out of any sense of need – far from it – but purely from curiosity. He had wondered what an expert – or one who posed as such – would make of him.

He had told the man . . . certain things. Oh, not much, by no means all, but enough to provide him with a working hypothesis. At the end of the session – there had been only one – the analyst had asked him a question.

'Do you know the clinical meaning of the word "affect"?'

Charon shook his head. He knew.

'It is a general term for feelings and emotions, particularly when they are attached to ideas or concepts.'

'Like good and evil?'

'Like good and evil.'

Charon had frowned. 'You think I don't know the difference?'

'I did not say that. You know very well. I'm just not sure you feel it.'

Charon was amused. 'I hope you're not calling me a psychopath,' he said lightly. He certainly hadn't been that generous with details. 'I've always understood that's the kind of word you people don't like to toss about.'

'You're right. We don't.' The old man had held Charon's gaze. His glance was not friendly. 'And no, I wouldn't call you a psychopath. The truth is I don't know what to call you. I have lived a long time and seen many things, some of them dreadful beyond telling. You are something new in my experience.' *And I would just as soon not see you again.*

The words were unspoken, but his meaning was plain, and for a moment Charon had felt a surge of anger. The old fool hadn't known what a risk he was taking . . . or perhaps he had?

Later, though, he had taken a more lenient view of their interview. All the supposed expert in the complexities of human nature had said was that he didn't know how to categorize the person he'd been talking to, and was it any surprise? How could any word begin to describe a man such as he? One who could, even as he did now, reflect so calmly and humorously on the ups and downs of life, the peaks and troughs, when death dogged his heels and the game was all but lost.

All but, yet not entirely, for Charon had a plan and already it was in motion. When in doubt, turn to the coaches. Smart fellas, the coaches, they knew there were only two things that mattered: winning and losing. And what was it they always said? It ain't over till it's over. Or was that one of the immortal Yogi's aphorisms? Charon frowned. He liked to get these small details right.

Meantime . . . meantime there were bushes ahead – he was approaching the rail bridge that crossed the river from Charing Cross, enjoying the soft cushiony feel of the snow underfoot, comfortable in the felt-lined après-ski boots he had purchased in a sporting goods store earlier that day – bushes that flanked a small park on his right. If he, Charon, were lying in wait for someone, observing yet unobserved, that was the spot he would have chosen to conceal himself.

As he walked past the spot he heard a faint sound. Was it the shifting of a branch? Something had moved – it was only a slight change in the pattern of shadows, but his eye had caught it and as he went by he was tempted to laugh out loud, because it was true, it was true, there was no one quite like him.

He went on . . . up the incline from the embankment on to the broad terrace in front of the Festival Hall and suddenly there were people around him again, a steady stream coming down the steps from the footbridge, men and women, but not many, they were mostly children, scores of them, boys and girls all hurrying towards the brightly lit hall where a long banner attached to the front of the building proclaimed *Concert of Carols.*

Without troubling to glance behind him Charon joined the crowd and seconds later he was standing in line at the café in the entrance of the hall, stamping his feet to get rid of the accumulated snow and drying his hair with a handkerchief. A young woman in the line ahead of him looked round.

'Goodness, what a night!'

Charon smiled at her. He had a wonderful smile, warm, and winning, and he knew it.

The young woman blushed. She was a dog, snub-nosed and overweight, a spinster for eternity, but he caressed her with his smile, watching her face glow, seeing the dream begin to take shape in her eyes . . . a chance meeting, a dark stranger . . . what a piece of work was woman.

'Please, miss, can I have a mince pie?'

'Please, miss . . . please, miss . . .'

Reluctantly the young woman turned to the line of girls in front of her. Charon glanced back at the entrance. The glass doors swung open and shut as people kept arriving. Out on the terrace a black-coated figure paced up and down.

He bought a cup of coffee. The young woman looked back hopefully as she shepherded her charges off and Charon followed them to a corner of the café. One of the girls said boldly, 'Are you coming to the concert?' It was the one who had asked for a mince pie first, a wiry redhead with a challenging expression.

Charon shook his head. He sipped his coffee.

'That's none of your business, Mary,' the young woman said. 'Don't ask so many questions.' She smiled at Charon.

'Why are you here, then?' the redhead persisted.

'Mary!'

Charon shrugged. 'Just passing through.'

The black-coated figure had moved to the end of the terrace and stood with his back to the river, surveying the front of the hall.

'What are you going to do?'

Charon put down his cup. He met the girl's gaze and saw her flinch. 'Terrible things,' he promised her.

Then in a second he was gone, walking quickly to the doors, going out on to the main terrace and then climbing a flight of steps to a platform above where the Queen Elizabeth Hall stood and beyond it, around a corner, the Hayward Gallery. Still moving fast – and not looking back – he went past both to a second flight of steps that led down to a broad paved walkway, which he crossed without pausing to a narrow stairway with steps made of steel that led to an underground car park. Out of sight finally, he stopped, and taking up a position just to one side of the steps, stood waiting.

Before long Charon heard the sound of footsteps, hurried at first, then slowing. He breathed easily. Patience . . . always patience. The footsteps paused at the top of the stairs. He heard the sound of a click, sharp in the silence, and pictured the knife gleaming in the half darkness. The man was coming down the stairs one step at a time. Step – pause. Step – pause. Charon stood relaxed, easy in himself. Everything came to him who waited.

The knife appeared first. The man held it a little in front of him, the blade pointing forward, palm under the handle in the prescribed manner. After the knife came an arm. Then a shoulder and a head—

Charon struck.

He caught hold of the wrist with one hand and the back of the man's neck with the other and held him – just held him – and though the man tried to struggle and lash out with his free hand he could barely move. The pain in his neck was close to paralysing. His breath came in whistling gasps.

Charon chuckled. He brought his lips up close to the other's ear.

'Relax. It's me.'

ELEVEN

'Rose? A man? Are you *sure*?' Addy was stunned.

'That's what I think.' Molly nodded. But she seemed hesitant, unsure whether she ought to be saying this. 'I wondered if you knew anything about it. I was hoping to pump you.'

Addy shook her head. She didn't know what to say. Too much was happening, and none of it made any sense. She couldn't take it all in.

First that business with the crazy dame, or whoever it was, breaking into Rose's house – Addy was still trying to process that.

'Must be a nutter.'

That was what the younger of the two cops had said. He had come over to the sofa, to play good cop – that was how Addy read it – while Molly was holding court with the other. A nutter? He could be right. Great word, too. Addy tucked it away for future use.

And then Molly's surprise at finding her there; it seemed Rose hadn't said a word to her about inviting Addy over for Christmas, nor about her trip to Paris. Neither of them knew what to make of that.

'I was just doing some shopping at Harrods and I thought I'd drop in,' Molly said.

But it was Molly herself who'd surprised Addy the most: the way she behaved. It would have been natural enough for her to show a little sympathy, make the right noises, go through the motions, et cetera. After all, poor little Addy had had an unsettling experience – that was how Molly would have put it, the Molly Addy knew from the past – but she'd gone beyond that, way beyond.

'This is disgraceful.' She kept repeating the word. 'Absolutely disgraceful. Are you implying that you don't believe Miss Banks? Are you suggesting that she made all this up?'

Actually the inspector – MacStupified by this time – hadn't implied anything so far as Addy could tell. He'd hardly got a word in. Molly had done the talking for both of them.

'I want to know if anyone is looking for this creature,' she had said. Tall, golden-haired, just dazzling as she towered over the poor guy. 'I want to know if she, he or it is still out there molesting other young women. I want the name of your superior.'

Jesus! It was like watching a shredder in action. Addy was beginning to think she'd misjudged Molly. The woman had balls. The younger cop had enjoyed it, too. He had stood next to Addy, grinning and sending her the occasional wink. Across the room, Sarah and Bill had stood listening, wide-eyed. This was better than cabaret.

Finally, the inspector had managed to speak, something about them needing a statement from Addy and maybe she could come round to the station tomorrow morning and . . .

That was when Molly took off.

Levitation! Addy could have sworn she actually *rose* off the floor. Several inches.

'Round to the station? Round to the *station*? Miss Banks will do no such thing. She's coming home with me – now. If you want to speak to her again, you can call at my house tomorrow. Is that clear?'

Must have been. Nobody said a word. Nobody even breathed. Except Sarah, who said in this little voice that she and her husband would be only too happy to put Addy up for the night if that was more convenient. Molly had turned to her.

'You're very kind,' she had said in a totally different voice. 'I can't thank you enough for all you've done, but Rose is my dearest friend and I wouldn't dream of letting anyone else take care of Addy.'

So that was settled, and Sarah had gone upstairs to collect a few things for Addy while Molly gave the cops her address and phone number, and since no one was stopping her any longer, Addy had got up from the sofa and walked around a bit and found that, bruises apart, she was OK. The working parts were still working; normal service was resumed.

They were just leaving when Molly said, 'Wait! I almost forgot. What if Rose calls from Paris?'

'She's got my cell number,' Addy had said. 'I can't call her because she's lost her phone. She told me in her letter.'

Molly thought for a moment. 'I'll leave a message for her here. If she returns later tonight she'll wonder where you are.' She wrote a note on the pad next to Rose's house phone and then stuck it up on the mantelpiece above the fire. 'She can't miss that.' Addy read the note. It said: *Rose, I've got Addy staying with me. Please get in touch with us as soon as you can. Molly.*

And then at last they were away, in Molly's car, and Addy was telling her story all over again because Molly simply couldn't believe it.

'A man dressed in an Arab woman's clothes?'

'I think it was a man. He was so strong. Gee, I don't know . . .' Addy was tired of telling the story over and over.

'Was he looking for something in the house?'

'Yeah, maybe . . . something, or someone.'

'Unbelievable.'

They hadn't far to go – Molly explained that Rose lived in Knightsbridge, while her own house was close by, in Chelsea – but the state of the snow-choked roads and the clogging traffic kept progress to a crawl.

'Here we are,' Molly said, pulling into the kerb. They had finally made it. 'Carlyle Square.'

'You're kidding.'

'What do you mean?'

Addy laughed. 'I had a boyfriend. His name was Carlyle – Bradford Carlyle.' She just loved the way life did that to you – suddenly caught hold of your sleeve and said, hey . . . remember?

'Was he nice?'

'Kind of.'

And thinking of Brad reminded her of Mike. He had her number, and he'd promised to call. Well, at least she'd have something to tell him – the best story in town.

No sooner were they in the house than Molly started acting like a mother hen.

'I'll show you to your room. I'm sure you want to go to bed.'

'It's only eight, Molly.'

'I think I'd better call my doctor.'

'I already saw a medic. He said I was fine.'

'But I'm sure you ought to rest. Addy, you've had a shock. You may think you feel all right—'

Addy grinned. 'Listen, if you really want to know how I feel, I'll tell you. I'm starving.'

'You mean – oh, God, what a fool I am. Of course, you haven't eaten. Look, I'll just show you to your room . . .'

And so Molly had taken her upstairs, and as soon as Addy was alone she had rushed to a mirror. She hadn't wanted to mention it, but the thought had been bothering her. How did she look? Because the chances were she'd be seeing Mike tomorrow or the next day, and what if she had a black eye or something worse? But the news was good . . . or reasonably so. There was the beginning of a bruise down the centre of her forehead where the edge of the door had caught her, but a little face powder would take care of that. Next she lifted her T-shirt and checked her stomach and found there was an angry red mark where the bitch/bastard had hit her. Unsightly to say the least, but then she didn't imagine they'd be getting to that sort of area right away, if ever. He *was* kind of old, after all, or she was kind of young, or something. But even if he hadn't come on to her exactly, he was interested. She could tell.

Addy washed her hands and face and then went downstairs, pausing to admire a modern chandelier that hung from the ceiling like a spray of jewels in the entrance hall, a foretaste of things to come perhaps, because it was plain just from the glimpse she stole of the sitting room that Molly had taste, even if it wasn't Rose's. It was richer, more opulent, but the rugs and paintings were great and she was warmed by the sight of the Christmas tree in the corner hung with tinsel and coloured lights. (Why hadn't Rose had a tree?) Addy was a sucker for Christmas.

She found Molly in the basement kitchen fixing supper, and as Addy came down she heard her speaking on her phone.

'Yes . . . here . . . tomorrow, then . . .'

She smiled when she saw Addy, who pointed at the phone. 'Rose?' she asked.

Molly shook her head. She switched off.

'I just wish she'd call one of us,' Addy said. 'Where the hell is she?'

'Paris, I imagine.' Molly put her head on one side as if she was expecting Addy to say something.

Addy shrugged. 'Even if Rose has lost hers, they've got phones in Paris. You'd think she'd want to check that I got in all right.'

She was starting to get a funny feeling . . . about Rose. About her not being home and not calling. Something wasn't right. She watched as Molly laid out their supper on the kitchen table: cold chicken and ham, salad, cheese, a bottle of wine. Addy was famished.

They sat down and Molly served her and then poured them each a glass of wine. She had shed her fur coat, revealing the nifty black outfit she had on underneath, a cashmere sweater with matching trousers, and for decoration a thin gold chain and pendant that picked out the colour of her hair and sort of carried it down in a single shining thread. Addy had always preferred dark hair – her own black curls suited her fine, though she wished sometimes that she'd gotten Rose's looks along with them – but she was thinking that blonde had its points, blonde was more glamorous in a way, when Molly dropped her bombshell.

She had leaned over the table, wine glass in hand, and said, 'All right, Addy. Spill it. Just who is this man?'

'Huh—?' Addy stopped chewing. 'What man?'

'Rose's man, of course. Who is he?'

And that was when Addy's jaw had hit the table. *Rose? A man? Are you sure?* And Molly admitted she'd been hoping to pump her for information.

'He lives in Paris, I think,' she said now, 'somewhere in Europe, anyway.'

'But how do you know?' Addy was dumbstruck.

'Intuition.' Molly giggled. 'No, more than that. Deduction.'

'Deduction?'

'All those trips Rose keeps making.'

'What trips?'

'You mean you don't know about them? I thought Rose told you everything.' Molly shook her head, baffled.

Addy was silent. She felt terrible. Like someone had cut a piece out of her. How could Rose do that? Not talk to her, tell her things?

Molly refilled their glasses. She'd stayed silent, too, though a couple of times she'd seemed to be on the point of speaking, but then changed her mind.

'Tell me about them,' Addy said. 'These trips.'

'They started a few months ago. Rose went to Paris twice, I remember, then to Amsterdam, and other places, too. Every few weeks she was off somewhere, visiting friends, she said.' Molly paused. 'That's what she told me, anyway. I didn't ask. It was as if . . . I don't know . . . as if she was afraid I might try and go with her.' Molly stared into her wine.

'And you never did?'

Molly shook her head.

Addy drank some of her wine. Her appetite had disappeared.

'But if she was seeing someone, why wouldn't she tell you?' *Or me.*

'I don't know.' Molly shrugged. 'Maybe I'm just imagining it.'

Addy didn't think so. It tied in with this feeling she had that something was wrong.

'Or maybe there's some reason she doesn't want to tell us, maybe there's something about the person . . . if it's a man, I mean.' Molly looked miserable.

'You mean, like he's married?'

Molly was silent.

'Something *else*?'

Molly finished her wine. 'Addy, all I know is that Rose has been acting strangely. It's not just the trips. It's something about her. I know she's not happy. You saw her in New York.'

'Yeah, but' – Addy was remembering the scene in the hotel room – 'she was still hooked on Uncle Matt, at least that's what I thought.'

'You didn't feel . . .?' Molly looked at her. 'Oh, God, I

don't know . . . you didn't think she might have been feeling guilty about something?'

'*Guilty?*'

Molly bit her lip. It was clear she didn't want to go on.

'You mean, like she'd betrayed him – Uncle Matt, I mean – with some other guy?'

'Oh, no.' Molly came to life with an angry shake of the head. 'That would be stupid. Rose was bound to meet someone eventually. No, I just wondered whether she had got involved with the wrong person. Or if she had done something – oh, Addy, I shouldn't be saying these things—' She broke off.

Addy waited. But Molly wouldn't go on. She looked wretched.

'What?' Addy urged her. 'Say it. If she had done something?'

'She was ashamed of.' Molly had turned pale.

Addy felt ill. She couldn't believe what she was hearing. Molly looked terrible too, white-faced and close to tears. What the hell were they doing, talking this way about Rose? She wanted to shout, bang the table, say it wasn't true. But she knew, she just *knew* something was wrong. Rose had never behaved this way before. She had always told Addy everything. So what had happened to make her change? Why was she keeping secrets?

And then Addy remembered.

'No, wait! She's going to tell me about it.'

'What?' Molly's face lit up.

'That's what she said in her letter to me.' Addy could remember it word for word. 'She was leaving for Paris and she'd tell me about it when we met. "Tell you all about that." It's what she wrote.'

'But that's wonderful.' Molly's face cleared in a moment. 'Why didn't you say so? Oh, God, I wish I'd kept my mouth shut. I shouldn't have said what I said.'

Addy reached over the table and took her hand, squeezed it. Molly was OK. A little over the top maybe, always coming on too strong, for Addy's taste at least. But she was Rose's friend and that was all that mattered. Together they'd sort this thing out.

She smothered a huge yawn. What a day! Suddenly she couldn't handle it any longer. She was beat. Exhausted.

Molly had spotted it. 'Bed for you,' she said firmly, making Addy smile because it reminded her of what Rose used to say to her when she was a child.

Ten minutes later she was tucked up in bed and Molly at the door was saying, 'Now if there's anything you need?' Back to being a mother hen, and Addy was shaking her head, no, and when the light went out she knew she'd be asleep in seconds.

Only she wasn't. She was still thinking about that time in New York, in Rose's hotel room, that stuff about Uncle Matt's photo and how Rose had stared at it and the line of poetry she had quoted. How did it go? Something . . . something . . . *desolate and sick of an old passion . . .* And it was true, thinking back now, the scene wasn't that easy to read. What had Rose meant exactly? Addy would have to ask her, was going to ask her just as soon as they got together, because enough of this shit, not telling people things, let's get it all out where people can see it . . .

And there was something else, some other thing that had happened between them in New York, something else Rose had said. What was it now? Addy was trying to remember, to dredge it up, and she almost had it . . . almost . . . almost . . .

TWELVE

Name: Grigor Grigorevich Klepkin. Codename: Gogol. Occupation: assassin.

Was there someone in Moscow with a sense of humour? Charon had often wondered. Either that, or a grudge. Some guy who had failed Russian Lit. back in high school and finally got his revenge?

Because other than Gogol there had also been Pushkin. *And* Tolstoy. *And* Chekhov. Killers all, if you believed their files, and although Pushkin and Tolstoy were no longer with us – both had gone to that great collective in the sky – at least the other two were still on the books. Nominally at any rate, though Charon had his doubts.

Gogol was cracking up. 'Touch me again and I'll kill you.'

Scary stuff, except the guy doing the threatening was backed up against the wall so hard you might have thought he was trying to make a hole in it. Of course, he still had his knife. But what was a knife to Charon?

'Put that thing away,' he said coldly.

Gogol rubbed his neck.

'Don't ever come near me with a knife in your hand.'

'How was I to know?' The hand with the knife waved back and forth. It wasn't threatening any longer, just making a point. (Puns yet. Charon chided himself. Really, he must try to take this seriously.) 'We had an appointment.'

'And you kept it. The knife . . .'

Gogol lowered his hand. The blade retracted with a faint click.

'In your pocket.'

Gogol obeyed.

'Report.'

It sounded great – all this military-martinet-cracking-the-whip routine – but in truth Charon was having a hard time keeping a straight face. It just wasn't his style. He much preferred the gentle approach. Walk softly and carry a big stick, in the immortal words of Teddy R, though with hands like Charon's, who needed a stick? But Gogol presented a problem. He was coming apart. The twitching cheek, the eyes that wouldn't hold still. And the fear: Charon could smell it. He wondered if he was making a mistake keeping him aboard. Surely the man was tired of life.

Mind you, he'd always known this might happen. Grigor Grigorevich Klepkin. It was years since their paths had first crossed, fortunately not fatally, since both were engaged in the same line of work, and Charon had taken the trouble to acquire a file on the Russian agent which had proved unusually enlightening. For a start there was the drinking problem – the file had much to say about that – and although Gogol had licked it, hadn't touched a drop in years by all accounts, everyone knew about alcoholics. And then there was the other thing . . . Grigor's little weakness. No, not booze, the other . . . well, every pig to his own trough, Charon had thought, but all the same it did seem to him – how should one put it – a little extreme? He had never understood why the Russians had kept him operational. A rotten apple was a rotten apple, after all.

But when opportunity had knocked and Charon realized that a prize lay waiting for the man who had the nerve to seize it, he'd discovered it was none other than this flawed fruit he would have to deal with. He remembered the setting well: a smoke-filled tavern in the Cypriot port of Limassol, the shock on Grigor's face when he realized who it was who'd just sat down at the table opposite him, bottle of *raki* in hand; the conversation that followed which had gone on late into the night.

The irony now was at the time Charon had had little hope that his companion of the evening would agree to his proposal and had a back-up plan ready should he refuse, one that would have involved an even earlier termination of Grigor Grigorevich's earthly existence. If he couldn't see reason, he would have to pay for it. There was more than one way to skin a cat. To his surprise, though, the other had agreed to join in the plan, and meeting the Russian's bleary gaze in the uncertain light of the seedy bar, Charon had read the despair in his eyes and seen him for what he was: a man at the end of his tether, one in search of a lifeline perhaps.

It was only by chance that the Russian was still breathing, still staying a step or two ahead of his pursuers. Aware of the change in their fortunes, he had reached Zurich on the same day as Charon. What they discovered there was what Charon had half suspected after his experience in Paris, and Gogol had taken it badly. Left to himself he might have self-destructed. It was Charon who had steadied him. Charon who had pointed out that the disaster was not final and planned their next moves. Charon who had given the orders.

Was giving them still.

'Report,' he said.

Gogol licked his lips. The dim light of the car park lent his cheeks an ashen tinge: a corpse in the making.

'The girl is here. I spoke to her.'

'You *what*—?'

The Russian flinched. 'I had to be sure. You don't understand – it's not easy keeping a watch on that place. The lights were on. I knew someone had arrived. I didn't know who.'

Charon was silent. He was thinking.

'What now?'

'We wait.'

'Is that all you can say?' Gogol's voice took on a whining note. 'Wait here, wait there. How much longer do you think it will be before—'

'Your people catch up with you?' Charon finished for him. 'My friend, we both have the same problem. Try to keep your nerve. Why should they know you are here in London?'

'Why should they not?'

Charon sighed. There it was again. What could you do? The man had a lousy attitude.

'Tell me,' he said. 'Out of curiosity, who do you think they'll send? Chekhov?'

Gogol nodded grimly.

Charon tried not to smile. It certainly had a ring to it. Chekhov versus Gogol. What would the coaches make of that?

'Listen to me,' he said, 'the girl is the key to this and now that you've introduced yourself, you'd better stay close to her. She will lead us in the right direction. The two of them are bound to meet, and when they do, we want to be there.'

The Russian stared at him through the darkness. He licked his lips. 'In that case we will have to dispose of her later – the girl, I mean.'

'As you say.' Charon inclined his head. 'Can I leave that to you?'

Give a dog a bone.

He lay on the bed listening to the sounds from the next room. The woman was entertaining a customer and he could hear them through the thin walls. He had seen her twice in the corridor – once yesterday, and again this evening on his return to the hotel. Blonde and heavy-breasted, she had too much flesh on her for his taste.

He thought about the girl in the mews. How she had stared at him, the look in her eyes.

What's the matter, bitch, don't you like my face?

He knew that look; he could guess what she was thinking.

The woman was saying something, murmuring, coaxing. The man grunted.

She was small and slight, the girl in the mews, hardly more than a child, and though a child would have been better, he thought about her and the way she had looked at him, and what he would do to her when he had her alone, what he was doing to her now as he shut his eyes and imagined her body between his hands, and the sound of breathing was loud in the next room and his own breathing raced along with it, and the bedsprings creaked faster and faster and the man cried out—

Gogol's body contracted in a spasm, and then slumped on the bed. The excitement drained out of him and as it evaporated the fear came flowing back; there was nothing but fear now.

He rubbed his neck. The muscles still ached from the pain of Charon's grip. But that was little compared with the torment he had suffered during those anguished moments.

He had thought it was Chekhov waiting to ambush him.

Chekhov with his hand on his neck.

Chekhov come to settle accounts.

Gogol shut his eyes. He could sense the presence of death. It was there in the room with him, lying silent beneath the bed. Death glared at him through the grimy windowpanes. It rose unseen with the smell from the clogged drain of the washbasin and mingled with the odours of sweat and stale scent that hung in the room like the musty reek of a long-sealed tomb.

The thought of his own extinction filled him with terror. But was life any better?

Pain, misery, death . . . these had been his offerings to others. The pleasures he had sought brought only despair.

Gogol rose from the bed. He went to the cupboard and took out a bottle of vodka. He had bought it two days ago. The seal was unbroken.

He put the bottle on the dresser and sat down on the bed. He looked at his reflection in the mirror.

What's the matter, bitch? Don't you like my face?

Despair was easily washed away. One drink, then another . . . one bottle, then another . . . and so it went on.

If he started now, he wouldn't stop.

Gogol stared at the bottle.

Perhaps it was better this way.

THIRTEEN

Fate. Providence. Call it what you will – Kimura was convinced that some unseen hand was guiding his steps. How else to explain the strange sequence of events that had led to his seeking refuge in the church, and to what had followed.

He had awoken before dawn, gnawed by hunger pains and conscious of an even more urgent problem that had to be dealt with.

Shoes.

Without footwear of some kind he could not venture out on the streets again. Yet if he waited in the church much longer he was bound to be discovered – and sooner rather than later, since it seemed unlikely that Christian priests kept office hours.

He could see only one solution. Wait for the priest to arrive and take *his* shoes.

But what if there were more than one?

Kimura did not doubt his ability to render harmless any number of holy men, but they would certainly report his presence to the police later on and give a description of him.

Unless he silenced them.

Traditionally, Kimura's calling left little room for scruples. Pity, if he felt it at all, was purely a private concern. But the thought of doing *that* in *this* place made him uneasy.

Returning to the vestry, he searched through the packing case of clothes again, but with no more success than before. Shoes were not among the items stored there. Next he considered tearing strips of cardboard off the case and binding them to his feet. The cardboard would soon become soaked in the snow – he realized that – and it would not be long before his feet were freezing again. But once outside he might encounter a lone pedestrian. The theft of a pair of shoes would seem bizarre, to be sure, but would hardly provoke any urgent police inquiries.

With the first grey light of dawn beginning to filter through the vestry window – and since he would need to see what he was doing when he constructed his makeshift footwear – he decided to turn on the light. There was a switch by the door and he pressed it down.

'Ha!'

A gasp of amazement escaped his lips when he saw what the sudden blaze of light had revealed. Right by his feet, lined up neatly against the wall with the toes pointing inwards, was a pair of boots.

With something close to reverence Kimura picked them up and examined them. They were made of some green rubberized material, knee-length and furnished with deeply scored soles like the treads of snow-tyres. Quickly he tried them on. Not surprisingly they were too big, but by adding another pair of socks to the three he already wore on each foot and tucking the trousers inside the boots he contrived to fill up the empty space.

Who did they belong to – the priest? Why had he left them there? Did he perhaps use them to work in the small garden at the rear of the church? Kimura had no answers to these questions. To him, the sudden appearance of the boots had an aura of mystery about it. He couldn't escape the feeling – no matter how irrational it seemed – that in some way, impossible to explain, the boots had been left there for *him*.

Although he was impatient to leave now, he spent a few more minutes preparing for his departure. First he replaced the priest's robes that had served him as bedclothes on their hangers and shut the cupboard door. His break-in would certainly be remarked, possibly reported, but he would leave nothing to indicate that he had spent the night there. Selecting a scarf and a pair of woollen gloves from the pile of clothes, he carefully folded the remaining garments and returned them to the packing case. Lastly, he collected the Arab woman's clothes and knotted them in a tight bundle for later disposal.

It was a few minutes after six by his wristwatch when he stepped out of the vestry door into the dark, snow-shrouded morning.

FOURTEEN

Addy woke to the sound of gentle knocking. She opened bleary eyes to see Molly's face peeping in.

'Sorry to wake you, my dear, but there's a detective downstairs. He wants to talk to you.'

'A detective . . . wha—?'

Oh, shit . . . that business last night . . . Addy rubbed the sleep from her eyes.

'Don't rush. I've given him a cup of tea. He's waiting in the kitchen. How do you feel?'

'All right . . . I guess.' Addy wasn't sure. She put a hand to her head and yelped. 'Jesus!'

'Is something the matter?' Molly opened the door fully and stood there, concern written all over her face.

'No, it's OK . . . just my head . . . is there a bruise?'

'I'm afraid so.' Molly winced. 'Can I get you something?'

'It's OK. I'll get dressed.'

Molly retreated, shutting the door behind her. Addy sat up, yelped again. This time it was her stomach. When she lifted the T-shirt she'd slept in, she saw the bruise there: it was a peach. Fucking Arab. She dressed quickly and after taking a minute to brush her teeth and dab a little face powder on her forehead – there was a small tub of it in the bathroom next to the soap and scent – she made her way downstairs to the basement kitchen where she could hear them talking, Molly and the cop.

'You can't be serious.' Molly was disbelieving. 'In *Harrods*, you say?'

She turned to look at Addy as she came down the stairs.

'You won't believe it.' It was plain Molly didn't. 'Tell Miss Banks what you've just told me.' She glared at the cop.

It was the younger of the two, the one who had grinned at her while his partner was having his sphincter reamed. He looked different this morning: serious.

'I'm told you haven't heard the news. The body of an Arab woman stripped of her clothes was found in Harrods this morning. The department store,' he added, in case she needed telling.

'No shit?' Addy was stunned. '*My* Arab woman?'

'We think whoever attacked you was wearing her clothes, most likely a man.'

'Jesus!' Speechless for once, she stared at him. 'You said her *body* . . . you mean he killed her?'

'It looks that way.'

'And then put on her clothes and . . . and broke into my aunt's house? *Why?*'

'We're hoping you can tell us.'

Addy just shook her head. Molly cut in.

'Haven't you upset Miss Banks enough?' she said. 'Do you have to keep on at her?'

The cop turned his head slowly to look at her. He was sitting at the kitchen table with a cup of tea in front of him, but as far as Addy could see he hadn't touched it.

'Excuse me?' he said.

'You said you needed her to sign a statement . . . well, for goodness' sake get on with it.'

Molly had moved into the attack mode Addy remembered from last night. Her voice had hardened. The cop eyed her coolly.

'I will,' he said, 'when I'm ready.' And then, in case she didn't get it, 'This is a police inquiry, Lady Kingsmill.'

'I'm well aware of it. And while we're on the subject, I'd like the name of your superior.'

'Detective Chief Superintendent Clarkson. You'll find him at West End Central. I'm sure he'll be glad to speak to you.'

The cop stared at her. Molly turned bright red.

'Just get a move on.'

Turning on her heel, she stomped up the stairs. He waited until she was out of earshot.

'Friend of yours?' he asked.

'Not exactly.' Addy grinned. She'd enjoyed the past few seconds. Theatre-in-the-raw. It was the first time she'd taken a good look at him, this young cop. He was lean and sharp-looking, with hair that was blacker than hers and olive-tinted skin that hinted at some Mediterranean blood.

'What happened to your buddy?' she asked. 'MacSomething?'

'Retired hurt. He didn't want to face her ladyship again.' He caught her eye. 'It looks like I've been landed with you.'

'I don't recall us being introduced.' Addy cocked her head on one side. 'I've watched plenty of British cop shows. Are you an inspector – a DI?'

'No, a sergeant. DS Malek. That's me.'

'What kind of name is that?'

'Lebanese. My dad came here to work in a restaurant. He married a local girl and ended up staying. Look, we ought to move on. I've typed out your statement here.' He pulled two sheets of paper from a file he had on the table in front of him. 'It's a summary of everything you told us last night. I'd like you to go through it. If there's anything you want to change or add, you can amend it.'

Addy did what he asked. There was silence while she scanned the two bits of paper.

'No, it's all here.' She looked up. 'Do I sign it now?'

'In a moment.' He'd turned serious again. 'I'd just like you to go over in your mind what happened one last time. You see, we can't think of any reason why this man – we're assuming it was a man – broke into your aunt's house. Are you sure you can't help us?'

Addy shook her head. 'I've told you everything I know.'

'As we see it there are two possibilities: either he broke into the wrong house . . .'

'Or?' Addy prompted him.

'He was looking for someone, and it wasn't you.'

'You mean my aunt.' She scowled. 'That can't be true. You don't know her. There's no way Rose would get mixed up with . . . with some crazy guy dressed up like an Arab – a killer, too.' Even as she spoke, Addy felt her heart give a lurch. The talk she'd had with Molly last night came back in a rush . . . all that shit about Rose's mysterious trips and had she met someone she didn't want to talk about, some man? 'You've got the wrong idea,' she insisted. But she wasn't so sure any longer.

He shrugged. 'Maybe, but as things stand, none of it makes sense. You do see that?'

Addy saw it all right, but that didn't make her feel any better.

'Have you had any contact with your aunt – since last night, I mean?'

Addy shook her head. 'I tried calling her phone. She told me she'd lost it when she wrote me, but I thought she might have found it before she went to Paris. No one picked up.'

'If you give me the number, we may be able to trace the phone, where it is, I mean, even if she lost it.' DS Malek's dark eyes were unreadable. Addy hesitated. Why did they need Rose's phone? Because they wanted to find out more about her, that was why.

'OK.' She wasn't entirely happy with the request, but she wrote the number down at the bottom of her statement and then signed the document in the space provided.

'You'd better put yours there, too – your mobile number. I may need to get in touch with you. And here's my card in case you want to call me.' He slid it across the table to her.

'Gee, thanks.' For a moment she wondered if he was flirting with her, then saw from his face that he wasn't. Fuck! She was turning into a basket case. First Mike, now this cop. Anyone would think she'd come to London just to get laid. 'If you find out where her phone is, will you tell me?'

Nodding, he gathered his things together and got ready to go. As Addy watched, he ran his fingers through his hair, pushing his forelock back. It had a habit of falling down over his forehead, making him look even younger. It was something she had noticed about him.

'What's your name, anyway?' She made it sound casual.

'I told you – Malek.'

'No, your first name.'

'Dave.' He smiled for the first time. 'And yours is Adelaide.'

'How'd you know that?' She snapped her fingers. 'But of course – you're a detective.' OK, so she was probably making an asshole of herself, but he was kind of cute. And just so he didn't miss the hint . . . 'My friends call me Addy.'

*   *   *

They spent the morning in a dither, she and Molly, both of them wanting to find out where Rose was, what had become of her, but not knowing how to go about it. Addy tried calling her on her cell again, but with the same result as before. There was no answer: no one picked up. As a last resort she called Rose's house phone and left a message on the answering machine. 'Rose, I really need to talk to you. I'm staying with Molly. Please call.' That was in case she got back from Paris and didn't notice Molly's message on the mantelpiece.

Molly made some calls of her own – to friends she and Rose shared, she said, people who might have news of Addy's aunt, but none did.

'They haven't seen or heard of her, not for more than a fortnight.'

Earlier, Addy had wanted to go back to Rose's house to collect the rest of her stuff and asked DS Malek before he left if that was OK.

'Not right now,' he had told her. 'Our forensic lads are going over it. Maybe later.'

'Is it worth the trouble?' Addy was surprised. 'He was only there for a few minutes, the guy who broke in, and I don't remember him touching anything.'

'Except you.' He had caught her eye and grinned. 'But that was yesterday and you're right, it didn't seem such a big deal. But now it's part of a murder inquiry, that's the difference.'

'You're sure he's the one who killed that woman in Harrods?' They had gone upstairs to the front door where Molly had joined them. She was listening.

'Hard to imagine it was anyone else.' Malek shrugged. 'It looks like he dragged her behind a screen in the beds department and did her there. Don't ask me why. She was with some other Arab women, but somehow they got separated. We've put out a call for witnesses.' He saw the look on Addy's face. 'I know, like I said before, none of it makes sense.'

He'd promised to call her when the forensic team was through so that she could return to the house to collect her things. Then, with a brisk nod to Molly, he'd gone on his way.

'I'm not sure I cared for that young man.' Molly's nose was still well out of joint (as the Brits liked to put it).

'He was OK.' Addy was more forgiving. 'Just doing his job.'

'Perhaps I was a bit short with him.' Molly bit her lip. 'It's this whole business, Addy. It's so upsetting. What's going on? Where's Rose?'

Addy couldn't have put it better herself.

Just then her phone rang and when she answered – hoping it was Rose – she found herself instead talking to Mike Ryker.

'Hey, there?' he said. 'How are you doing?'

'You wouldn't believe it if I told you.' Addy shot a glance at Molly, whose eyebrows had gone up. She shook her head. *No, it's not Rose.*

'Trouble?' He sounded genuinely concerned.

'Yeah . . . kind of . . .'

'Do you want to meet? How about dinner tonight?'

'Could we make it a drink? Somewhere in Chelsea? I'll explain when I see you.'

Molly was listening, her brow grooved in a faint frown.

'Why not? I'll think of a place and get back to you.'

He hung up. Addy took a deep breath.

'It's a guy I met on the plane,' she explained. 'I kind of liked him. He wants to meet up.'

'Good for you.' Molly beamed her approval. 'But stay close. In case we hear from Rose, I mean.'

'That's why I suggested somewhere nearby,' Addy replied.

She was pleased Mike had come through so quickly. She'd half wondered if he'd even bother to call. Now if only Rose were here . . .

FIFTEEN

'Think of it, Ryker. The glory that was Greece, the grandeur that was Rome, the wonder of the Renaissance, and then the beginning of mankind's long struggle upwards by way of the Enlightenment and the near miraculous discoveries that science and technology have brought to the world. And where has it taken us – tell me that – what has it led to?'

Bela Horvath paused as though as he actually expected a reply, though Ryker could see he didn't. This was just his schtick.

'The Age of Greed.'

Bela spread his hands. 'I'm sure you're familiar with that statistic they keep quoting – the one about half the world's wealth being in the hands of one per cent of the world's population. If you have any doubts, look around you. We sit among them – the filthy rich.'

That much at least was true. You couldn't mistake them, Ryker thought, the older men in their five-thousand-dollar-plus suits, hair barbered to a millimetre, the wink of gold in their cuff links when they lifted a hand to summon a waiter; the younger ones more carelessly attired, shirts open at the front, the better to display the gold chains resting on their tanned chests – hey, a good tan in winter was a sure sign of moola – and the young women who leaned forward to catch every word they said, eyes avid. They wanted a piece of it, too: the money. Not that the restaurant didn't reek of it: snowy linen, silver cutlery, crystal glass, soft-footed waiters. They spoke a language all their own, and it wasn't tuned to peasant ears.

Bela, though – the guy on his own was worth the price of admission. A legend in his lifetime – or so Ryker had been told – Hungarian by origin, but American now (albeit of an exotic strain) thanks to the twenty years he'd put in with the CIA before he'd joined Safe Solutions, which might or might not be the biggest security company in the world – Ryker wasn't sure – but was certainly the most hated, being referred to openly by its competitors, and with no intent at humour, as the SS. Bela was their man in London, the guy who was going to put him in the picture, which was just as well since Ryker still didn't know what the fuck he was doing there.

His host, meantime, was studying the menu. It had been brought to the table by one of the soft-footed crew who was standing there, head bowed in a suitably servile pose.

'I'll start with the gravlax, but *a la Danoise.*'

'*A la?*' The waiter looked anguished.

'With a dill and mustard sauce, tell the kitchen, and a spoonful or two of caviar. What about you, Ryker?'

'Soup, I guess.'

'Soup?' Bela looked as though he'd been shot between the eyes. 'If you must.' He sighed. 'I see you have sea bass on the menu.' He was talking to the waiter again.

'It's one of Monsieur Antoine's specialities, sir.'

'What about you, Ryker? Will you join me?'

'Can they manage a steak and fries?'

Ryker had said that just so he could see the rabbit-in-the-headlights look on his host's face, and it appeared on cue. Not that Bela needed any help in the looking weird department. His black hair, which had to be dyed, was plastered down flat on his scalp like an old movie idol's and his dark eyes never blinked. Or so it seemed to Ryker, who knew as well as the next guy that everyone's eyes blinked, but Bela Horvath still made him think of a lizard on a rock: patient, motionless, tongue ready to zap any passing fly.

'Ah, money . . .' He wasn't done yet. 'How it soothes the savage breast. What balm it brings to troubled souls. But as always there's a catch. Do you know what it is?'

Ryker didn't.

'There's never enough of it. That man sitting directly behind me – the baldy with what looks like a severe bowel blockage – has substantial holdings in two of the biggest pharmaceutical companies on earth. According to *Forbes* magazine he's worth eleven billion dollars and this offends him, because he claims it's closer to twelve. Now any normal man should be more than content with eleven billion dollars. I mean, what can you do with twelve billion dollars that you can't do with eleven? But the rich are not normal. As a famous writer once observed, they are different from you and me. And of course they are not born this way. They acquire the disease, or should I say addiction, for which there is no known cure. Once they have made their pile, all they can think of is making more. And as I said, it's never enough. Ah, my gravlax . . .'

He paused for a moment to study the artfully arranged confection on his plate.

'So think money while I order our wine, Ryker, colossal amounts of it. And then turn your mind to things Russian.'

'*The Russians?*' Ryker blinked. He hadn't seen this coming.

Bela didn't respond at once. He was busy, talking in low tones to the sommelier who had sidled up to their table, wine list in hand.

'Those champions of the proletariat.' Satisfied, he turned back to his guest. 'The great toilers. They're the newest addition to the ranks of the stinking rich, and my goodness how quickly they've taken to it. Since Vladimir and his merry men got to work back in the nineties, they've managed between them to extract more than three hundred and fifty billion dollars from the economy and tuck it away in safe investments in the West. Their proclaimed justification for doing so was to protect Mother Russia's wealth from predatory hands following the collapse of Communism and the ensuing chaos under the late but not greatly lamented Boris Yeltsin. However, since all the money went into accounts or investments controlled by them, one can draw one's own conclusions; all, that is, except for a sizeable portion that ended up in the hands of local hoods. You may not believe it, but quite a number of these recently reformed comrades didn't know how to handle a cheque book, let alone a credit card, and were forced to turn for help to their home-grown mafia, who had no such problems and were well situated to render assistance, at a price of course, as a result of which, as we all know, Russia is now to all intents and purposes a criminal state. This gravlax is excellent by the way.' Bela chewed thoughtfully. 'How's the soup?'

'Fine. Go on.' They were still nowhere near the point as far as Ryker could tell, if there was any point to this Hungarian rhapsody.

'Now, as you may have heard, much of the loot went into real estate here and elsewhere. But it wasn't long before the ugly words "money laundering" were heard and since these shrewd *muhziks* knew it would not be wise to put all their eggs in one basket, a fair proportion of the pillaged funds went into shell companies scattered about the world. Of course, to carry this off they needed the help of bankers here in the West, people who knew how to bury the money in offshore accounts, using their own private network of lawyers and accountants who would lend their signatures to the paperwork involved for a fee, thus hiding the real owners' names. It's one of these gentlemen, a Cypriot by the name of Nico Stefanidis, who is the reason behind your visit to London. The story I'm about to tell you begins with him.'

Hooray! But couldn't they just cut to the chase? Ryker shifted restlessly on his over-padded chair. He had to wait while Bela sipped his wine and murmured his appreciation of it.

'Exquisite. Drink your soup, Ryker. Don't let it get cold.' He paused to collect his thoughts. 'Stefanidis, then . . . Nico of that name: he managed a small family bank in Limassol, one that barely showed up on the radar and was attractive to the Russians for that reason, but even more so when they realized what a jewel they had unearthed in his person. The man was a genius. I'm not exaggerating. One day they should put up a statue to him. We all know about conjurers who pull rabbits from hats. Nico was the man who knew how to put the bunnies back in the headgear without anyone guessing how the trick was done. The Russians sent him their money, great wads of it, and Nico did his magic, dispatching it to the four corners of the earth, from Panama to Paradise Island and beyond, leaving no trace behind. He didn't run it through his bank, you see: he created something different, parallel, a ghost bank if you will – the Russians could never figure out how he did it and neither can we – but it was as though the money vanished for a while and then reappeared where it was supposed to be in some far-off account, under a false name, but with a password attached to it that was known only to the person to whom it belonged. Magic, as I say, and the Ivans loved him for it. They began sending him more and more of their cash.'

Bela paused. Ryker sensed they were getting close to it now: the moment of truth.

'There was a problem, though.' His host sighed. 'What the Russians didn't know was that Nico's personal life had turned to shit. His wife had announced she was leaving him. She was joining her lover in Rio. What lover? It was the first Nico had heard of it. Oh, and taking their three kids with her.' Bela shook his head. 'The poor guy – he'd just seen his world blown to bits. Someone was going to pay for it. And as fate would have it, just then he happened to be holding a bigger pile of money than usual, sent to him by his Russian chums for discreet disposal: perhaps he'd been otherwise occupied worrying about his private life, but it had built up to a little over a billion bucks.'

'Come again!' Ryker's jaw dropped.

'Didn't I say . . . didn't I tell you? Think *billions*. These guys had been siphoning oil and gas money out so fast it was a wonder they didn't choke on it. Nico was going through the usual motions getting ready to send it off to its final destinations when he had what they call an epiphany. Either that or it was a message from on high.' Bela shrugged. 'Maybe God spoke to him and said, "Nico, don't be a schmuck. Think of yourself for once."'

'You're not telling me he stole it – the billion?' Ryker couldn't credit what he was hearing.

Bela shook his head. 'He wasn't that crazy. No, he wanted it all to be straightforward and above board. He was a banker, for Christ's sake, not a thief. He wanted a deal, and he'd come up with what seemed to him to be a perfectly reasonable proposal. He would put the details – where the money was going, the names of the accounts with new passwords he'd created, everything in fact that was needed – on to a memory stick and then tell the Russians it was there waiting for them. All he wanted in return was a measly ten million dollars. Only one per cent, no more – it probably seemed quite fair to him given the miracles he'd performed on their behalf, something they could easily afford. Once they agreed to pay up, the memory stick was theirs. Otherwise, they could whistle for their money.'

Bela started to shake in his chair. He couldn't contain his mirth.

'Just think of it, Ryker, try and picture the scene. Here they were, these big shots – *siloviki* they call them in Moscow, heavy hitters, not to mention their mobster pals with their fucking tattoos – and all of them having to take it up the ass. You'd need a heart of stone not to split your sides laughing. They say Vlad the Impaler was one of those who got burned.'

'Putin?'

'It's what I heard. I can't swear to it. But Nico, God bless him, had made a fatal mistake.' Bela's sigh was regretful. 'They'd paid him well in the past for his services, and if he'd asked nicely they might even have given him the ten mill. But Nico had had changed the rules, he'd gone and threatened them, and these were guys you do not fuck with. One of them, the biggest loser by report, just happened to be the current head of the FSB, the Foreign Intelligence Service – that's the old KGB to you and me – a mean son of a bitch called Alexei Gurov. He was charged with the job of getting their money back. Sure, he told Nico, they'd pay him the ten mill, but given that the guy he sent to Cyprus to close the deal was a hitman with a well-deserved reputation as a torturer, a sicko by the name of Grigor Klepkin, it was dollars to dimes poor old Nico wasn't long for this world, which proved to be the case, though not quite in the manner Gurov had anticipated. When Klepkin reached Cyprus, he called back to say that someone had got there ahead of him. Nico's body had been found floating in Limassol harbour and some very unpleasant things had been done to it.'

'And the memory stick?'

'Was nowhere to be found.' Bela shrugged. 'All the Russians had left to hold on to were their dicks, and once they'd got over the shock, a swarm of FSB agents descended on Limassol and started combing through every inch of Nico's business dealings, every dot and comma, looking for a clue as to where the money might have gone, but it was no use. They couldn't find a kopeck. Nico had outsmarted them. What made it worse was they couldn't figure out who the guilty party was either: who would have had the balls to pull a stunt like that.'

Bela sighed.

'They kept on looking, of course – for both the money and whoever it was who had ripped them off, but six months went by without them getting any closer to cracking the mystery. Then they caught a break: an anonymous tip-off in the form of a typed message that was slipped into the letterbox of the Aeroflot office in Amsterdam and which you can bet very soon found its way to Moscow. It didn't mince words either, this *billet-doux:* it told them straight out who had pulled the heist and where at least one of them could be found.'

'*One* of them?' Ryker seized on the word.

'It was a two-man job,' Bela explained. 'But what really burned the Russians was the discovery that one of the pair was their own Grigor Klepkin. He was the one who'd done the business on Nico, persuaded him to part with the stick – I told you he was a torturer – but then he'd stepped back and acted the innocent, joining in the hunt for the money, never giving his comrades a hint that he was in on the scam. He happened to be on assignment in Istanbul when the tip-off reached Moscow and it wasn't long before he received an order to return home ASAP.'

Bela chuckled.

'Maybe Gurov was just too mad to think straight. But he should have remembered his history. Ever since the days of Stalin and the Cheka, every Russian agent has had it branded on his soul that an urgent summons to return to Moscow without explanation almost invariably meant curtains. It was as good as a death sentence, and Klepkin didn't hesitate. He dropped out of sight the same day, and hasn't been seen or heard of since. Until yesterday, that is, when he was spotted here in London. One of my people saw him boarding a Tube train at Blackfriars.'

'Jesus!' Ryker was struck dumb. 'But wait a minute – you said there were two of them.'

Bela nodded. Emptying his glass of wine, he signalled to the sommelier.

'And now we come to the painful part,' he said. 'I regret to have to tell you the gentleman in question is one of ours. *Was*, I should say, we got rid of him a year ago, but that meant nothing to the Russians. As far as they were concerned this was down to us, and Safe Solutions had better come up with an answer.'

'So who is he?'

'You haven't been with us long, have you, Ryker?' Bela brushed an imaginary piece of lint off his cuff. 'That's one of the reasons you were chosen for this job. Your face is new. Still, word spreads. Have you ever heard the name Charon? . . . One moment . . .'

Bela Horvath raised a finger. On the point of firing off his next question, Ryker was caught with his mouth open. The sommelier had materialized from nowhere like ectoplasm and was standing by their table.

'The Chateau Margaux you recommended was excellent.' Bela addressed the man. 'We'll have another bottle. But this time we'll go for the Premier Grand Cru. Why shouldn't we spoil ourselves? White wine with fish is a myth in case you were wondering.' This was for Ryker's benefit. 'Red goes just as well with it.' He peered at his guest. 'Is something troubling you, my friend?'

'Charon . . .' Ryker finally got the word he was choking on out. 'Is that a *name*?'

Bela smiled. 'I see the Classics passed you by. Charon was the ferryman of Greek mythology. He carried the bodies of the dead across the River Styx to the underworld, but only for a fee, hence the practice employed by the ancients of slipping a coin between the lips of their nearest and dearest once they'd expired. Our Charon likes to leave his mark in the same manner, from which you might well deduce he's yet another sick puppy, but that's by the by.'

'What's his real name?'

'He was born James Meredith Hatton in the city of Pittsburgh some forty or more years ago, or so he asserts, but how can we be sure? He's a man of many aliases, many passports – some we know about, some we don't – and I wouldn't even hazard a guess as to what he might be calling himself now. Charon was the code name he chose when he worked for the CIA years ago and I dare say he still uses it. It's how I think of him.'

'And he's the one who stole the memory stick?'

'With Klepkin's help, as I said, but Charon was the brains behind the scheme, and the Russians knew it. The man had a reputation. Nico's little scam was a poorly kept secret. Word of it soon spread – it was just too good a story – and it couldn't have been long before Charon got wind of it and saw there were rich pickings to be had. Don't ask me how he talked his partner in crime into the heist, but if Klepkin had refused to go along with it I've a feeling he wouldn't have left Cyprus alive. Charon was going to get his hands on that memory stick no matter what. So you can imagine how pleased Gurov was to think he would at least get his hands on *him*. The tip-off the Russians received told them where Charon would be on a certain day – this was only a fortnight ago – it was an apartment in Paris. They set a trap for him.'

'And?'

'Ah, there you are!'

The sommelier was back. Bela went through the rite of sniffing, tasting and then swirling the ruby liquid around his mouth before giving his approval for their glasses to be filled. Ryker kept his eyes shut. He was counting up to ten.

'Where were we? Ah, yes, the rendezvous in Paris.' Bela's dark eyes shone. 'Now you're probably wondering where the memory stick had been all this time. The answer as far as we know was in a safe deposit box in a bank in Zurich. Charon apparently felt it was the best place to leave it until the hunt for whoever had stolen it had died down. But he was expecting to have it delivered to him in Paris.'

'So he turned up, did he?'

'As promised, but in his own inimitable fashion – which is to say not as expected – and the upshot was the Russians lost two of their operatives, a man and a woman, and never even caught sight of their target. Now they were seriously pissed, and we knew we had to do something – and fast.'

'But why? You told me we'd fired him. How was it our responsibility?'

Though it hardly needed smoothing, Bela ran a hand over his hair. 'As I remarked, you're new to the firm, Ryker, and perhaps they failed to tell you when you joined that we're not simply in the security business. Our brief, if I can put it this way, is a little wider than that. We call ourselves Safe Solutions, but our brochure doesn't mention the other benefits we offer carefully vetted clients. "Extreme solutions", I would call them, and the Russians have been among our most loyal customers in that respect. After all, they couldn't go on dropping spoonfuls of polonium into the mouths of anyone who rubbed them the wrong way or decorating their doorknobs with a dose of nerve agent. Think of the scandal. Outsourcing – that was the answer, and Safe Solutions were there, ready to offer help when it was needed. And don't look so shocked. I've seen your record. Unless I'm mistaken you've been involved in black ops before.'

Ryker shrugged.

'The Russians were among our best customers, as I say, and best paymasters, too, and now they are threatening to pull the rug from under our feet if we don't help sort out this problem for them. Reputation is all in this game, Ryker. Lose that, and very soon you'll find yourself sitting in a house of cards. Word spreads quickly, and to make matters worse before this all kicked off, we lost another prime client in Asia, and the same person was responsible in both cases.'

'You mean this guy Charon?'

'The truth is the man was proving worse than the plague. We thought we were done with him after he was fired. We thought he'd disappeared for good and all, but the fucker always did have something up his sleeve and sure enough he's come back from the dead as it were to stick it to us.'

Spittle had appeared on Bela's lips. He wiped it off carefully with his napkin. Ryker reflected on what he'd heard.

'So you want me to waste him?'

'Christ, no!' His host exploded. 'Put that thought from your mind. The Russians don't want him dead, not yet. They want their money back first, and they'll take him apart one finger at a time and then move on to his other body parts if they have to; the same goes for Klepkin. Finding him is Moscow's business: Charon is ours. We've reason to believe he's also in London, and though it's unlikely you'll come across him, if you should happen to, just call it in.'

While he was speaking he had reached into his pocket and pulled out a photograph.

'Take a good look,' he said, sliding the print across the table to Ryker. 'Then give it back to me.'

Ryker studied the photo. 'Not a bad-looking guy, but no special features I see. He could be anyone.'

'That's our Charon, a *tabula rasa,* and as if that weren't enough he also has a gift for altering his appearance.' Bela reclaimed the photograph and put it back in his pocket. 'I've a crew waiting here ready to take him if and when he shows his face. I want to wrap him up like a Christmas turkey and hand him to the Russians. We could do with a feather in our caps right now.'

Bela sat back with a sigh. He needed a breather. The baldy with the bowel problem was studying his check, Ryker noticed. Whatever he saw there wasn't making him any happier.

'So what am I doing here?' he asked.

'Your job, nothing more.' Bela roused himself. 'I know you haven't been fully briefed. I'll give you the full picture now. But remember, you're to do exactly what I say – don't step outside the parameters you've been given. Don't try to be a hero: that could prove fatal.'

He studied the other man's expression.

'You're not happy, are you? Look, Ryker, I know you're a tough guy. I've read your file: Marine Recon, two Silver Stars, I'm impressed. But you're in a different sort of game now, one you're not familiar with. These two guys we've been talking about, they're killers. Keep clear of them – Charon in particular. I've known the man for years – he's a charmer, and about as trustworthy as a rattlesnake. Before you can count to three, he'll have you eating out of his hand. But be warned: he's lethal. You never know when he'll strike.'

He glanced up in time to see a pair of waiters heading towards their table, each carrying a plate. They deposited the platters in front of the men, removing the gleaming silver lids covering the food with a theatrical flourish. Bela acknowledged the performance with a wave of his hand.

'And now, for heaven's sake, relax, Ryker.' His smile was benign. 'We must enjoy the good things in life while we can. Eat, drink and be merry – isn't that what the philosophers say?'

'So I've heard.'

Ryker wondered how his host had come by the story he'd just related. Was it down to his old CIA ties? What bothered him more, though, was the suspicion that he'd just been played.

'For tomorrow, we die.'

SIXTEEN

'*S uzume . . .*'

Kimura breathed the name. It meant 'sparrow' in his language and just for a moment she seemed close to him. He could sense her presence in the quiet of the empty restaurant and imagined he could hear her soft voice.

'*Beloved . . .*'

It was the word she had whispered in his ear when they made love, a miracle in itself, not only that such a word could be spoken to *him*, but that he could be loved by anyone, and particularly one such as she.

What had brought her back was the rich broth he was sipping, a spoonful at a time. It was the first proper meal he had eaten in days and the familiar flavours had carried with them a rush of memories, some sweet, some bitter beyond bearing.

He had come upon the restaurant by chance. Since quitting the church before daybreak, his wandering steps had taken him across a wide park into another area of the city, one less elegant and therefore less peopled by the rich, of a kind he was seeking where he might find a place to hide . . . and wait. He had paused twice: the first time at a bank where he had changed the different currencies he was carrying into sterling. Along with his book of maps – his *London A–Z* – his wallet was the only thing he had salvaged from the garments he had left behind after stripping the Arab woman of her clothes. His second stop had been at a shoe store where he had bought a pair of trainers to replace the ones he had been forced to abandon. Although the boots he had come across in the church had been a godsend at the time, he had soon found them clumsy, a weight on his feet, and was glad to be wearing proper footwear again.

Although the day had been long and for a time fruitless, it had brought him some encouragement at least. One threat to the goal he had set himself had been removed. Earlier that afternoon his eye had been caught by a headline as he walked by a newsagent's shop: *Harrods Murder: Japanese Held*. According to the story in the paper – which he had slowly worked his way through, puzzled by many of the words, but finally making sense of the whole – the police had received reports from several witnesses that shortly before the body of a woman was discovered in the furniture department, a number of Japanese had been observed charging through the crowded store apparently in pursuit of another man. Acting on 'information received', they had subsequently arrested four men staying in a rented Air BnB flat in a district called Clapham. Although there was no indication that they had been directly linked to the Harrods crime, Kimura was relieved to read that they had been found to have entered the country illegally using 'false travel documents' and would appear before a magistrate the following morning. It was clear that Leather-coat and his crew would be out of action for some time and even if no further charges were brought against them, they would very likely be deported.

He'd been surprised, though, to find there was no mention of his own violent act. The house he had broken into was only a few minutes' walk from the store. Compelled to think of an explanation, in the end he had reasoned that if the police had not made it public, it wasn't because they hadn't connected it to the discovery of the body – Kimura was sure they had – but rather because they could make no sense of it.

As for the house itself, owing to his rash act he would have to keep clear of it, at least for a while. Yet it remained his only lead. Word of its link to the woman he sought had been passed to him by a former colleague, a man he had once counted as a friend, but one who, according to the iron rules they both lived by, should have killed him when he had the chance. Instead he had provided Kimura with this vital piece of information, along with a chilling message.

'Move quickly, brother. If I can find you, so can others, and they are close.'

In flight from that moment on, he had crossed two continents, arriving in London, a city he had never visited before

– and never thought to see – only to find that his pursuers were on his heels.

But with the house and its presumed occupant his only means of achieving his end, he would have to keep a watch on it somehow. Surely the woman would come hurrying back from wherever she was once she heard that her home had been broken into. It was the natural thing to do. But if she failed to appear, there was still the young girl to consider as a last resort. Who was she? Why was she there? These were questions to which he would have to find answers.

Luckily the police had no worthwhile description of him to circulate. The Arab woman's clothes he had worn had covered him from head to foot. Neither the girl nor the man who had arrived later had seen his face. Depending on what the police learned from the men they had arrested, and it would not be much, they might not even know that he, too, was Japanese. But he couldn't take that chance and he resolved that once he had found a place to stay he would keep out of sight as much as possible during daylight hours.

However, before he could put this resolve into action – he was still tramping the snow-choked streets, narrower and more crowded in this less fashionable area – his eye had been caught by a word in Japanese script and above it the same word in Western lettering: *Rakuzen*. It meant the joy of dining and although it was only a little after five o'clock and the place empty, he had gone into the restaurant and found a middle-aged woman of his race busy wiping the tables and laying them with chopsticks and cutlery. She had begun to explain in Japanese that they would not be open for another hour at least, but Kimura had cut her short. Prefacing his words with a respectful bow, he had appealed to her for help.

Chance had brought him to London – a city he had never visited before – and for the moment he was stranded there and in sore need of a place to stay for a few days; a room would suffice. Could she perhaps advise him on how to proceed? It was not a question of money: he could pay his way. But given that he had no luggage and had temporarily mislaid his passport, a hotel was out of the question.

Whether she had believed him, or whether she had simply

been touched by the spectacle he presented – the clothes he wore, rough trousers, a stained sweater and a coat at least a size too big for him with missing buttons, looked like what they were, cast-offs – he was nevertheless a fellow countryman and she had asked him to wait while she consulted her husband. Presently an older man wearing an apron and wiping his hands on a dish rag had appeared from the kitchen. Polite greetings had been exchanged between the two, after which Kimura had repeated his request and the man had replied that a cousin of his who lived nearby had a room in his house that he occasionally rented out and might well be willing to offer this unexpected visitor a bed. He would enquire.

Unused to meeting with such consideration – the world he lived in had never been other than harsh and pitiless – Kimura had wondered at the couple's behaviour, which seemed to come only from a desire to help. They had asked no questions; they had simply sought to ease whatever pain it was that weighed on him that they either saw in his eyes or simply guessed at.

And yet the sensation was not entirely new to him. He had known it once before, that other world where love ruled and kindness dwelt, but for such a brief time that now it seemed more like a dream; and like a dream for ever lost.

At the woman's urging he had sat down at a table in a corner of the restaurant, and presently the man had returned with the news that his cousin had accepted Kimura as a tenant, and also with a bowl of the broth that Kimura was drinking now. He was preparing a beef teriyaki for him, the man had explained, but it would take a little while, and in the meantime perhaps their visitor would like to taste the soup in which it would be cooked.

What he could not have known, this caring man, was the effect his simple act of generosity had on the tattered figure sitting slumped at the table – overcome by exhaustion, Kimura was struggling to stay awake – who had straightened at his approach and then bowed his head in thanks as the bowl was placed in front of him. At the first sip of the broth – *dashi* it was called in his language – Kimura was flung back into the past (it happened in a moment) to a room steeped in the same rich aroma that filled his nostrils now, and to the sight of a young woman bent over the small stove where a saucepan stood, her smooth brow grooved in concentration, a spoon in her hand, as she slowly brought the savoury liquid in the pan to perfection.

Early on in their time together – so fleeting it was that just the thought of it now pierced him like a *tanto* blade – she had realized that he wanted to know how she created this miraculous broth that transformed each evening meal they shared into an experience that lingered at the back of the throat like a gift from the gods and was the prelude to what followed when they lay down together on the narrow bed and he held her slender body in his arms. And so she had showed him: first *kombu*, kelp seaweed, must be added to the water that was heating, then *katsuobishi*, shavings of fermented tuna. This was the basis of the dish, she explained, though other things could be put in to further enrich the taste – fermented soy beans, called *miso*, and *koji*, which he had learned was a fungus, and *mirin*, too, a rice wine milder than *sake*.

He had listened, fascinated as much by the solemn look in her deep brown eyes as by what she was telling him, as she explained that this was a taste superior to all others, not like the flavours common to all cooking, not salty or sugary, not bitter or sour: it was the best and most delicious of all tastes. And it had a name, a name that for Kimura during the short months they were together had come to embrace the whole of the small world they had made for themselves and which bore all the sweetness of life he had never known before, a name that fell from her lips like a blessing.

Umami.

SEVENTEEN

Addy checked the guest bedroom. Had she got everything she wanted? She'd never properly unpacked at Rose's house, just taken a few things she would need out of her bags when she had left to stay with Molly. Both were lying open on the bed the way she had left them and she wondered if the cops had looked through them when they were here, but thought not. There'd have been no point.

Dave Malek had called her on her mobile just before she had left Molly's house to meet Mike Ryker for a drink. He had told her the forensic squad was through with the house and she could go back any time to collect her stuff.

'Did they find anything?' she had asked. When she got there she had discovered traces of their presence on the wooden banisters going upstairs – a faint dusting of fingerprint powder.

'Not that I know of,' Malek had told her. 'But we'll need a set of your prints for matching purposes. I'll come round tomorrow and get them. Or you could look in at Chelsea nick. It's not far from where you're staying. Just mention my name. They'll do it there.'

Chelsea nick! Matching prints! Addy had felt like she was in the middle of one of those British cop shows she'd watched, and she enjoyed the little prickle of pleasure it gave her; she just wished it wasn't anything to do with Rose's continuing absence. There'd been no word from her all day.

'I just don't understand why she hasn't called,' she'd told Molly. 'Even if she's still stuck in Paris she must know I've arrived by now.'

The pub Mike had chosen for them to meet was close by, off King's Road, the same as Carlyle Square, but further up the street near Sloane Square.

'It's only a ten-minute walk, but I'll drop you there if you want.' Molly had been like that all day, anxious to help, but Addy had declined the offer with thanks.

'It's stopped snowing,' she said. According to the radio that they had listened to over breakfast the worst of it was over, though there would still be what the forecaster called occasional 'flurries'. 'I could do with the exercise.'

What she hadn't said – and felt guilty over – was that she didn't want Molly deciding once they got there that she might just as well stay and have a drink with them. Addy wanted Mike to herself.

Walking up the snow-covered sidewalk towards Sloane Square, looking for the street where the pub he'd suggested was located, she'd wondered how the evening would play out. Would he make a pass at her? And did it matter that he was so much older. What did a guy like that see in a girl her age? Apart from the obvious, of course, but maybe that was it – the obvious – and why did she have to complicate everything by picking it to pieces? Come to think of it, couldn't she have worn something a little sexier under her coat than jeans and a sweater? If life was some sort of race, then she was falling behind. Addy was convinced of it. Two! Wasn't it about time she hit three? And didn't they say you could learn a lot from older guys?

It hadn't taken long for her to get the answers to these questions and she was still kicking herself as a result: her and her big mouth. Mike had been waiting when she got to the pub, and it gave her a lift to see him sitting at a table in the corner checking his phone. There was something about him – poise, she decided. He was one cool commodity broker, but tough looking at the same time. You could see it in his face, and that scar on his temple only served to underline the impression. It didn't do any harm either that he was also the best-looking guy in the room, or so Addy told herself as she made her way through the noisy crowd of drinkers to where he was sitting. He had surprised her by getting to his feet. Men didn't do that any more.

'Addy . . .' He pulled up a chair for her.

So how had she handled things? Flirted a little maybe? Given him the kind of come-on that suggested she was just waiting for him to make his move? She was an actor after all. She knew how to play a part. Had she handed him his cue?

Not even close: the fact was she'd blown it. Dived straight
in and given him a breathtaking account of last night; told
him about the man she'd thought was a woman breaking
into her aunt's house and smacking her around, dragging her
up the stairs, the cops, everything.

And, of course, he'd reacted. Who wouldn't?

'Were you hurt? Have they caught the man? Addy, this is
terrible.'

He'd been the very soul of concern. You would have
thought he was her big brother. No, worse than that: her
fucking *father.* He'd told her he had a daughter her age in
her sophomore year at Bryn Mawr, and if anything like what
had happened to Addy had happened to *her* . . . And then
he'd patted her hand.

Actually *patted* it.

And he hadn't quit there. Before she could stop him he'd
begun telling her *his* problems . . . the ex-wife he was still
scrapping with who tried to keep them apart, him and his
daughter. Would Addy like to see a picture of this lovely child
of his? Would she hell.

'Look, we'll have to make this brief, Mike. I've got to
go and pick up my bags from my aunt's house. I'm staying
with this friend until Rose gets back from Paris, or wherever
she is.'

It had been a ploy to get away from him, to put an end to
the evening. She hadn't really intended going back to Rutland
Mews, not till tomorrow, and she wasn't planning to collect
her bags, just get a few things out of them that she needed.
She was sure Rose would turn up sooner or later and she could
move back in with her. But Mike wouldn't hear of it. There
was no way he was going to let her go on her own, especially
after what had happened to her, and nothing Addy could say
would make him change his mind. Besides, he had a car – it
belonged to the old roommate who had lent him his flat. He
could drive her there and then drop her off later at her friend's
place. Having dug herself into a hole, Addy had been forced
to go along with the plan and as soon as they'd finished their
drinks they had set off. She'd wondered if he'd be able to find
his way to Rutland Mews – whether he knew his way round

the city – but it turned out he had satnav in his car and it wasn't long before they were sitting in the car outside the mews entrance with the engine running.

'Look, I'll just slip down to the house and get what I need,' Addy said. 'I won't be long.'

'There's no hurry.' Mike had been looking for a parking space. 'I'll find somewhere.' It was clear he didn't want to leave her on her own.

'No, really.' Addy had settled the question by opening the door and climbing out. 'I'll only be a few minutes.'

Leaving him there, she had hurried down the snow-covered cobbles, noting when she got to Rose's house that the lights were out at Sarah and Bill's house opposite. She remembered what Sarah had told her – they'd be away for Christmas. Unlocking Rose's door, she had gone straight upstairs to the guest room where her stuff was and, having emptied one of her two bags, she put the stuff she wanted in it, leaving the rest to lie there on the bed.

Ready to leave now, she paused at the head of the stairs. Better check on Rose's room first. The cops would have been in there too. Dumping her bag, she went to the door and peered in, switching on the light as she did so. Nothing had changed: nothing was disturbed. The photograph of the two of them still stood where Rose had left it on the bedside table. She was reaching for the light switch when her cell phone rang and she plucked it out of her pocket.

'Hullo?'

'Addy?'

'*Rose!*' She couldn't believe it. 'Is that you?'

'Who did you think it was?' Rose's laugh didn't sound right. 'I just wanted to hear your voice, Bear. Tell me what you're doing for Christmas. I may have a surprise for you.'

'*Where* are you?' It was all Addy could think of to say. She just knew something was wrong.

'Here in London . . . where else?' Now Rose was trying to sound casual, but Addy wasn't fooled. 'We've had all this snow. How are things in New York?'

'*New York!* Rose, I'm standing in your goddam bedroom. You invited me over, remember?'

There was silence the other end . . . just the sound of Rose's breathing. Then a terrible cry.

'Oh, no!'

The terror in her aunt's voice was like a blow. Addy was struck dumb. When she opened her mouth to speak, nothing came out.

'What do you mean, I *invited* you?'

'I got a letter from you, and an air ticket. People here said you'd gone to Paris for a few days. We thought the snow had stopped you coming back.'

'What people?'

'Sarah from across the road, and Molly. She came round to the house, Molly did. That was yesterday. She thought you'd be here.'

'Oh, Christ!'

Should she tell Rose about the man who'd broken in? Would it make things worse?

'Tell me where you are.' She tried again.

But Rose wasn't listening. 'So it was you who switched the lights on. Have you been staying here, in the house?'

'I told you – Molly looked in. When she found you weren't here she took me off to stay with her. I just came by to . . .'

'Listen to me.' Rose's voice had risen to a shriek. 'Do exactly what I say. Turn the lights out, all of them. Wait for me.'

Before Addy could reply, she hung up.

Paralysed, for a moment Addy could only stare at her phone in her hand. Then, springing into action, she flipped the light switch in Rose's room and then the one in the passage leading to the stairs. The lights in the sitting room downstairs were still on. The switch was by the front door. Stumbling down the stairs, almost tripping on the bag she had left there, she made it in seconds flat. The room was plunged into darkness. Hardly daring to breathe, she waited.

A faint noise reached her ears. It was coming from outside, sounded like running footsteps. Then a key turned in the door which opened and a dark figure slipped inside.

'Addy?'

'I'm here . . .'

Addy found herself caught in a fierce embrace. Rose's cheek

was pressed to hers. She got a whiff of her so-familiar perfume, but only for a second. Then Rose drew back and Addy caught a glimpse of her aunt's face in the faint light from the window. Her eyes were wide and staring. This wasn't the Rose she knew: she looked more like a madwoman.

'Rose, I . . .'

'Not now.' The words were hissed in her ear. 'We've got to get out of here.'

Rose had left the door open. She put her head out, checking the mews, looking first one way, then the other. Addy could feel her heart pounding in her chest. What was this? What was going on, for fuck's sake?

'Can't you tell me *anything*?' she whispered.

'Later.'

Rose stepped outside into the mews. Addy followed. The narrow street was empty, but there were lights on in most of the houses. Rose had already begun walking towards the entrance at the head of the mews and Addy saw she was toting a small travel bag.

'Where were you?'

'Across the way.' She spoke in the same urgent whisper. 'Sarah and I have keys to each other's houses. I came here to pick up some things. When I went out I saw you come into the mews. I didn't know who you were so I went in there and watched. I saw you go into my house, but your back was to me.'

'But Rose, *why*?'

Addy broke off. She had just spotted Mike coming through the arched entrance to the mews. He was hurrying towards them, hands buried in his coat pockets. Rose had seen him too and she stopped.

'Who's that?'

'It's all right,' Addy assured her. 'That's Mike. He brought me here.'

'Who is he? Where did you meet him?' The questions were fired at her like bullets.

'On the plane coming over. We sat next to each other.'

'On the *plane*—? Oh, Addy!' Rose sounded as though she were in pain. She stared at the approaching figure.

'Rose, *please* tell me what's wrong?'

At that moment Addy caught sight of another figure, a man. He had materialized from the shadows at the side of the narrow alley and was following in Mike's footsteps walking even quicker than he was, covering the ground with long loping strides, his footfalls deadened by the mantle of snow covering the cobbles. Even at a distance and even in the uncertain light coming from the houses on either side, which was the only illumination in the narrow alley, she recognized him. She saw who it was.

'Look out!'

Her shouted warning brought Mike to an abrupt halt. He was only a few paces away.

'*Behind you!*'

He turned, but too late. The bat was on him. They came together face to face, body to body, and as Addy watched in horror she saw Mike suddenly buckle and sink to his knees in the snow. For seconds that seemed to stretch into an age he knelt there, and then slowly fell forward landing face down in the snow.

'*You bastard—!*'

Without thinking Addy dropped her bag and ran towards him ignoring Rose's cry behind her: '*Stop – come back.*'

Before she even reached Mike, however, the bat had a stepped around his body and was facing her. Addy saw he had a knife in his hand, the blade dark with blood. The sight brought her to a halt and they stood facing each other, neither of them moving for an agonizing second or two. Addy could see from the look on his face what he meant to do next, but as he moved towards her, Mike came to life. Still prone, he managed to lash out with his foot, catching the bat on the ankle, making him stumble, and as he turned, knife raised, to stab again, Addy hurled herself at him, grabbing him round the neck with one hand, clawing at his eyes with the other. It was no use. With an abrupt twist of his body he threw her off and without pausing drove his knife straight down into Mike's back.

Lips drawn back in a snarl, he turned to deal with Addy, who had scrambled to her feet. But before he'd taken a step towards her he was struck from behind and lurched forward, losing his footing in the slippery snow and tumbling to his knees. Addy saw it was Rose who had charged into him. Her face stark white in the snowy light, she kicked him in the back, knocking him flat on his stomach, meanwhile screaming: '*Run, Addy, run!*'

Before Addy had time to react – she wasn't about to run anywhere, she was going to help Rose – she saw the bat scrabble for the knife that had fallen from his fingers and roll over on to his back. At the same moment Rose flung herself on to him, and like a dreadful scene from a movie – there was no stopping it – Addy saw her aunt land full on the upturned knife.

'*No!*' she screamed.

The two of them lay there unmoving for what seemed an eternity. Then the bat thrust Rose's body off his and got to his feet. He fixed his gaze on Addy, who had been turned to stone. What he meant to do then she never knew because while all that was happening the mews had burst into life. There was a man standing in an open doorway two houses up. He was shouting.

'I'm calling the police now, do you hear me?'

He turned and disappeared inside.

Then a second man followed by a woman came running up the mews from beyond Rose's house. He was wielding what looked like a golf club.

'You . . . you!' he shouted.

The bat hesitated. He had his knife pointed at Addy, but now he was looking over his shoulder at the man who was approaching. Then a woman called from an upper window nearby. 'I see you, I see you!' she cried.

The blade of his knife retracted. Addy heard the faint click. Without a word, he turned and ran, heading for the entrance to the mews, long legs pumping, his black coat flapping on either side of his body so that for a moment he looked like he might suddenly take flight, a giant bat. Addy didn't wait for him to disappear. Before he had reached the entrance to the mews she was down on her knees beside Rose. The snow around her aunt's body was turning black with the blood that continued to spread. She was moaning faintly.

'Rose . . . Rose . . . can you hear me?'

She was in despair. She didn't know what to do. Should she try and turn her over? Leave her as she was?

'Can someone call an ambulance?' Desperate, she cried out for help.

'I'll do that.' It was the woman who had shouted from the window.

'Is she badly hurt?' The man with the golf club had come running up to them. His wife, if that was who she was, knelt in the snow beside Addy.

'It's Rose,' she told the man.

'What about him?' His words made Addy look up for a second. The man was pointing at Mike who hadn't moved from the spot where he lay.

'Someone bring a towel, please.' The woman kneeling beside her called out the request. She seemed to know what she was doing. 'We should turn her over.'

Together they gently rolled Rose on to her back and the woman undid her coat, drawing it back to expose the widening stain in the white cable-knit sweater Rose was wearing, the scene now lit by a flashlight which someone in the small crowd that had gathered around them was holding. A towel was thrust into the woman's hands. Pulling Rose's sweater up, exposing the wound beneath, she pressed it to her stomach. 'We must try and stop the bleeding,' she said.

'Oh, Rose!' Addy had never felt more helpless in her life. As she murmured the words she saw her aunt's eyelids flutter.

'Addy . . . my darling . . .'

'Why did you do it, Rose?' She held the loved head in her lap. '*Why?*'

Rose's lips moved. Addy bent closer.

'Don't . . . don't . . .' Her panting breath all but drowned the words out.

'What is it, Rose? What are you saying?'

Somewhere in the night, far away but drawing closer all the time, a siren sounded.

EIGHTEEN

'**M**iss Banks . . . Miss Banks?'

Addy looked up. She'd been sitting there she didn't know for how long – head bowed, staring at the floor in front of her, her mind a blank. All she could see was Rose's face and the blood on the snow.

The woman standing in front of her was Asian; she wore a blue hospital smock stretching down to her ankles and a cap of the same colour on her head.

'My name is Dr Ranjit. You are Mrs Carmody's niece, yes?'

Addy nodded.

'I am sorry to have to tell you, but your aunt's condition is giving us cause for concern.' Her brown eyes offered sympathy. 'She lost a lot of blood before they got her to the hospital and we've been unable to stop the bleeding. She has internal injuries and we are about to operate on her to try to repair the damage. Unfortunately she is in a very weak state.'

'Can I talk to her?' Addy pleaded.

'I'm afraid not.' The brown eyes grew sadder. 'The operation will start in a few minutes. I must get back.' She hesitated. 'Even when it's over your aunt will not be able to speak to you for some time. It might be best if you went home to rest and then returned in the morning.'

Addy shook her head. 'I'm staying.'

They had given her a room to sit in, glass-walled on one side so that she could see people passing in the corridor outside, doctors and nurses and occasionally a uniformed constable. One of them was sitting in the passage outside the intensive care unit a little further down, which was where Rose would be placed after the surgeons were done with her. There was a desk in the room and Addy was sitting in the chair facing it, but turned round so that she could observe the comings and goings in the passageway outside.

She had wanted to go with the medics after they had loaded

Rose into the ambulance at the mews but the older of the pair, the one in charge, had told her it wouldn't be possible.

'We've tried to stabilize her,' he said, 'but she's very weak and we'll have to keep working on her in the ambulance. Sorry, luv, but you'll be in the way.'

They had briefly checked Mike's body, which lay where he had fallen a few yards away, and after pronouncing him dead had got on with attending to Rose.

'The police will see to it you get to the hospital,' the medic had assured Addy before the ambulance took off, siren wailing.

She had stood for a while after that, gazing down at Mike's body, unsure what it was exactly that she felt. Shock, she supposed. She had never seen a dead person before and it struck her, bizarrely then, that on stage people died all the time and just lay there until it was time to get up and go to the dressing-rooms.

It was the waiting that was hardest. The police when they came had been in no hurry to take her where she needed to be. The first to arrive had been two young coppers in uniform, a man and a woman. Other than asking her what had happened – the who and the how and the when – they had left her to herself while they busied themselves clearing the snow away and marking the spot where Mike's body lay on the cobbles with tape and then beginning the job of questioning the other residents of the mews who had gathered around to find out what they had seen.

Pretty soon more police had arrived including four detectives, one of them Malek. They had conferred for a few moments and then Malek had come over to where she was standing by Mike's body.

'I'm so sorry about your aunt, Addy.' He had held her gaze. 'I'll drive you to the hospital now. We'll talk there.'

As they left in his car a second ambulance had arrived to collect Mike Ryker's body and take it to the mortuary.

'Did you know him?' he asked, and Addy had nodded.

'He brought me here. I was supposed to pick up my stuff. He wanted to tell me about his daughter, but I couldn't take the trouble to listen.'

'What are you saying?' He didn't understand.

'Never mind.'

There was no point trying to explain how she felt, she didn't know herself. It was like she was two people, one of them speaking and carrying on normally, the other watching, and she knew that at some point she would have to wake up from the spell she was under and take a grip on the present. But not yet, she wasn't ready. All she could do was stare out of the car window as they made their way through the snow-covered streets to the hospital.

There, at reception, she had learned that she couldn't see Rose yet.

'She's receiving emergency treatment at the moment,' the nurse at the desk told them. 'You'll be told as soon as there's any news on her condition.'

She had let Malek lead her to the room where she was now and it was while she was sitting there on her own, head down, staring at the floor that Dr Ranjit had brought her the news about Rose.

Now Malek was back. He pulled up another chair close to hers. Somewhere in the midst of the fear that gripped her – the thought of Rose fighting for her life had thrust all other thoughts from her mind – Addy was aware that he was treating her gently, as though she were fragile, as though he didn't wish to cause her any further pain. But he also wanted answers. Before he could start, though, a uniformed constable knocked on the door and came in. He was carrying two bags with him. Malek went over to have a word with him. He took the bags from the man and put them on the desk.

'These were lying in the snow near where your aunt was,' he told Addy. 'We want you to take a look at them – the contents, I mean, and tell us if there's anything that strikes you as unusual.'

'The big one's mine.'

She got up and opened the bag for him to see what she'd put in, clothes mostly.

'You can go through it if you like. The other one belongs to Rose. She had it with her.'

Malek opened the zipper on the overnight travel bag Rose had been carrying.

He pulled out the first object that came to hand and held it up for her inspection. Addy took it from him.

'Grumble . . .'

'I'm sorry?' Her whisper had barely carried to him.

She was silent, remembering. What was it Rose had said that day? 'I'm going to keep him for ever. Wherever I go, he goes.' And as though the words held a hidden power, the memories they brought in their wake shattered the spell she was under, bringing her back to the moment, releasing her tears.

'Oh, Rose . . .' Hugging the tattered body to her chest, she burst into deep, racking sobs.

Shocked, Malek reached out a hand to comfort her, but then quickly withdrew it. Giving her a chance to collect herself, he went slowly through the contents of Rose's bag and by the time he was done Addy's tears had dried.

'I gave this to Rose years ago.' She held the bear close to her. 'She took it with her wherever she went.'

'You can keep it,' he reassured her. 'We don't need it.' Then, clearing his throat like a signal that things were about to change, he resumed his seat facing her. 'I'm sorry, Addy, but we have to move on. Let's start at the beginning. Did you know your aunt would be at the house?'

She shook her head. 'Like I told you, I went there to collect some things. Rose called me on my cell. She thought I was in New York.'

He waited in vain for her to explain.

'Then, if it wasn't your aunt who invited you to London, who did?'

Addy could only shrug.

'It really threw her though. I could tell from her voice. But I already knew something was wrong. You see Rose and I were . . .' But she couldn't finish the sentence, couldn't say that Rose was the person she loved most in the world and felt closest to and now she didn't know if that last bit was even true any more. What had Rose been hiding from her?

'Did you ever trace her phone?' All she could do was put a question to him.

He shook his head. 'There was no signal. She must have

dumped it. The battery was probably dead. She used another phone to call you. We took a look at it. There are no leads we can use.'

She told him how Rose had been keeping watch on her house from across the way.

'Was she afraid of something . . . or someone?' he asked.

'She must have been. But she didn't say what or who.'

'She didn't tell you *anything*?' Malek was disbelieving.

'There wasn't time. We were only in the house for a minute. She said we had to get out at once. All I know is she was scared, really scared.' Addy could see he wasn't satisfied with her answer. 'We'd just left the house when I saw Mike coming towards us. He'd had to park his car. It really shook Rose seeing him there. She wanted to know who he was, where I'd met him.'

'She thought he was part of whatever was going on? Is that what you're saying?' Malek seized on the point.

'Maybe. But then I saw this other man. He just appeared out of the darkness. He must have been hiding. I recognized him and called out a warning to Mike.'

'You *recognized* him?'

'It was the same guy who called at the house last night when I was there – this was just before the thing with the Arab woman. He was looking for Rose.' She saw the expression on his face. 'I know, I didn't tell you about him before, but there seemed no reason to at the time. All he did was ask if Rose was there and said he'd be back the next day. It had nothing to do with what happened afterwards.'

Malek's raised eyebrows suggested otherwise.

'OK . . . I see what you mean . . . but there could be a connection.' She was starting to get a headache. 'He's Russian, by the way.'

'How do you know that? Did he tell you?'

He was pushing harder. He wasn't getting what he wanted from her.

'It was his voice. I'm good at accents.' She wasn't going to explain how being an actor helped. If he didn't believe her that was his problem. 'I already gave a description of him to the cops who got there before you.'

'You said he looked like a bat.'

'That was because of his eyes, the way they stuck out.'

He wanted to know about the attack next, how Mike came to be killed and Rose so badly hurt. She'd had to take him through it step by step right up to the point where Rose lay bleeding in the snow and she was calling for an ambulance.

'Let me see if I've got this right.' Malek frowned. 'This man's attack on your friend Mike was deliberate, and from what you say he was coming for you next. But the stabbing of your aunt – that sounds accidental. He had his knife pointed up and she landed on top of him. Is that correct?'

Addy had had to go back to the moment, to an image she was trying to wipe from her memory, when Rose had come to her aid and thrown herself forward on top of their assailant.

'I don't know. Could be.'

'And there's one other thing I don't understand.' The frown had deepened. 'Why did you shout a warning to Mike? What made you do that?'

Addy needed time to fashion her reply. Her headache was getting worse.

'When he called at the house last night, the bat, there was something about him, the way he looked. It scared me.'

'But you didn't think it was worth telling us that when we questioned you later?'

Well, pretty fucking obviously not. Addy could feel her hackles rising. Did she have to admit it? And couldn't he stop with his questions? All she wanted now was to know how Rose was, what they were doing to her, and she'd been on the point of making her feelings clear when the door opened and a man looked in. He caught Malek's eye. They went out into the corridor together and stood talking for a minute. She saw Malek make a phone call.

'Your friend Ryker – didn't you say he was a commodity broker?' he said, coming back into the room.

'That's what he told me.'

'According to a card we found in his wallet he was a "security consultant", whatever that means. He was employed by a big American company called Safe Solutions. They have an office here in London. Does that mean anything to you?'

Addy shook her head.

'I've just spoken to their duty clerk. He doesn't know anything about it, says he's never heard the name Ryker. We may have to wait till tomorrow to find out more.'

She said nothing.

'Addy, we can't just leave things this way.' He sat down in front of her again. 'Are you sure you've told me everything you know?'

Before she could reply the door behind him opened again. This time it was Dr Ranjit who stuck her head in.

'Miss Banks, come quickly!'

Addy leaped to her feet. Ignoring Malek's cry of 'Addy, wait!' she ran to the door and followed the doctor who was already hurrying back down the way she had come, talking over her shoulder as they went.

'The internal injuries she suffered were even worse than we thought. We were doing our best to repair the damage, when her heart gave out. They're trying to resuscitate, but I'm afraid we're losing her.'

Holding Grumble close to her chest, Addy stumbled after her through a pair of swinging doors and then through another pair and she saw they were in the operating room with a crowd of people, nurses and doctors, all of them wearing masks and they were standing around a bed and when Addy tried to go forward, force her way through the crowd, Dr Ranjit held her back.

'Wait.'

Addy stood rooted. It was just like the movies. What she knew was called a crash cart was placed by the bed and a man was holding two defibrillators, one in each hand. She heard him say 'Clear!' and when the others stood back he pressed the pair of paddles to the body on the bed and Addy saw for the first time that it was Rose who lay with her front bared, and the bloody wound that was either where the bat had cut her or the result of the surgery she was undergoing, or perhaps both, was plain to see. Her body jumped from the electrical shock and then lay still. The man with the paddles made a sign to a nurse who upped the charge on the monitor. 'Clear!' He said it again, with the same result. They went through the routine a third time and then the man said something in a low voice which Addy didn't hear. But she knew from watching this kind of scene on television, and with a finality that turned her heart to ice, that he was declaring the patient dead.

There was nothing she could do now and she stood patiently in the circle of Dr Ranjit's arm while the nurses disconnected Rose from the tubes attached to her body and then covered her wound. Placing her arms close to her sides, they drew a sheet up over the length of her body leaving only her head uncovered.

'Now, if you wish,' Dr Ranjit murmured in Addy's ear.

She went forward to the bed and looked down at the still figure for long minutes, consigning to memory every inch of a face that she knew as well as her own, one she had loved for as far back as she could remember, and without reserve.

Then, because she couldn't stand to gaze at it any longer, she bent and kissed Rose on the forehead, just once. When she turned to go she found Dave Malek standing behind her.

'Come, Addy.' He took her hand. 'I'll take you home.'

NINETEEN

Like a cellist drawing a chord from his instrument, Kimura ran the stone down the edge of the steel blade. The movement produced a high, keening note, not especially pleasing to the ear, but comforting nonetheless. He had been repeating the same action for nearly an hour, first on one side of the sword, then the other, and although it was well after midnight he was ready to continue for as long as necessary until the edge was razor-sharp.

The room where he sat cross-legged on the floor was furnished in the Japanese style, but with little imagination and with the kind of prints that might have come from a catalogue: Mt Fuji, inevitably, two paintings of birds on the wing, and one larger than the rest that showed a great blue wave about to break, a picture Kimura knew was famous and by an artist whose name he surely ought to know but had long since forgotten. The basin in the corner was hidden by a screen on which a geisha garbed in colourful costume was depicted. What was welcome, though, was the bed, a simple futon laid out on the matting-carpeted floor, on which for the first time in many days he had passed a long night's sleep free of dreams.

The house where he'd found sanctuary – a modest two-storey dwelling – was less than ten minutes' walk from the restaurant where he had eaten and on ringing the doorbell he had found the owner, a simply dressed man well into his seventies to judge by his appearance, awaiting his arrival. After a brief exchange of courtesies he had been shown to his room on the top floor by a woman he assumed was the man's wife. Warned perhaps by the owner of the restaurant, they had not burdened him with enquiries, seeming to accept his shabby appearance and lack of any personal effects as perfectly normal and requiring no comment. But there was something more, and it had not escaped Kimura's notice: a nervousness that translated into a desire to please. It wasn't respect exactly; it was rather a fear of offending, which told him that exiles though they were – he knew from the restaurant owner that the couple had been resident in London for thirty years – they had recognized him for what he was. Either that or they had been forewarned by the restaurant owner, in which case it meant that none of them were deceived, they had not forgotten the position that men of his kind had once held in society. Men whose blood line went back centuries to the time of the samurai and who in spite of all the laws that had been passed in the interim outlawing their very existence still pursued their ancient profession in one guise or another: men to step aside from.

Rising early that morning, he had made his way to a small sporting goods store where he changed his uncomfortably large overcoat for a padded jacket well supplied with pockets and also bought a woollen cap of the kind favoured by skiers. Dressed now in clothes very like those worn by others about him and aware from the mingling of races he'd observed on the crowded pavements that his own appearance would excite little interest, his earlier fear of discovery had receded and instead of returning to the house and spending the day indoors as he'd planned, he continued to wander the streets.

He had no immediate goal in mind. Eventually he would have to return to the house he had broken into to see if the woman he sought had returned. But he intended to wait for at least a day so as to give the police time to complete their investigation. Although he would have found it hard to put into words, he was still possessed by the conviction that in some way he was fate's instrument and nothing that had occurred in the past two days – the extraordinary chain of events that had followed his escape from his pursuers, the fact that he was still at large and free to pursue his goal – had altered his growing certainty that some unseen hand, divine or otherwise, was guiding his steps. How his quest would end was still uncertain, but he was waiting for a sign, and late in the morning, when his wanderings had led him to an area crammed with small shops, most of them dealing in antiques of one kind or another – and centred around a street with the unusual name of Portobello – he stopped outside a store in one of the side streets leading off it to gaze at the collection of old weaponry displayed in the window.

It was the swords that had caught his eye. They were of various kinds – sabres, scimitars, needle-thin rapiers – and he had stood gazing at them for some time while an idea slowly took shape in his mind. Eventually he had gone inside.

'You have Japanese swords?'

He had directed the question at a bald-headed man who was sitting behind the glass-topped counter reading a newspaper with the aid of a pair of spectacles perched on the end of his nose, and who had looked up with an enquiring glance when Kimura had entered.

'As a matter of fact, I do, sir.' The man had risen to his feet with some difficulty, easing what looked like stiffened joints. 'I keep them in the back. If you would wait a moment?'

Disappearing through a curtained doorway, he had returned presently with two lengthy cardboard boxes, which he laid on the counter. Removing the lid from one of them with a flourish, he stood back.

'There you are, sir. Beautiful, isn't it? They were craftsmen in those days.'

Kimura had removed the curved, single-edged blade from the box and held it up to the light. Just as he thought! This was no *katana* dating from the Shinto period, or even the one that followed (both famous for the skill of their sword-smiths); this blade had not been made from the specialized steel used then – *tamahagane* it was called – nor had it been treated with the wet clay slurry which, after heating and quenching in cold water, caused the steel to be hardened so that later it could be ground to the finest razor's edge. This was a weapon dating most likely from just before the Second World War when all Japanese officers had been obliged to wear a sword and numerous blacksmiths with no knowledge of traditional methods had been recruited to produce the weapons. Proof of it could be found in the government stamp on the tang, something no true craftsman's sword would ever have carried. But it was a katana nonetheless, and though the edge was blunted and the steel rusted in places, properly prepared it would serve the purpose he had in mind.

Some haggling had followed. The shopkeeper, thinking he had a fish on his hook and a valuable article to tempt him with, had pressed for a price well in excess of the sword's true value. Given his uncertain command of English, it had taken Kimura some time and trouble to set him right, but in the end they had come to an agreement and he had purchased both swords for a total of thirty pounds.

His money would run out eventually, but the thought did not trouble him. He was confident matters would come to a head well before then and the important thing was to be ready when they did. With his purchases tucked under his arm he had set off at once to return home, pausing only at a hardware store where he bought an emery stone and a bottle of oil. By early afternoon he was back in his room and at work on the first of the swords.

TWENTY

D S Dave Malek cupped his hands and blew on them. Unlike Addy, he wasn't wearing gloves. They had paused for a few seconds by a pond as they walked through the snow-covered park. Busy with duck life it was patrolled by two swans and they watched as the pair, like galleons in full sail, went coasting by in line astern.

'It seems Bela Horvath was the only person in Safe Solutions – the only one here in London – who knew about Ryker's assignment. Apparently it was his idea, and he set it up with the help of their New York office.'

'And Mike was told to pick me up on the plane?'

'To get to know you.' Malek glanced at her. 'Horvath thought it would be the quickest way to locate your aunt – maybe the only way. Or so he said.'

'And I fell for it.' Addy felt an overwhelming urge to kick something, starting with herself. She settled for glaring at a couple of kids who came belting down the path on a toboggan – one riding, the other pushing – yelling at the tops of their voices and forcing them to skip aside. 'I thought he was flirting with me. How dumb was that?'

Since waking from a drugged sleep earlier that morning, the memory of all that had happened the night before had lain like a lead weight on her heart. The feeling was one she could hardly put into words. Her life would never be the same: it was as simple as that. The world had shifted in its orbit; it was no longer the same planet. It was a world without Rose.

There was anger, too.

'How the fuck did this happen?'

She had muttered the words aloud as she lay in bed staring at the ceiling; staring at nothing.

What had Rose got into? Why was she running for her life – and from who? Was it that Russian psycho? Or was there more to it? And what about the crazy who had broken into Rose's house the night before, the one dressed like an Arab? Was he part of it too? The questions had buzzed around in her head like a swarm of angry bees, and it was partly to put a stop to them – to bring some order to her thoughts – that she'd forced herself to get up and go downstairs, only to find there was another interrogation awaiting her there.

'Addy! At last!'

Molly had been pacing the kitchen like a caged tigress and Addy could hardly blame her. She herself had been in no condition to talk when she'd got back from the hospital. Still clutching Grumble, it was all she could do to stumble from the police car to Molly's door, helped by the hand that Malek had put under her arm. Once inside he had taken over, deflecting the barrage of questions Molly fired at them – on hearing them arrive she had burst out of the sitting room into the hall, demanding to know where Addy had been, what was going on (it was one o'clock in the morning) – but getting no change from Malek.

'Addy can't talk to you now,' he had told her. 'She must get some sleep. Let her go to bed.'

It wasn't the first time they'd locked antlers and Molly had let fly.

'How dare you? This is my house. You've no right to speak to me that way. I warn you I intend to lodge a complaint with your superiors.'

Unruffled, Malek had stood his ground. 'I'll explain every-thing to you,' he had told Molly. 'But leave Addy out of it.'

There apparently being no comeback Molly could think of, she had turned on her heel and flounced back into the sitting room. With a nod to Addy and a murmured, 'Get some sleep', Malek had followed her.

Addy remembered dragging herself up the stairs and collapsing into bed, but nothing more, and on finding Molly waiting for her in the kitchen this morning she had felt some remorse. It must have been tough being told about the tragedy that had overtaken her friend by a detective – and one she seemed to have a strong aversion to – when the person she really wanted to talk to had left her in his hands without a word. Addy had done her best to make it up to her, but the effort it took – the pain of going through it all again up to the moment when Rose had lost her fight for life – cost her and finally she'd had to quit.

'I'm sorry, I can't talk about it any more . . . please . . .'

'Forgive me. I shouldn't have pressed you.' Molly had been contrite.

But sitting there in the kitchen, her breakfast untouched, Addy had felt despair take hold of her again – just picking up a cup of coffee seemed too much of an effort – and it had come as a relief when the doorbell rang and Molly said, 'That will be that detective, I expect, wretched man. He said he'd be round again today.'

Her prediction proved right and it came with a bonus. No sooner had Molly ushered Malek into the kitchen than she'd announced that she'd be going out for a while. It seemed his presence was more than she could endure.

'There are some errands I have to run. And we must think about the funeral.'

The prospect was one Addy couldn't bring herself to contemplate, and she'd been relieved to have Malck there as a distraction and to deal with the business that had brought him back, which turned out to be the matter-of-fact process of taking her fingerprints for matching purposes, followed by a further statement they needed from her dealing with the events of the night before. Doing it that way – in a flat question-and-answer manner – was easier and they got through it facing each other across thc table with Malek taking down her words on a laptop, looking up now and again to make sure that she was OK.

'I'll get it printed at the station. You can sign it later.'

Folding his laptop, he'd sat gnawing at his lip.

'There've been developments since last night.' He caught her eye. 'Information's come our way that I feel you have a right to know. I'm not authorised to tell you, so I'd appreciate it if you keep it to yourself.'

'As in not tell Molly?'

He had grinned. 'That'd do for a start. But what do you say we go for a walk?'

'In case she comes back, you mean?' Addy had summoned up a grin herself.

'Battersea Park's not far away. You look as though you could do with some fresh air.'

'We called on him first thing this morning. Bela Horvath has been running the London branch of Safe Solutions for the past three years. Their offices are located in Canary Wharf. He said he was ready to fill us in on what Ryker was doing here and some other stuff too that he thought we ought to know about. I went over there with my chief super. He'd decided he'd better handle the interview himself. They're a big organization, worldwide, and with friends in high places.'

He and Addy had driven across the river. It took only ten minutes to get there from Molly's house in Carlyle Square, but Malek was already well into his story by the time they reached the park.

'I might as well tell you we don't have much time for them in the Met – Safe Solutions, I mean. I'm told they're known as the SS. They've got their fingers in a lot of pies, some of them bordering on the illegal, and those are just the things we know about. But they have powerful clients and good contacts where it counts. Horvath himself is quite a character. I hadn't met him before, but I'd heard about him. He's ex-CIA and knows how to pull strings.'

Addy felt better in the cold air. The sky was still overcast but the threat of further snow flurries had passed. She was wearing a padded jacket and a white woollen skiing beanie with a red bobble on top. Malek was clad in an overcoat that had seen better days and had a plaid scarf wrapped around his neck. When he wasn't playing with his forelock, trying to push it back from his forehead, he walked with his hands buried in his coat pockets.

'He told us your aunt came to see him a few weeks ago with a request for protection from a man she thought might do her harm. She said his name was Philip Moreau.'

He eyed Addy hopefully, but she shook her head.

'I've never heard of him. Why didn't she go to the police?'

'Because that wouldn't have helped. We can only offer

protection to people when there's clear evidence that a threat exists, and, for reasons of her own, your aunt wasn't in a position to supply that.'

'Why not?'

'I'll tell you in a second.' Malek paused. 'But let me explain about Ryker first – how he fits into this. Horvath said he offered your aunt round-the-clock protection since that was what she wanted. He had her house watched twenty-four seven and assigned two men to accompany her whenever she went out. It cost a lot, but she was insistent. A fortnight ago she gave them the slip. She had an appointment at her hairdresser's and while the two men waited for her outside she left by the back door.'

'Why?'

'Horvath has a theory about that, which I'll get to. But in the meantime, he'd discovered she was in more danger than even she realized and he knew they had to find her as quickly as possible and put her in a safe place until the situation was dealt with. They'd been looking into her background and found out that you were the person closest to her. Their New York office was handling that side of things and they learned from one of your friends that you were going to London to spend Christmas with your aunt, which seemed unlikely, given that she'd vanished. What made you come, Addy?' He looked enquiringly at her.

'I got a letter from Rose inviting me, only it wasn't from her.'

'An email?'

'A typewritten letter.'

'But it had to be a person who knew you were close to your aunt?'

Addy was silent. It still burned her to think how she'd been made such a fool of.

'And by someone who had the same idea as Horvath.'

'What do you mean?' She scowled.

'Horvath didn't know what was behind your trip, why you were coming to London, but he thought you were the one person who might lead them to your aunt. That's why Ryker was on the plane.'

'And I fell for his line.' Addy smouldered. 'You said there was a situation that had to be dealt with. What did this Horvath guy mean by that?'

This time the wait was longer. They had reached the top of the park and begun to circle round, following the path where the snow had been trampled and made walkable. Malek's frown indicated he was having trouble formulating whatever it was he wanted to say.

'Horvath told us a story that sounded far-fetched.' He found his tongue at last. 'But from the few checks we've been able to make, it seems to hold up. This is a whole other world, Addy, with some bad people in it, and I'm sorry to have to tell you that your aunt was caught up in it. It'll be best if I tell you what Horvath told us. Then you can tell me if any of it sounds familiar. By the way, we have a line on the man who killed her now – and you were right, he's a Russian, name of Grigor Klepkin. The description you gave us of him matches the one we got from Horvath and it's been circulated to all police stations. But the story's more complicated than that. It has to do with this man Moreau. He and Klepkin were working together, and if Horvath's story is correct, he's the one who got your aunt involved.'

'So who is he?' Addy demanded.

'Hard to say. All we really know is it's not his real name. Horvath recognized it from his time with the CIA. It was one of several used by an agent they had working for them then, a man who went by the code name of Charon. It was how Horvath made the connection – how he knew that your aunt was in real danger.'

'Why so?'

'He said this man Charon was something of a specialist, and when we asked what that meant, he said he carried out the kind of work that wasn't talked about. It wasn't even supposed to happen, officially. Then he said he'd leave it to our imaginations to figure out what that meant.' Malek shrugged. 'My guess is the man was a licensed killer, an assassin, but they don't want to say so.'

Addy looked away. She didn't know how to deal with all the feelings that washed through her, the pain they brought.

But she wasn't going to lapse into tears. She was going to get to the bottom of this. She owed it to Rose. She turned to face him and saw his eyes widen in surprise.

'Did I say something?' he asked.

It must have been the look she was giving him, she thought: the one that scared men.

'What was this story you got from him? Just tell me.'

'I know it must seem hard to credit. We didn't believe it ourselves until we checked with MI6. They told us there'd been a rumour going around Moscow for some time giving those in the know a good laugh. Horvath heard about it from his contacts in the CIA. It was about some big shots, important men, friends of Putin, who'd had a fortune stolen from under their noses by a couple of smart operators. A billion dollars was the figure he mentioned, if you can believe it. The theft took place in Cyprus and involved a banker who was working for the Russians. He'd put the money into a number of different accounts along with the passwords to them and loaded it all on to a memory stick. Then he told the Russians he would only give them the stick if they paid him ten million dollars. The poor guy was murdered for his pains. Charon and his Russian chum left his body floating in a harbour.'

Malek studied Addy's face, trying to gauge her reaction. They had stopped at a café in the middle of the park and bought mugs of coffee. Addy watched as a bird landed on one of the empty tables nearby and began picking up crumbs.

'What made the joke even better was that it was money the Russians had stolen themselves, filched from the state. And like Horvath, MI6 had also heard that this man Charon was one of the two.'

'Who just happens to be Moreau, the man Rose was afraid of?' Addy had followed the tale with difficulty. It was full of twists and turns. 'What I don't understand is how she met him. Does Horvath know that?'

'I don't think so. But she said Moreau had told her he worked for the CIA, which didn't surprise Horvath. He said it was exactly the kind of deception Charon would have employed – and that he almost certainly managed to persuade

her she was doing something for her country by placing the
memory stick in a safe deposit box in Zurich.'

'Yes, tell me again about that.' Addy shook her head. 'It
just doesn't ring true. I can't see Rose doing that. I don't see
her being fooled that easily.'

Malek looked uncomfortable. 'According to Horvath, this
Charon bloke is attractive to women. He called him "a
charmer". I don't know about your aunt's personal life, whether
she had someone . . .' He trailed off when he saw Addy shake
her head again.

'Her husband died a year ago; he was killed in a plane crash.
She was alone after that.' More than alone, Addy thought:
despairing.

'So she might have fallen for him?'

Addy said nothing. She was remembering the scene in the
hotel room in New York when Rose had quoted the poem
about being 'desolate and sick of an old passion' and Addy
had thought she was talking about Uncle Matt. But maybe it
was this new love, if that was what it was, and maybe she'd
been trying to break free from an old attachment that still
had a hold on her. Yes, and feeling guilty about it, just as
Molly had said. But then she recalled the look Rose had given
her in New York when they were talking about Macbeth and
Addy had wondered if there were people who were just plain
evil. What did that mean?

'I don't know,' she said. 'But if so Rose never talked about
him, not to me.' It hurt her to say it. 'But she couldn't have
known that they'd murdered that banker and stolen the stick
from him. Rose would never have gone along with something
like that.'

'Maybe.' Malek seemed less certain. 'But at some point
she must have discovered what was on the memory stick
and that he'd been lying to her. Otherwise why go to Horvath
for protection? She even knew that the Russians were
involved.'

'How can you be sure of that?' Addy challenged him. She
was going to defend Rose, no matter what. 'And why did
Charon give her the stick to take to Zurich? Why not do it
himself?'

'Because according to Horvath he didn't want to be caught with it. He couldn't be sure the Russians weren't on to him already. If the stick was in a box in a bank in Zurich they'd have had to take him there to open it and that would have given him a chance to escape. He could have told the bank he was being robbed. It was the smart thing to do. He wanted to wait until the trail had gone cold and after six months he decided it would be safe to take possession of it. But he was still lying low, which was why he wanted your aunt to collect it for him.'

'You say Rose knew the Russians were involved. Have you any evidence of that?'

'She told Horvath that she'd already given Moreau's name to the "authorities". But she was afraid he would find her before they could track him down, which was why she needed protecting.'

'Well?'

Malek looked unhappy. 'She wasn't being truthful, Addy. What she'd actually done was shop Charon to the people he'd stolen the money from and she was hoping they would take care of the problem for her. She was supposed to hand the stick over to him in Paris, but instead the Russians were waiting at the apartment where they were due to meet. Somehow Charon got away – leaving a couple of bodies behind him, if Horvath's to be believed.'

Addy shut her eyes. She didn't know how to deal with this . . . Rose getting tied up with a cold-blooded killer? Malek was right. This was some other world he was telling her about.

'But if Horvath was protecting her, why did she choose to disappear?'

'He thinks he may have frightened her when he asked her about the memory stick. She knew there were people ready to kill to get their hands on it. His guess is she panicked, thought she'd be better off on her own.'

Malek crushed his empty paper mug and dropped it into a trash can. Spilling her coffee on the ground, Addy followed his example. She just couldn't put anything into her stomach right now.

'We've been able to trace some of her movements.' They walked on. 'She stayed in three different hotels in the Paddington district, only spending a few nights in each. And she booked a flight on Christmas Day. It might have been the first one she could get a seat on with the airlines jammed. No one flies on Christmas Day.' He looked at her. 'She was going to New York, Addy. My guess is she wanted to be with you.'

Addy blinked back the tears. *Oh, Rose* . . .

'What about the memory stick? Where is it now?'

'As far as we know, still in that bank in Zurich. Your aunt told Horvath she had left it there. It certainly wasn't among the things she brought with her in that bag, and it's not in her house either. We had some men go over it again this morning. But there's no reason to think Charon knows that. If he's here in London, which Horvath thinks is likely, it must be because he thought she had the stick in her possession and he was hoping to get it off her. From what you told me I don't think that Russian meant to kill her. It was an accident. But he had to get rid of Ryker, whoever he was, and you too, before he could take her. But he failed, and now Charon must know he's playing a losing game. With your aunt gone, his only hope now is to lie low and hope the Russians don't catch up with him.'

'What about the police?' Addy scowled. 'What are you doing?'

'Well, we're looking for Klepkin, and if we find him he'll be charged with murder. He'll get life.'

'And Charon?'

Malek shrugged. 'Look, Addy, the truth is if he walked into a police station today we couldn't arrest him. What could we charge him with? Stealing a billion dollars from some Russian crooks? If that's a crime, no one's reported it, and somehow I doubt they will.' He snorted. 'We've no evidence to suggest he's broken the law in England.' He looked at her. 'There's the law, Addy, and then there's justice . . .'

'And they're not always the same thing. Thanks for the lesson, Dave.' She glowered. 'What about that business in Paris? Didn't you say he killed two people?'

'According to Horvath, the Russians never reported it. They

removed the bodies and cleaned up afterwards. They don't want the police involved; they want to handle this business themselves. And get their money back, of course, but that'll only happen if they can get hold of the memory stick.'

'Did Rose tell them she'd left it in the safe deposit box?' she asked.

'Who can say?' He shrugged. 'But even if she did, they can't claim it. Your aunt would have had to be there to open the box – either her or Moreau, whose name must be on it too. So he's the only person who can open it now. But if the Russians know about it, they'll keep watching that bank till doomsday. Charon would be a fool to go anywhere near it.'

He glanced at his watch. They had walked the full circle of the park and were back at the gate where they had come in.

'Maybe Rose never put it in the box,' she said. 'Maybe she just threw it away.'

'What? A billion dollars?' Malek shook his head. 'Can you imagine anyone doing that?'

TWENTY-ONE

'C ome on, Addy, you've got to eat something. How about a sandwich?'

Dave Malek peered at her face as though he were trying to read something that was written there. They were sitting in a pub where he'd taken her after learning that she hadn't had any breakfast that morning and wasn't planning on lunch either.

'Or a Scotch egg?'

'What the fuck is that?'

The pub was in Clapham, just next door to Battersea, he'd told her, and was nothing like the place where she'd met Mike. That had been populated by the kind of people you might expect to find in a gossip magazine: smartly dressed and talking with the kind of braying notes that Brits of a certain class, like Molly, for example, seemed to favour. Addy's sharp ear had caught their tony accents and tucked them away for future reference. The walls of this pub were lined with photographs of soccer teams, draped with tinsel as a gesture to Christmas, and the drinkers were a rougher lot – some of them in workmen's clothes, and with a good ethnic mix – and it seemed Dave was known to quite a number of them. There'd been waves from the bar when they came in and a loud call. 'Watch it! Copper in the house!'

'You live around here?' Addy had asked, and when he'd nodded she'd thought in the strange, disconnected way she couldn't shake off that if things were different, she might have been wondering at this point if he was going to suggest that they go over to his place and . . . and so on. But all that seemed an age away now.

When they were still in the park, he'd said he had something more to tell her, but maybe she'd had enough for one day and wanted to go home and rest. Faced with a choice between answering more of Molly's questions and simply listening, she'd agreed to the alternative suggestion.

'Tell you what – I'll get you a nice roast beef sandwich,' he said, and before she could stop him he rose and went to the bar, returning a minute later with their drinks: a beer for him and a glass of red wine for her.

'Sandwiches on the way.'

He studied her again.

'I won't say I know how you feel, Addy. But try not to torture yourself. None of this was your doing. You've been dragged into it much the same way as your aunt was.'

Since this was just what Addy had been feeling – that somehow she was to blame for Rose's death, if only she hadn't rushed up the mews to help Mike, what followed might not have happened – she wondered how he had guessed. If nothing else, he was turning out to be an interesting guy: sharp, but with a human side, and just now he was treating her with kid gloves, as though he'd taken the measure of her grief and knew what the situation called for. At any other time . . . but there was only this time – now – and she didn't know if it would ever end, this feeling she had of irretrievable loss.

'You said you had something more to tell me?'

Before he could reply, a hand reached between them. It was holding a plate with two thickly cut sandwiches on it. A face with a wide grin crowned with dreadlocks paused for a moment beside hers. 'Enjoy.'

Malek picked up his sandwich. 'Come on, Addy. I want to see you eat. Bite. Chew. Swallow.'

She couldn't help it. She had to laugh, and then did as she was told. It was the same as it had been with Mike – he was treating her like a big brother, but somehow she didn't mind. His dark gaze was fixed on her.

'Cops' eyes,' she said. She'd managed a swallow, and found to her surprise that he was right – she felt better for it.

'What . . . what do you mean?'

'They look at you differently. Everyone says so. It's true, isn't it?'

He considered the question over a swallow of beer.

'I suppose so.' He shrugged. 'You pick it up on the beat. I was in uniform before I joined the CID. You're taught to look for things that aren't the way they should be – doors, windows, cars, people too. It's a hard habit to break.' He took another sip. 'So how am I looking at you?'

But Addy just shook her head. She wasn't ready for it, wasn't up to flirting if that was what he was doing and didn't know when or if she would ever feel that way again.

He went on looking at her for a moment longer and then nodded, as though he understood.

'That other thing we learned from Horvath . . .' he began.

The change of subject took her by surprise and she half choked on the piece of roast beef she was swallowing.

'Yes, what was it?'

'We told him about the person who broke into your aunt's house the first night you were there and asked him if it was connected in any way to her. We said we were pretty sure from witnesses in the store that the man was Japanese and that it seemed he was fleeing from four other men, also Japanese. Horvath didn't know about it – we'd kept the story out of the press – but he guessed at once who the man was. He even gave us a name. One second . . .'

Malek reached into a pocket and drew out a notebook. Opening it, he riffled through the pages until he found the one he wanted.

'Kimura,' he read out. 'Hideki Kimura.' He passed the book over to Addy. 'He'd been employed as a bodyguard by a Japanese gangster, a big shot in the Yakuza. You've heard of them?'

Addy nodded. She stared at the name.

'Apparently Kimura ran off with a young girl that this boss was grooming to be his wife, or maybe just his mistress, I don't know – they do things differently in Japan – but the thing is Kimura pinched her from under his nose and the two of them fled to Singapore.'

'Why there?' She gave the notebook back to him.

'Because, according to Horvath, the Singapore government runs a very tight ship, and although this Yakuza boss would like to have sent a crew of his thugs after them, he knew there was no way they would escape the notice of the police there. So for the moment he was stymied.'

Malek drained his glass of beer and waved to the barman for another.

'Kimura meantime hadn't been idle. He knew they couldn't stay in Singapore indefinitely. It was too close to home. He had South America in mind as a place of refuge, but he wasn't sure he could handle the arrangements on his own. It would mean coming out of hiding. And so he turned to Safe Solutions for help.'

'He knew about them?'

'More than that: he had once worked – if you can call it that – with one of their people, a joint operation so to speak. It was some Yakuza business in Hong Kong. Horvath claims he doesn't know what was involved – he hated having to admit that those gangsters were once clients of his firm – but I doubt he was telling the truth. The interesting thing is the man Kimura was partnered with was none other than our friend Charon.'

'I thought you said he worked for the CIA.' Addy had been listening closely.

'That was before. According to Horvath, he went freelance after he left them and Horvath claims he was shocked when he joined Safe Solutions to learn that they had been using Charon for the odd assignment. He says he warned his superiors the man wasn't to be trusted but they wouldn't listen to him. Anyway, since Charon already knew Kimura, he was offered the job – an "extraction" Horvath called it – which involved getting both Kimura and his lady friend out of Singapore and on a plane to Buenos Aires without anyone noticing it.'

Malek paused to reflect. 'They should have listened to Horvath. Maybe Charon felt he was wasting his time with the firm. They were paying him on a job-by-job basis, but the money wasn't big and he'd come up with a plan of his own. He'd got in touch with the Yakuza boss and discovered he was willing to pay a king's ransom to get the girl back. They struck a deal.'

Addy winced. 'What about Kimura?'

'As Horvath understood it, Charon was given a free hand.

If the chance came to remove him from the picture, well and good, if not, he could be left for others to hunt down and kill. Nice people, huh?' He caught her eye.

'So what happened?' Addy took a swallow of her wine.

'Charon screwed up. He had no problem making contact with the pair in Singapore and started setting up their escape as planned. But once he'd got Kimura out of the way on some pretext, he went to the apartment block where they had a room and cornered the girl. I don't know what he intended doing. Horvath thought he was probably going to drug her. He may have had some help on hand. Drug her and whisk her out to the airport where a private jet would have been waiting. But the girl must have sussed what was going on. She cut her throat.'

'Oh my God!' Addy gasped.

'So it all fell to pieces and Charon had to make himself scarce. He knew Kimura would be out for his blood, and the Yakuza, too, most likely. And to make matters worse, Safe Solutions finally realized Horvath had been right all along and severed their ties with him. Not that it did them any good: the Yakuza boss held them responsible, and according to Horvath they lost him as a client. Charon had to lie low after that and he didn't surface again until he learned about the scam that Cypriot banker had pulled on the Russians and decided to get the memory stick for himself. Horvath said he didn't know how he and Klepkin got together, but when all was said and done, they were birds of a feather and probably knew each other. He said what Charon needed was a whole new identity, the kind that cost a great deal of money to manufacture, but with the Russians on his trail and with Kimura and possibly the Yakuza as well closing in, it was just a question of time before they caught up with him.'

He fell silent. He was watching Addy, waiting for her reaction.

'That must be about the time he met Rose,' she said.

Malek nodded.

'But Kimura couldn't have known about her.'

'Horvath's not so sure. It's obvious he was bent on tracking Charon down and somehow he must have learned about your aunt's connection to him. They had worked together before, remember. Charon himself had vanished – even Horvath didn't know where he was – but your aunt was reachable and Kimura may have thought he could find him through her.'

Malek pushed his forelock back.

'At least we know now who we're searching for when it comes to that Arab woman who was murdered, though since he was wearing a mask when he broke into your aunt's house, we still don't know what he looks like. But we've messaged the Tokyo police, asking them to send us a photograph of the bloke. They must have him on record. But it still doesn't get us any closer to Charon.'

He took a long swallow of his beer.

'What really puzzles me, though, is why he's still alive – Charon, I mean. I've never heard of anyone so many other people want to see dead.'

'Moreau?'

Molly stared wide-eyed at Addy.

'Are you sure that's the name?'

'Positive. The police think he might have been a friend of Rose's, someone she met in the past few months. They want to talk to him.'

Addy didn't like the fact she was lying to Molly, even if they were only small fibs. But Malek had been insistent. The police didn't want the whole story about Charon and his connection to Rose made public. He had raised the subject while they were driving back to Molly's house from the pub.

'Look, I know I said not to mention any of this to Lady Kingsmill, but you could try that name on her and see if she recognizes it, say he's someone we'd like to interview. I gather she and your aunt spent a lot of time together.'

'They were friends.' Addy's acknowledgement had been grudging. She didn't like to think that Molly might have known things about Rose that she didn't. 'But she told me she'd seen less of her in the past few months. Molly thought she might have met someone she didn't want to talk about.' Addy felt she had to say it.

'A man?'

'Molly thought so. Rose was travelling a lot at the time, she said, and she didn't seem to want company.'

Malek's next move had taken Addy by surprise.

'You can also show her this photograph.' He had reached into his pocket and handed her a print. 'It's a picture of Charon taken some years ago. Horvath told us not to put too much faith in it. Apparently the man has a habit of altering his appearance. You can keep it. We've made copies.'

The photo was a head and shoulders shot of a man staring blankly back at the camera. It could have been a passport snap, Addy thought. He had fair hair and regular features, but nothing in the way of a distinguishing mark. 'I don't know him,' she said. And then, 'Did Horvath show it to Rose?'

'He never got the chance. He only put two and two together – figured out what it was she'd got herself into and that this bloke Charon was part of it – after she'd disappeared. That was why he was so worried, he said, why he wanted to find her. He knew her life was in danger.'

Now Molly sat frowning. They were in the kitchen. Expecting Addy back for lunch, she had taken a quiche out of the freezer and put it in the oven. Addy saw if she didn't want to feel even more guilt about not saying what was really going on and what the police had discovered about Rose, she would have to sit with her and eat some of it.

'Moreau . . .' Molly repeated the name. Her frown stayed fixed. She was gnawing at her lip. 'It rings a bell? I'm trying to remember . . . what's his first name?'

'Philip.'

'Yes, that's it.' She nodded. 'It was in Paris, I remember now, but months ago; one of the last trips Rose and I made together, before . . . before she started going off on her own.'

She stared at Addy with unfocused eyes.

'I'd spent the afternoon shopping. Rose had gone to see an exhibition, a retrospective . . . some famous painter, I forget who. We'd agreed to meet at La Coupole. Rose was there when I arrived. She was sitting with a man and she told me they'd met by chance at the exhibition.'

'And it was him – Moreau?'

'That was the name.' Molly nodded. 'He said he was French

Canadian. I was rather intrigued. He was quite good-looking, not in a movie star kind of way, but attractive all the same, and I couldn't help noticing it was the first time I'd seen Rose animated in the presence of a man – since Matt died, I mean. Later I teased her about it and asked if she'd found a new beau. She laughed it off, but the next day when we had a plan to visit Versailles, it turned out she had invited him to join us. I shut up after that. I was just praying Rose had found someone she liked, someone she was drawn to, and I kept hoping she would mention him when we went back to London, that perhaps they had made a plan to meet again.'

'And?' Addy prompted her.

'I never heard any more about him. But it was just around that time that Rose started going off on her own and after a while I began to wonder if she'd met someone – not him, someone else – a man she didn't want to tell me about. We still saw a lot of each other, but somehow it wasn't the same. I felt she wasn't really there any more, with me, I mean . . .'

Her voice trailed off. She had noticed Addy taking something from her jacket pocket.

'Malek asked me to show it to you.' Addy handed the snapshot to her. 'He thinks it could be Philip Moreau.'

Molly laid the photograph on the table in front of her and bent over it. She sat like that, staring at it, for what seemed like for ever.

'There's a resemblance.' She spoke at last. 'But I remember he had dark hair, and it was combed differently.' She went back to gnawing at her lip. Addy held her breath.

'I'm sorry, Addy.' Molly looked up. 'As I say, it looks like him, but I can't be certain.'

Though she'd been more than half expecting it, Addy still felt a shock on hearing the words. She looked away. How could Rose have been so blind? Why had it taken her so long to see what kind of man she had got involved with? Questions she would never find an answer to now.

Later, when they went upstairs to the drawing room, Molly showed her a copy of the evening paper she had brought back with her. Rose's picture was on the front page under a headline in heavy black print: *Knightsbridge Killings: Two Americans*

Dead. It was an old photograph, which she recognized from the time when Rose had worked for a New York publisher. The residents of the mews had been interviewed by reporters. Her own name was mentioned: *Adelaide Banks, Mrs Carmody's niece from New York, had been with her aunt when the attack occurred.*

'The press will be looking for you, Addy dear. You must stay here with me. Don't worry if they find out – I'll keep them at bay. But we ought to go over to Rose's house at some point and collect the rest of your things.'

'The police searched it again this morning,' Addy said. 'Malek told me.'

'What on earth are they looking for?' Molly was puzzled.

'I'm not sure.' Addy bit her lip. She realized she'd been careless. Dave had asked her to keep what he'd told her to herself.

'Is it something important?' Molly persisted.

'Must be, I guess.' Addy could only shrug. She knew she mustn't let on about the memory stick. 'But whatever it is, he said they hadn't found it.'

TWENTY-TWO

I t was after ten before Bela Horvath was finally able to leave his office in Canary Wharf and go home. It had been a trying day, but luckily he lived only ten minutes' walk away in one of the high-rise apartment blocks that formed part of the sprawling development that had grown up around what until quite recently had been the capital's tallest building, its commanding presence still dominating the skyline overlooking Limehouse Reach.

Informed overnight of the death of one of the firm's employees, he had not been surprised when a pair of detectives had called on him that morning wanting to know who Michael Ryker was and what business he'd had in London. Had the circumstances been otherwise, he might have reached out for help in dealing with this troublesome question. In accordance with the firm's usual practice, he had taken pains to cultivate several high-ranking officers in the Metropolitan Police, a policy that had paid off when it came to smoothing over irregularities in the behaviour of certain of the company's clients, some of them celebrities with habits that might well have landed less fortunate offenders behind bars, others who were out and out criminals requiring at the very least a blind eye turned to what might be laughingly called their 'lifestyles'. But murder was murder; there was no getting around it, and Bela knew better than to try appealing to any higher authority to intervene on his behalf.

In the event, the interview had taxed his ingenuity to the limits. He had had to abandon any thought of pleading ignorance: to say he had no idea why one of his employees together with an American lady of apparently spotless reputation should have been fatally stabbed within minutes of each other. The detectives would never have bought it. Better by far to give them a good story. It was a technique he had learned during his time with the CIA. The more complex, the more incredible a tale, the more likely it was to be believed, providing it had a kernel of truth. And since Bela was aware that rumours of the theft of an unusually large sum of money and consequent humiliation of various high-ranking personages in Moscow had been circulating in the intelligence community for some time, he knew that the police would have no difficulty in confirming the fact. Once swallowed, the rest was easily digested, and Bela took pride in the fact that most of what he had told the pair was true. If he had sailed close to the wind it was with a certain confidence in his powers. After all, he had done this sort of thing before, and on occasion when his very life had been at stake.

Unfortunately that had not been the end of it. There were still his superiors in New York to be appeased and the calls and messages from that quarter had been flooding in since the early hours. Ryker's mission to London had been his idea, and while New York had approved it, they were yet to be convinced that the violent fashion in which it had ended could not have been avoided. There was still work to be done in that quarter, and in truth Bela had grown weary of it all, the endless business of explaining and placating. He deserved better, and had good reason to believe that a future as bright and orgiastic as any dreamed up by a paperback author awaited him. But a problem had cropped up overnight, and now the enterprise he was engaged in had run into difficulties. At least he feared so, and was anxious to have his doubts resolved at the earliest possible moment.

It was something of a relief then to put the worries behind him for a while at least and take refuge in his apartment, which was on the tenth floor of a fifteen-storey block, to pour himself a glass of *palinka* – the fruit brandy for which the country of his birth was famed, and from the taste of which he had never weaned himself – and then to open the glass doors that gave on to a small balcony, where he could catch a glimpse of the river below and the great expanse of lights beyond it. Standing on the small deck with the world spread out at his feet he found – as was so often the case these days – that his thoughts were straying back to the past, to the strange course his life had taken; to the winding road it would have been impossible to foresee that had brought him to this spot.

Born in a thatched cottage in the middle of the great Hungarian plain, he had been the fourth of four sons of a farmer whose losing battle with the soil had condemned his family to a life of penury and whose leaky ship had only been kept afloat by his wife, Bela's mother, a woman of iron will, whose advice to her last son had been to leave the village where they dwelt for good and seek his fortune elsewhere. Though aged only fifteen, he had contrived to live by his wits thereafter, first as a street boy and sometime thief in Budapest, later as the protégé – though *discovery* might have been a better word – of an American diplomat who Bela only later learned was contracted to the CIA. It was this man who had spotted the same gifts in the young boy that his mother had divined and by degrees Bela had found himself drawn into the secret world, which, even now, though he had finally abandoned it for another, better paid profession, he still felt part of.

His life had taken an eventful turn and, in the years that followed, he had risked it more than once in the service of his new masters, acquiring as he grew older a variety of skills and the mastery of several languages. Something of an exotic figure among the purposely colourless ranks of the monk-like community he had joined, he'd become known for his unorthodox methods and something more valuable: a cool head in a crisis. Yet though he had prospered, eventually obtaining American citizenship along with a senior position on the East European desk at Langley, he had always known that he was not one of them – not in their eyes – he was 'our *Magyar*', an interesting character with a fascinating background. He knew for a fact that many of them dined out on stories about him.

And so finally he had had enough and taken his leave of the Company with a capital *C*, as it was known, to enter the private sector, where his particular talents were valued at least as highly as before, but better rewarded, and again he had prospered. But it was not enough. Simply put, he had yearned to rise higher, so high in fact that one day he could look down on them, the ones who in spite of all he had achieved continued to patronize him, their pet 'Magyar', the ones who had never entirely trusted him and let him know it: the ones who, one day from a great height, he would finally piss on.

But now the situation had changed. Or had it? He would soon find out.

Quitting the balcony where the cold air had begun to bite, Bela went back into the sitting room and refilled his glass, pausing to lift it in a silent toast to a photograph that stood on a glass-topped table next to the drinks cabinet and bore the grainy black-and-white image of a woman with thinning hair and a set jaw. It was his only memento of his mother and of far greater importance to him than the photograph that stood beside it of his late wife, a pale blonde lady of impeccable WASP lineage who Bela had thought, in his innocence, might gain him access to the private sanctums of the great from which he had always been excluded. The unlucky woman had contracted cancer at an early age and died after only ten years of what had been in all senses a barren marriage.

He looked at his watch: it was ten thirty. He was expecting a visitor and wanted to be ready for their meeting. Quitting the sitting room for a moment, he went into his study next door and retrieved a Glock pistol from the top drawer of his desk. A slimline model, it felt light in its polymer casing and fitted easily into his jacket pocket. It was simply a precaution, he didn't expect to have to use it, but given the unpredictable nature of his late-night caller it was good to be prepared. As he shut the drawer, the house telephone rang. He picked up the receiver.

'Yes?'

'There's a gentleman to see you, sir.' It was the night porter calling from the lobby downstairs. 'A Mr Zhukov.'

'Send him up.'

A smile crossed Bela's lips. His visitor was known for his peculiar sense of humour and perhaps the name of a famous Soviet war hero appealed to his taste for the absurd. He went out into the hall and unlocked the door, leaving it open just a crack. Then he returned to the sitting room and took a seat in an armchair, one of a pair facing each other. Presently he heard the front door shut, then footsteps. A man, not immediately recognizable, entered the room. Dressed all in black, he had grey hair and Bela saw he was limping.

'Dear me, how you've aged.' His tone was ironic.

'You, on the other hand, haven't changed a bit, Bela. I don't know how you do it.'

Charon's smile was warm and engaging.

'Let's not beat about the bush. This whole business has turned into a disaster. What can that fool have been thinking of? We needed the woman alive.' Bela gave vent to his feelings.

Charon shrugged. He had shed his coat and was walking about the room, prowling rather: despite his limp he moved with the languid grace of a big carnivore.

'I blame myself,' he said. 'I should have kept Klepkin on a tighter leash. He was told to restrain her, nothing more. It was just a question of making her see reason. The man's become an embarrassment. He's drinking again. The police will be looking for him now. They must have a good description of him.'

While his guest was speaking, Bela had risen and gone to the drinks cabinet.

'You used to drink whisky,' he said.

'And still do.' Charon seated himself in one of the armchairs. He caught his host's eye. 'There's no need for you to worry,' he said. 'Klepkin's convinced we cooked up this scheme on our own. But he's afraid if he's arrested, the British police will eventually hand him over to the Russians, not that they would. But try telling Grigor that.'

Bela handed his guest his drink. 'You have a solution in mind?' He sat down facing him, and as he looked into Charon's eyes, he was reminded uncomfortably of a moment years ago when he had glanced into a tiger's cage – in the Berlin Zoo it was – and found the beast standing close up to the bars regarding him. He had never forgotten its gaze, which was tranquil, impartial, uninterested – and utterly chilling. He shook his head to clear it.

'A solution?' Charon examined the contents of his glass. 'Oh, I think so. It's time.' He looked up. 'Is Chekhov in town?'

'He is.'

'With a crew?'

'Of course.'

'Do you have his number?'

Bela nodded.

Charon reached into the pocket of his jacket and drew out a piece of paper. Leaning forward, he handed it to the other man.

'I suggest you give him a call. Say you have it on good authority that his quarry will be at this location at around ten o'clock tomorrow morning.'

'How can you be sure?' Bela glanced at the slip of paper.

'We're due to meet. I told him I would have some good news for him.'

Bela raised his eyebrows but said nothing. He took his phone from his pocket and tapped out the number. It was quickly answered and he began to speak in Russian. Charon waited patiently until the conversation was ended and Bela had rung off.

'He naturally wanted to know where the information came from. I said a confidential informant. He wanted to know if we'd made any progress in tracking you down. I said I had alerted all our branches to be on the alert for any sighting of you.'

Charon grunted. He swallowed the last of his whisky.

'And one other thing you might want to bear in mind.' Bela put his phone away. 'It seems your old friend Kimura is here as well. He broke into Mrs Carmody's house two nights ago. It sounds as though he's managed to connect her to you.'

'Now that is unfortunate.' Charon frowned.

'He was masked at the time so the police have no description to go on. But all things considered it might be as well if we got this business wrapped up as soon as possible.'

'I quite agree.'

Bela studied his visitor. 'The hair comes from a bottle, of course, but the limp . . . it's very convincing.'

'I had a special shoe made with a slight lift. I use it on occasion. Together with the hair and an accent of some sort I can provide any witness with a set of images easy to recall.

Elaborate disguises are nearly always a mistake. The trouble is they look like what they are . . . disguises.' Charon smiled.

'Another whisky?'

'Thank you, no.'

Bela rose and went to the drinks cabinet. He refilled his glass.

'I suppose I know you better than anyone, though that's not saying much. But I was thinking about you today, remembering the first time we met. Vienna, was it? You were wearing some rough kind of tweed jacket and one of those hideous Tyrolean hats with a feather in it. You looked like a country bumpkin in town for the day.'

'I remember . . . the *grafin* with the cocaine habit . . . what became of her, I wonder?'

'The next time I saw you it was in Bucharest. I don't remember how you were dressed, only that it took me a full minute to recognize you. I simply didn't know who you were.'

'I'll let you in on a secret, Bela.' Charon stretched. 'I have the same problem myself.'

Horvath emptied his glass. It occurred to him that he was drinking too much. Twenty years they had known each other and he had never lost his sense of how dangerous this man was.

'To business then: I've persuaded the police that the stick is in the bank in Zurich. Of course, Klepkin will tell the Russians otherwise and that he doesn't know where it is. Am I right?' He glanced at Charon, who nodded. 'You say it's here in London? But now that the woman is dead, how can you possibly be sure?'

'Calm yourself.' Charon yawned. 'I'll have it in my hands shortly.'

'But are you certain? It wasn't among Mrs Carmody's belongings. According to my police sources they searched her house again today. They were looking for it. I'm sure they examined her clothes, the linings and so on, and her shoes as well. They're not fools.'

'Let me say again: I know where it is.' Charon took a deep breath. 'Do you mind if I get some air? It's rather stuffy in here. The heating . . .'

He rose and went over to the glassed doors and opened them.

'What a view!' He spoke from the balcony. 'My word, you've done well for yourself, Bela. Are you sure you want to give up your job? I've always thought it a pity Safe Solutions arrived so late on the scene. If I'd been a younger man I might have applied for a permanent job with them. The things you people get away with! How do you explain it?'

'That's easy.' Horvath's laugh was hollow. 'Look at the world – pick a country, any country, ours if you like – look at the people who are running it. You have to wonder what stone they crawled out from under. Believe me, our services are much in demand.'

'A sobering thought.'

'Like a billion dollars.' Bela had risen to pour himself another drink, but then changed his mind and put his glass down. He came over to join Charon. 'Divided by two of course, which I must admit is a good deal better than three.'

Charon backed off the balcony. Bela moved forward to close the doors.

'But not as perfect as one.'

Charon's whisper sounded in his ear.

'What?'

His voice was cut off as his neck was trapped in the crook of Charon's arm. As he reached for the pistol in his pocket his wrist was pulled into an iron grip and thrust up behind his back. In a moment he was being forced forward on to the deck outside.

'Don't understand . . .' Pushed up against the balustrade, choked by the arm around his neck, he could barely speak.

'You will, Bela, you will.'

Letting go of his hand, Charon bent swiftly and took a grip of his thighs.

'You've got time.'

Hoisting him up in one movement he held him balanced, teetering like a seesaw on the bar of the balustrade.

'. . . time . . .?'

'It's a long way down.'

He tipped the body over. A diminishing scream punctured the night air.

Charon leaned over the balustrade. He cupped an ear.

'That music has a dying fall.'

Charon could feel his heart racing like a turbine engine: his nerve ends tingled with the thrill of it.

'Divided by *two*? What can you have been thinking, Bela Horvath? You knew me better than anyone. You said so yourself.'

Stepping back, he wiped the handle of the door with his handkerchief, shut both of them and then retrieved the glass he'd used, took it to the kitchen, washed and dried it and then replaced it in the drinks cabinet. Had he touched anything else? Perhaps the wooden table by the chair where he'd been sitting? He wiped the surface carefully, and did the same thing to the front door handle as he went out.

He took the elevator down to the second floor and then walked down the stairs into the lobby, which was deserted. The door to the outside was open. No doubt the night porter had heard the scream and gone out to investigate. Charon had taken note of the CCTV camera mounted in the lobby and was careful to keep his face turned away from it. Without haste he walked out into the forecourt. Stars were beginning to appear in the night sky. The clouds were clearing. A small group had gathered away to his left in front of the building. He heard a woman's cry, but paid no attention to it, walking towards the river, limping towards the river, a grey-haired man, too old and too handicapped to offer any assistance.

TWENTY-THREE

L ooking down at the expanse of trampled, soiled snow – he was on an upper level of the National Theatre, leaning over a parapet that overlooked the broad walkway running alongside the river below – Charon was reminded of a scene he had witnessed years before on a dry, dusty plain in Africa. Tanganyika it was, the Serengeti Reserve.

He had offered his companion at the time a choice of holiday destinations. She had plumped for a safari, and in due course they had found themselves perched on a low hillock looking down at a herd of wildebeest with only a guide for company. A grizzled settler-type wearing soiled khaki – the words *white hunter* came to mind – he had the purplish nose of a drinker, a face the colour of mahogany and a vocabulary so limited it was all they could do to get a word out of him. Sign language had seemed to be his sole means of communication.

Without warning, he had pointed, and, following the direction of his nicotine-stained finger, Charon had noticed a slight difference in the colour of the grass below and a little to one side of the hill where they were sitting in the sparse shade of a thorn tree. Peering hard at the spot through his field glasses, he had eventually made out of the shapes of two – no, three lionesses. They must have been lying there for some time since he had not noticed their approach through the waist-high grass.

As he'd watched, the group had begun to stir. First one, then another of the animals had risen and begun to move off in a leisurely manner, though in different directions, their slow passage making little impression on the swaying grass, leaving the last of the trio alone and unmoving.

The herd had also begun to stir, though not in a noticeable way, there were no signs of panic among them, but like a ripple on the surface of an otherwise still pond, a shared feeling seemed to pass through the scattered herbivores and they began gradually to move off. Meantime, the two lionesses had quietly disposed themselves around the back of the herd, but keeping their distance, not ready yet to spook their prey, simply setting themselves up for the action that was to follow.

Only then did Charon spot their target. It was one of the cows near the edge of the herd. At first glance there seemed nothing wrong with her, but when you looked closer, you could see she was moving a little awkwardly – a torn muscle perhaps – not limping exactly but hampered in some way.

The lone lioness rose to her feet. She began to move forward, crouching low, crawling through the barely stirring grass. As though connected to her by some invisible medium, the other two began to advance at the same time, drawing closer to the herd, which by a similar shared instinct broke suddenly into a run, all but one galloping away across the dusty plain, leaving only the injured animal in their wake, struggling to keep up, but almost at once falling behind. At the same instant the crawling lioness rose to her full height and like a tawny arrow shot from a bow burst out of the tall grass. Coming at the straggler from the side, she easily caught up with it and then sprang on to its back and, with claws and teeth sunk in its neck, dragged it to the ground.

The kill had sent a thrill akin to an electric charge racing through Charon's veins – for a moment he had sensed the claws, *his* claws digging deep into the unresisting flesh – and with the memory now fresh in his mind and something of the same excitement starting to build in him, he watched the three men he'd been observing for the past ten minutes slowly adjust their positions on the terrace below. Curly, Larry and Moe he'd named them, and stooges they were, creatures at the beck and call of a fourth man who was sitting at a table behind the plate-glass windows of a café some way to the left of where Charon had posted himself apparently reading a newspaper.

'Anton Pavlovich . . .'

Although it was some years since he'd last set eyes on the Russian agent whose codename was Chekhov, Charon recognized the balding, stocky figure seated beside the window. The scene was set. It remained only for the ringmaster to give the signal.

Chekhov folded his newspaper and rose, buttoning his coat.

Curly was first to react. Tall and stooped, he had been standing not far from where Chekhov had been sitting, studying a pillar covered with posters advertising forthcoming attractions – for rather longer than was necessary. As he turned away, the second of the trio, Larry, balding and bull-shouldered, rose from the stone bench where he was seated almost directly below Charon and stretched luxuriously like a man tired of sitting and ready to move on. His gesture in turn triggered a reaction from Moe, the smallest of the three, who was dressed formally in a business suit and coat and carried an attaché case. He had been standing further along the walkway, glancing at his wristwatch every few minutes as though expecting someone to join him. Now he shook his head in apparent exasperation, making it clear he would wait no longer.

In fact, their prey had arrived some minutes earlier. Charon had spotted Gogol's meandering progress as he came along the walkway from the bridge and even from a distance it was clear the man had been drinking. Twice he had bumped into pedestrians coming the other way, seemingly unaware of their presence, and although he appeared vaguely alert to possible danger, glancing behind him now and again, his movements were clumsy, uncoordinated: the straggler in the herd. The paved surface of the pathway, though much trampled, was still covered with snow and slippery enough for Gogol to have fastened one hand to the rail bordering the river as he walked alongside it. Meanwhile, with the weather clearing, it seemed Londoners along with the inevitable tourists were making the most of the opportunity to stretch their legs or simply bask in the spells of intermittent sunshine that broke through the scattered clouds overhead, and although the terrace below where Charon was standing wasn't crowded it had remained busy for the half hour or so that he had been waiting there.

Following the directions Charon had given to him, Gogol had taken up a position almost directly below and in front of Charon, who had added a close-fitting woollen cap to his appearance and wrapped a large scarf around his neck which, pulled up as it was now, covered the bottom part of his face. In addition, he had provided himself with a camera and had spent the time he was waiting apparently taking snaps of the river and the buildings lining it. Now he fixed his gaze on Gogol, who was standing with his back against the railing, head bowed, and with the brim of his black felt hat pulled down low so as to hide the bulging eyes, which half the police force in London must now be on the lookout for, or so Charon surmised.

With the pieces all in place, Chekhov had quit the café and come out on the terrace. Standing with his back to Gogol, he was apparently checking his phone, but Charon could see that his lips were moving and he was speaking into the lapel of his coat. At least one of his crew – the thick-set one who had been sitting on the bench below – had what looked like a hearing aid in his ear and Charon assumed the other two were similarly equipped. All three were moving in Gogol's direction now, making their slow way through the strolling throng, none of them seeming to have any particular purpose in mind.

The next act would be choreographed and Charon felt he could have penned the script himself had he chosen to. The Russians were good at this sort of thing. The three men would group themselves around Gogol, none of them too close, none of them looking at him. Once in position they would go into action.

One of their number, most likely Larry, the heavy-shouldered one, would jostle their victim, pushing him off balance for a moment, long enough to distract him while a second – Curly perhaps – jabbed a hypodermic needle loaded with a knockout drug into his neck. As he collapsed suddenly to the ground, panic would ensue among those nearest to him. Cries for help would be heard. The first two would be down on their knees trying to render what help they could while the third, Moe, showing more presence of mind, would already have his phone out while announcing to the world that he was calling for help.

Later, those who had witnessed the incident would comment admiringly on the speed with which an ambulance had arrived in the road behind the theatre and on the calm and efficient way in which the two medics who had run in carrying a stretcher had dealt with the unfortunate man lying prone on the cement, transferring him into their vehicle after only the briefest delay and driving him off at speed, siren wailing.

So much for the script, but Charon had a scenario of his own in mind, one that had occurred to him during the last few minutes and which had been brought on by the sight of Gogol standing where he was by the hand rail bordering the river. It was a long shot, but worth trying (and something of a *coup de théâtre* if he could pull it off). And he could also claim if he cared to that he'd be doing the man a favour considering what lay in wait for him at the hands of his captors.

But the question remained: how would Grigor react? Even given the right incentive, would the lab rat respond as expected? It was a field in which Charon, all modesty aside, quite rightly regarded himself as an expert. People were predictable. He had always said so. It was just a matter of pressing the right buttons. Speaking of which . . .

He took a phone from his pocket and tapped out a number. He watched as Gogol reached for his own phone.

'*Da?*'

'It's me, Grigor. You're in trouble.'

'What . . . what . . .?'

'I just got here and saw Chekhov. He's over on the other side of the terrace near the café. He's got his back to you. He has a crew with him. See the tall one to the right of you? And the big man in front?'

Gogol swore in Russian, his gaze switching from side to side.

'Oh, and the little man with the briefcase – he's one of them.'

More swearing. Gogol stood rooted to the spot, the phone pressed to his ear: a cornered wildebeest.

'Don't let them take you, old friend. You know what will happen. You'll tell them the truth, but they won't believe you, not till they've broken every bone in your body, and that's just for starters. There's nothing I can do to help. Look behind you.'

'*Behind?*' The word came in a gasp.

'The river . . .'

Charon watched, fascinated. Had it worked? For a moment, he thought not. Then all at once Gogol spun on his heel, and clutching hold of the railing dragged his body up on to it. The three men who were near now saw what he was about to do and began to barge their way through the crowd. One of them, Larry, the biggest, lunged forward, knocking a young couple walking hand in hand aside, but he was too late. Not hesitating for a second, Gogol hauled himself over the railing and vanished.

There were screams now; people flocked to the edge of the terrace and leaned over the rail to peer down. Chekhov's crew were lost in the crush.

Charon hurried to the end of the parapet where the view was clearer. His sometime partner had vanished for the moment, but presently he caught sight of Gogol's head and his desperately flailing arms. He was being swept along by the muddy current and stayed afloat for only a few seconds. First his head sank beneath the surface, then his arms until finally there was nothing to be seen except for a small black object that spun round and round as it continued on its way downstream. It took Charon a moment to recognize what it was: a black felt hat.

The moment called for a suitable epitaph and he had one ready.

'Sweet Thames, run softly . . .'

TWENTY-FOUR

I t was Rose in her dream, but not the Rose she'd known: this was the Rose she had glimpsed for a second in the uncertain light of the hallway before they went out into the mews. Rose with her eyes wide and staring, mouth twisted in anguish. Rose on the edge of madness.

She was speaking to Addy, trying to tell her something; her lips were moving, but no sound came out, and Addy felt helpless. Trapped in the deep silence of the dream, she struggled to break through the invisible barrier that kept them apart, but try as she might she could get no closer to her aunt and then the dream ended as dreams did and she woke with a start and lay shaken and sweating.

The Rose in her dream wasn't Rose. She knew that. People didn't come back from the dead with grim warnings for the living. That was all crap. Most likely it was her own subconscious' way of trying to tell her something and to fool her into thinking that if it was Rose talking to her, she just might believe there was something she had forgotten or hadn't understood.

Which was?

Addy had no idea, and the struggle to recover it kept her tossing in bed for what felt like hours. It took for ever to get back to sleep, and when she woke next morning, with a solitary beam of sunshine showing through a crack in the curtains, she found that for once she was able to remember her dream in detail. It hadn't melted away as they often did. Something was nagging at her, something important; it was there at the back of her mind, some idea she couldn't quite get a hold of.

Waking later than usual, she went downstairs to find that Molly had left her a note on the kitchen table.

Had to pop out for an hour or two. Breakfast roll in the oven if you want it. Have you had any thoughts about the funeral? Christ Church and St Luke's are both nearby if you want a religious ceremony. I could arrange that for you. Otherwise there's the Golders Green crematorium. Let me know what you want. Molly

Addy was glad she could have breakfast on her own. They'd had dinner together last night and Molly had been in overdrive, going on and on about Rose, reliving the last few years, the things they had done together, and then wondering what had gone wrong in her friend's life. Was it this man Philip Moreau? Was he behind it? Or was it someone else, some other man they didn't know about? It was Molly's way of trying to deal with the tragedy, Addy supposed, to talk it to death, and she felt bad about not being allowed to tell her that Philip Moreau wasn't Philip Moreau; he was some badass killer that Rose had somehow got tangled up with, and would she please just shut up. What Addy wanted was quiet; a chance to ponder, to put all the pieces together, to think it through. No wonder then, with all that in her mind, that her sleep had been so disturbed. Perhaps her dream had been nothing more than the backwash of her waking thoughts. Yes, maybe . . . but Addy didn't think so. There was something else there, hidden in the tangle of half-formed ideas, a stray thread she hadn't grasped yet.

She had just taken the roll Molly had left her from the oven when her phone rang.

'Hi there.' It was DS Malek. 'Have you heard the news? That bloke I mentioned yesterday, the one who told us all about Charon and Moreau and the memory stick, the Safe Solutions guy, Bela Horvath – he fell off his balcony last night.'

'He *what*?'

'Ten floors down. Fell or was pushed. I thought I'd better tell you, and to warn you again not to talk to anyone about this. We don't want what I told you yesterday to get into the newspapers until we can find out what's going on.'

'*Pushed*, you say?'

'He had a visitor last night, a Russian. The hall porter can't remember his name, but said he had an accent. He ran outside when he heard the commotion and didn't see the man leave. But it must have been just after Horvath hit the ground. His visitor was caught on CCTV, but he kept his face hidden, and he was also spotted walking away.'

'Could it have been the same man who killed Rose . . . what's his name?'

'Klepkin? We don't think so. It sounded like an older man. One of the witnesses said he was limping.'

Addy was silent. She was staring at a calendar that was hanging on the wall. There was something about it . . .

'Addy? Are you OK?' He sounded concerned.

'Sure.' She pushed the thought, whatever it was, from her mind. 'I was just thinking. It's all part of the same thing, isn't it? It's to do with that memory stick.'

'I would call that a reasonable assumption.' He laughed drily.

'So what is going on, for Christ's sake?'

'I wish we knew. But don't tell anyone I said so. We can't have the public thinking the Old Bill is baffled.'

'Especially when it's true.'

'And no sharing any of this on social media.'

'You're talking to the wrong canary. Facebook is just a word to me and I tweet not.'

His laugh was unaffected this time.

'Have the press tracked you down yet?' he asked.

'Not so far. Molly had a couple of calls yesterday. They must have found out she knew Rose. She told them she thought I was staying with friends in London, but wasn't sure where or with who.'

'Have you thought about the funeral?'

'Jesus! First Molly, now you – can't you guys give me a break?'

He chuckled. 'Are you always this combative?'

'Combative! That's a big word for a homicide dick.' But she laughed. 'I guess I am. I'm told I scare people off.' She meant men, and she was testing him, but he didn't bite.

'I thought I'd better tell you, we haven't released your aunt's body yet. The post-mortem won't be done till later today. There are usually delays around this time of year. I'm afraid the funeral will have to wait till after Christmas.'

'That's OK, but I want to go to Rose's house and start clearing up. Are you done with it?'

'As of yesterday,' he said. 'But we've told one of our mobile units to keep an eye on the place. If they think anyone's there, they might knock on the door. I'll make sure they're alerted. Just tell them who you are.'

Actually clearing up wasn't what Addy had in mind, not yet. She would do that later, after the funeral, which right now she didn't want to think about. She just wanted to be on her own in the house, to feel Rose's presence in some way, and not have Molly there with her, because if she mentioned it, Molly was sure to want to come along.

Molly. Addy knew she meant well and wanted to help, but the truth was they'd never really hit it off. Even now, with Rose's friend doing her mother hen bit, making out that nothing was too much trouble and if there was anything Addy wanted she had only to ask, Addy still couldn't warm to her. It was hard to put her finger on exactly why, but there was one thing she had no doubt about: Molly didn't care for her either and never had. It was one of those things, oil and water, and it was like that with some people and the opposite with others; DS Malek, for example. She'd felt easy with him from the start, they'd connected, and you couldn't explain it any more than you could explain why Molly Kingsmill had always set her teeth on edge. At first Addy thought it might be a simple case of jealousy. She'd been too posses-sive of Rose, she knew that. But there were other currents at work between them, and Addy wondered if Molly felt the same. Maybe they had both sensed a quality in the other they couldn't relate to.

It was something to ponder, and as she took an Uber ride up to Knightsbridge Addy turned the question over in her mind. Maybe it was just one of those things, and she should let it go. There was the funeral to be got through, and Molly would want to be part of that. Difficult days lay ahead and Addy knew she would have to behave like a grown-up, accept all the help that was offered and keep her feelings to herself.

Did she have to go on staying with her though? What would Molly say if she moved out? The truth was she wanted to be in Rose's house, to spend these last days with the ghost of the person she had loved most and was now gone from her life for ever. Would Molly understand that?

It was a question she couldn't answer and one that took on a new and disturbing aspect when she reached her destination. The mews was deserted – a lucky break, the last thing Addy wanted that morning was have Rose's neighbours telling her how shocked they were by what had happened, how fond they had been of Rose, how much they would miss her, all of which Addy would have believed, Rose having been the person she was – but as she walked down the cobbled way she noticed where the snow had been cleared around the places where the bodies had lain and wondered if she wasn't making a mistake returning to the scene.

The feeling only gained strength when she entered the house, which was like an ice-box – the cops must have turned off the heating when they left – and though she got it going again she had to keep her coat on as she wandered through the rooms that now seemed so empty, stripped of the life that Rose must have breathed into them and that she had imagined the evening she'd arrived. And although the police had treated the place with care – they had left nothing lying around – the signs of their search were there to see: two of the drawers in Rose's small writing-desk in the corner of the sitting room had been left half open, and the books they must have pulled out from the shelves hadn't been pushed back properly. Rose's clothes, too, had been searched, as she discovered when she went upstairs to the bedrooms. Although they were still on their hangers some of them were askew and Addy found part of the lining in one of Rose's jackets torn and hanging loose. It was obvious they'd been searching for the memory stick.

The bag her aunt had had with her when Addy last saw her – the one she had carried Grumble in – was lying on the bed, open. She had brought the bear with her and now she put him back where he belonged, on the throne of pillows at the head of Rose's bed. She had as good as made up her mind that she would move out of Molly's house and come back here.

Returning Grumble to his proper place was like putting down a marker to that effect.

Before quitting the bedroom Addy looked inside Rose's bag and found that apart from a few clothes and toilet articles there was only her aunt's MacBook, which she knew the cops must have checked for any clues it might contain and found nothing, otherwise Malek would have told her; at least she hoped he would.

She opened the small computer, and after giving it a minute to boot up, she checked it herself. Her guess had been right: there was nothing, just a list of bills paid and other household stuff and a file dealing with tax records. Nor was there anything of note in Rose's emails, which seemed mainly from friends, some of them familiar to Addy, some not. The name Philip Moreau didn't appear anywhere, and though it might have been found in Rose's phone, it wouldn't be the one she had had with her when she died, the one the police had checked. It would have been in the one they had not been able to trace: the one Rose had lost or perhaps dumped when she was on the run.

She switched the computer off and was just putting it back in the bag – she would deal with it later – when her own phone rang. It was Molly calling.

'I was expecting to find you home when I got back, Addy. Where are you?'

'At Rose's house. I thought I'd start sorting things out.'

Aware that she wasn't being entirely truthful, Addy scowled at her reflection in the wardrobe mirror. She was sitting on Rose's bed.

'Do you want some help?'

'Not at the moment, thanks. I'm not going to be here long. I thought I'd leave most of it until after Christmas.'

Shit! She shouldn't have mentioned Christmas. It was only two days away and, just as she'd feared, Molly came in on cue.

'I meant to say, I thought we'd just have a quiet meal on Christmas Day. What do you think? Neither of us is exactly in a festive mood.'

'That's sounds fine, Molly.' Her and her big mouth – she'd

been hoping simply to ignore the occasion this year, pretend it wasn't happening.

'And there's something else. I've just had a call from a friend of Rose's. I wonder if she ever mentioned him to you. His name's Peter Flynn. He's an actor, an Irishman, a good bit older than Rose, but a very nice man. They met at a dinner party somewhere and Rose took to him. Oh, not in the romantic line, that's not what I mean.' Molly giggled. 'As I say, he was a good bit older than she, but he was very agreeable company. The three of us used to have lunch together now and again. Anyway, he read about poor Rose in the newspaper and called up to say how shocked he was and also that he'd noticed your name in the report and wondered how he could get in touch with you. There's something he wants to tell you.'

'Like what?' Addy was intrigued.

'I don't know. He was rather mysterious about it. Apparently he saw Rose not long ago and they had a drink together, which was news to me – I had the impression she'd been avoiding her friends. I tried delicately to find out what it was she had said to him, but all he would say is that he has something to tell you. It sounds strange, I know, but I assure you he's perfectly respectable. Would you like his number?'

'Please.'

Addy grabbed a pad and pencil from the bedside table and wrote down the number Molly gave her.

'He said you could call him any time this afternoon, but not this evening as he'd be working. He's appearing in a play in London.'

Thinking about what she had just been told, Addy felt a stab of guilt. Molly kept trying to help, and she knew she ought to feel more grateful. The very fact that they didn't really get on was a point in her favour, Addy thought, a sign of good character. It was how adults behaved, or ought to behave, and maybe she should take a lesson from Rose's friend and make a little more effort herself, offer to help with their Christmas dinner, for example, at the very least buy her hostess a present as a way of saying thank you for all she had done.

She called the number Molly had given her. It was answered on the second ring.

'Peter Flynn speaking, who's that?'

'I'm Addy – Adelaide Banks. Molly said you wanted to talk to me.'

'Addy! I'm so pleased you called. My dear, I can't tell you how distressed I was to hear what happened to poor Rose.' The voice was soft and musical, the Irish accent unmistakable. 'I can only imagine how terrible you must be feeling. I know how much Rose loved you, how close you were. Truly, I can't find the words . . .'

'That's very kind of you, Mr Flynn . . .'

'Peter, please . . .'

'Had you known her long?'

'For about a year. We met last winter at a dinner party and we saw quite a bit of each other for a while. I'll make no bones about it – I thought she was enchanting. We used to go to the theatre, sometimes Molly would come with us. I have such warm memories of them both.'

Addy hesitated. 'Memories . . . you mean all that stopped?'

It was his turn to pause. 'I don't know how to say this, Addy, but suddenly Rose seemed to change. She wasn't around any more for one thing. Mind you, she was travelling a lot then, which may have had something to do with it, but even when she was here I didn't see that much of her and when I did she seemed reserved . . . withdrawn . . . not like the Rose I'd known. It's hard to explain.'

Addy waited. She wanted him to go on, but he stayed silent.

'There was something you wanted to tell me?'

'It's what Rose said to me the last time we met. I'm not sure I understood her—' He broke off. Addy could hear noise in the background, what sounded like other voices. 'Addy, I'm sorry, but we're in the middle of rehearsals here. Can we speak again later?'

'Rehearsals? Yes, of course.'

'I've just had an idea. You're an actress, aren't you?'

'We say *actor* these days, Peter.'

'I stand corrected.' He laughed richly. 'Look, I'm appearing in a production of *Twelfth Night* at present. It's playing at the Globe Theatre on the South Bank. I'm sure you've heard of it.'

'You bet.'

'How would you like to see this evening's performance? I can get you a ticket. Then when it's over, we could talk, and if you like I could also show you the theatre proper – I mean the Globe itself. It's not used in winter, because it's open to the elements and too cold. We're performing in the smaller closed theatre, but I thought you might like to see the main one as well. It's a reproduction of Shakespeare's Globe. You won't have seen anything like it before.'

He paused, awaiting a response.

'Is something the matter?' He sounded anxious.

'Oh, no.' Addy was searching for the right word. 'I'm just . . . overwhelmed.'

'We'll meet this evening then. I'll leave a ticket for you at the box office. There's a pub called the Anchor a few steps down the river. You could have a drink there or a cup of coffee after the performance and when everyone's gone home I'll give you a call and you can come and join me. The theatre's locked up at night, but you'll see there's a courtyard beside it behind some locked gates with the stage door beyond that. I'll leave the smaller gate open so you can come in. I'll tell you then what Rose said. I'm not sure I really grasped what she meant, but you may have a better idea.'

'Can you give me a hint?' Addy said.

'Well, let me see . . . it was so odd, I didn't know what to make of it—' He broke off. Addy heard more noises. 'Yes, yes, I'm coming.' He wasn't talking to her. 'Look, Addy, I'm sorry, I can't talk now.'

'No, that's OK, Peter.' Addy swallowed her disappointment. 'You can tell me this evening. I'll see you then.'

She went downstairs. The house was starting to warm up and she took off her coat. Before coming down she had fished Rose's MacBook out of the bag again and googled Peter Flynn. Wikipedia had a piece on him – he was in his early sixties and a well-known character actor, on this side of the pond anyway. They also had a photo of him – several, in fact. Rosy-cheeked, with a full head of grey wavy hair and a wide smile, he looked like what Molly had said he was – a nice guy.

Although her thoughts were elsewhere, she busied herself for a few minutes straightening the books in the bookshelves. Looking around, she saw that the note Molly had left for Rose was still standing on the mantelpiece. Addy took it down.

Rose, I've got Addy staying with me. Please get in touch with us as soon as you can.

Rose had never got to see it. Addy wondered what Peter Flynn was going to tell her. She had liked the sound of his voice with its pleasant Irish lilt. The accent was one she had a particular fondness for. She had even tried it herself once or twice at drama school and found the rhythms weren't that tough to copy, though you had to be careful not to exaggerate them.

Quit daydreaming, she scolded herself. She sat down on the sofa. She was here to try and figure out how this whole godawful shitstorm had come about. So Rose had met a man she was attracted to a few months back and somehow he had managed to draw her into his criminal world, and though it seemed improbable on the face of it, Addy knew that if the person who had played such a part in her life, who'd been more like an older sister or even a mother than an aunt, had a weakness, it was rooted in her nature – she was too trusting – though Rose wouldn't have called it a weakness. For her, love and trust were the same. She made no difference between them.

She had told Horvath that the man she had met, who called himself Philip Moreau but was also known as Charon, claimed to be working for the CIA, and Addy could understand that if Rose had been strongly drawn to him, she might easily have seen that as a reason to do certain favours for him, perform some seemingly innocent tasks.

But if she had discovered at some point that what the memory stick held was of no imaginable importance to her country – that it was just a squalid theft she was involved in – she must have had her suspicions already. Otherwise why look at it in the first place? Were there other, worse things she had learned about this 'Philip Moreau'? Had she come to realize he was a killer, and if so, how had he managed to blind her to his true character? Although Rose's nature had been open and, yes, trusting, she had not been a fool (except maybe a fool for love). There had to be more to it than that. Addy felt she had all the pieces of the puzzle in front of her, yet somehow couldn't fit them together. The picture kept eluding her.

Her phone rang again. This time it was Malek.

'Just checking,' he said. 'How are you doing?'

Another mother hen!

'I meant to call you this morning.' Addy couldn't deny she was pleased he'd been thinking about her. 'Molly says she can't be sure that was Philip Moreau in the photo you gave me, the one Horvath said was Charon. She said his hair was a different colour and combed some other way. But it could be him.'

He whistled into his phone. 'The plot thickens.'

'But I still can't see Rose falling for this guy the way she did. Why she couldn't see through him.'

'Didn't someone once say that love was blind?'

Addy sighed. 'Maybe you're right,' she said. 'It's how she was with Uncle Matt. She fell for him in a big way, and maybe it happened again. Maybe she was waiting for it to happen. Maybe she *wanted* it to happen.'

'And according to Horvath, this Charon bloke has a way with women.'

Addy didn't respond. It was something she didn't want to think about. 'Do you know yet whether he was pushed – Horvath, I mean?'

'We know he had a pistol in his pocket. That seems to suggest he wasn't too sure about his visitor. There's something else, too, but I'm not sure I should tell you about it. I've told you too much already.' His tone was teasing.

'Oh, come on. Who am I going to spill to? Molly?'

'The river police fished the body of a man out of the Thames an hour ago. He was spotted jumping into the river, an apparent suicide. He had a Belgian passport in his pocket, but what's interesting is that according to the coppers who pulled the body out he had big bulging eyes, "just like a bat's", they said.'

It was Addy's turn to whistle. 'Sounds like him – Klepkin.'

'Could be. But keep it to yourself. Look, I have to go. I'll leave it to you to figure it all out.'

'I'm looking for an answer I find convincing,' Addy said.

'Then look at it in a different way.' He chuckled. 'That's what my dad always says. Turn it upside down. Would you believe he's sometimes right? Bye, Addy.' He hung up.

Thanks a lot. Turn it upside down. That was a big help.

Addy put her phone back in her pocket. She stared at the wall opposite where a framed colour photograph hung. It was a study of a windswept beach – looked like Nantucket – where the spume from breaking waves was flying about in the air like torn lace. Away in the distance a couple were walking hand in hand, a woman and a small girl, and the woman's hair was blowing in the wind, and although it was too far to see who they were, Addy knew it was Rose and her and that the person taking the snapshot had most likely been Uncle Matt.

Then she found herself remembering the feeling she had had the day before when she'd woken up and remembered Rose was dead. How it seemed the world had shifted in its orbit, how it wasn't the same any longer, everything was out of sync, and she wondered if that was how Rose had felt when they took her up into the mountains, the Sierra Nevada, and showed her where the plane had crashed and asked her to identify Matt's body, and what she had said to Grandpa later: 'I think I went crazy for a while.'

Hanging next to the photograph was a painting, a print rather, which Addy remembered having seen with Rose the last time she visited New York. They had gone to an exhibition – at MOMA or the Whitney, she couldn't recall which – a display of works meant to fool the eye. She struggled for a few moments trying to remember what they were called . . . it was something like 'Trump' – oh, no, Jesus, not him! *Trompe*, that was it, a French term, *trompe l'oeil*: paintings designed to deceive the viewer, and Rose had liked this one particularly. It looked like a window in the wall that opened to show the Grand Canal in Venice at sunset. But it was an optical illusion. It wasn't what you thought it was. Rose had found they had a print of it in the museum shop and bought it.

Had something like that happened with her and this man
Moreau or Charon or whatever he was calling himself now?
Had she thought she was looking at one thing and found out
too late it was another? Had she . . .?

Addy stopped dead. It was like her mind had hit a brick
wall. The feeling was close to physical and she clutched her
head, which all of a sudden was bursting – though not with
what she'd been thinking a moment ago.

Now it was a new idea, just one that seemed to hammer at
her temples: a single shattering thought.

'Oh, Jesus . . . oh, *no!*'

TWENTY-FIVE

Kimura blew on his hands and then buried them in his coat pockets. Although the day was clear and sunny, a cold wind had got up and the air was filled with stinging bits of ice from the crusted snow covering the ground. He was keeping his distance from the girl who was walking some way ahead of him, head bowed, staring at the path in front of her. He had noticed she wasn't following any particular route in the park, just wandering about, and the opportunity was there for him to approach her, but so far he had held back.

How could he frame the question he wished to put to her? His English was so poor. How to explain his need for an answer? He would have to admit his guilt, acknowledge that it was he who had broken into the house and assaulted her three nights earlier. How would she respond to that? He had no way of knowing, but once he had put the question to her, there would be no turning back. What if she simply decided to report their conversation to the police?

He could prevent her from doing that of course, but at what cost? He knew the girl was innocent – she had no part in this – as innocent as the young woman he had loved, and whatever happened he wouldn't raise his hand against her. Yet he hesitated. Although he continued to believe that some unseen power was directing his steps – that he would eventually track down his quarry – the day had begun with an evil omen.

Unwilling to trouble the elderly couple who had given him shelter for anything more than the room they had provided, he had gone out that morning to have breakfast at a nearby café and on his return had noticed a stack of newspapers standing on the hall table ready for disposal. On top of the pile was yesterday's edition and the headline had caught his eye: *Knightsbridge Killings: Two Americans Dead*. There was a photograph of a woman under the headline and when Kimura read the name printed beneath it, he froze.

Rose Carmody. There could be no doubt. The murders had taken place at the same address he had gone to. She was the woman he had come to London to find. Could it be the Devil's work? Kimura was ready to believe it.

He had taken the paper upstairs to his room and read the report carefully. According to 'police sources' there was no apparent explanation for the double-murder, with no motive for either having been discovered. At the very end of the story was a line to the effect that Mrs Carmody's niece had been with her aunt when the attack occurred. She must be the girl who had been in the house when he broke in: his last remaining lead. If anyone could point him in the right direction now, it was she.

He knew then there was nothing for it but to return to the house in the mews. Even if the police were in the vicinity, he had to discover if the girl was still there. The longer he delayed it, the more likely it was she would disappear. According to the newspaper report she lived in New York. How long would it be before she returned home?

His decision made, he had set off at once, crossing the same great park he had navigated a few days earlier – he had since learned it was called Hyde Park – returning to the broad busy road where the department store was so as to be able to follow the same route he had taken to the mews on the fateful evening of his arrival, but more cautiously this time, alert to any sign of police activity in the area, and had reached the entrance to the narrow cul-de-sac without incident.

There he had paused for some minutes, delayed by the sight of a small van that was drawn up outside a house at the end of the mews. Kimura had waited while the driver delivered several packages to a man who had come outside and then backed his van up to the entrance and driven off. About to enter the lane, he was halted by a further development. The door to another house had opened and a young woman had come out into the street. She had a white woollen cap in her hands and as she raised it to her head he recognized the dark curls she was about to cover and realized it was the young woman he had assaulted, the one he had come to find.

Instinctively he had drawn back out of sight and as he did so he noticed there was a car approaching from behind him, driving slowly along the street. It was a police vehicle with lights on top and he had reacted in the only way he could by walking towards it in an innocent manner, looking straight ahead and paying it no attention. When he had finally glanced round it was to find that the car had stopped at the entrance to the mews and one of the two uniformed policemen inside it had got out of it, cap in hand. As Kimura watched, he had placed the cap on his head and stood where he was. A second later the girl had appeared and they had exchanged a few words, after which the man had got back into the car and driven away. The girl had then set off herself, walking down the street away from him.

Kimura had followed her at a distance and found she was leading him back to Hyde Park by a different route. Presently he had found himself treading the same path he had taken earlier that morning, though in the opposite direction, but not for long. She had soon turned off on to another and thereafter he had continued to trail her at a discreet distance as she wandered on, pausing now and again to look about her at the wide and largely unpopulated expanse of snow-covered parkland, even turning around to gaze back in his direction, as though uncertain where she was, and then, having seemingly regained her bearings, carrying on in the same aimless fashion.

It was clear to him she was distracted, deep in thought, and he was on the point of steeling himself to approach her – it would serve no purpose to hang back any longer – when she stopped in her tracks once again and as though struck by an idea stood staring at the ground in front of her. Kimura hesitated. What should he do now? Continue on his way and when he caught up with her try to start a conversation? He knew how flawed his English was. How could he begin to explain to her who he was and why he wanted to speak to her? He had come to a halt himself, unsure what to do next, when he saw her turn around and stare back along the way she had come. He felt her eyes on him.

There was a bench close to where he was and he was

on the point of sitting down there and waiting to see what she would do next when she moved again, but no longer in the direction she'd been going. She was coming straight back along the path towards him.

TWENTY-SIX

M ovies were about images. That was what people remembered.

Addy had heard it said once by some famous director in an interview he'd given on radio. She couldn't remember his name, but he'd maintained they weren't really about the plot or the dialogue or even the stars who appeared in them: they were about *images* and directors should never forget it. What people remembered when you mentioned this or that film was a moment, or certain moments, scenes that might have lasted no longer than a few seconds but were engraved on your memory, carved in stone. Like the sequence in *Blade Runner*, for example, when the dying replicant released the white dove he was holding and said all that had happened to him, all the marvels he had witnessed in his short life would be lost in death. That was what you remembered, and only then did you start recalling the story; or maybe you didn't; maybe that single image was enough to stand for the whole movie.

The scene Addy remembered when the realization had struck her so hard in Rose's house had been from an old and quite frankly crap movie whose title she had long since forgotten and which she'd viewed on television late one night. There were these men, soldiers of some kind, who were driving across a post-apocalyptic America in an armoured car through a world that was out of kilter – the sky was the wrong colour and rent by bolts of lightning, the sun was glaring, nothing felt right – and the explanation given was that the recent nuclear war had knocked the planet off its axis. It was why everything was cockeyed. And then at some point in the story the earth had shaken itself like a dog coming out of a pond – the whole planet had vibrated – and suddenly everything was back to normal: the sky was blue, the lightning had stopped and the sun was shining the way it ought to.

It was that single image of things righting themselves that had come to her as she'd stood clutching her head, trying to bring order to the thoughts that were suddenly rampaging around like wild things in there.

Was it really that simple?

The flood of fresh ideas – a whole new way of looking at this – was so intense that she'd had to get out of the house, which suddenly felt claustrophobic, and with no better idea in mind she had found her way up to Hyde Park which, with the help of a map she had discovered in the house, turned out to be only a few minutes' walk away. The bracing cold air was what was needed to clear her mind and she'd gone back to the beginning, to the moment when she had received the letter supposedly from Rose, when things had started to go haywire, and began to put the pieces together. The more she thought about it, the crazier it seemed, yet the strange and unnerving thing was the further she went along that road the more the pieces seemed to fit.

Or was this just one of her fantasies?

Addy knew she liked making up stories about people she met or glimpsed, creating whole fictions for them, which she played out in her mind like books or movies. It was a habit from childhood, a game she and Rose used to play, something to while away the time on a long car journey, say, or when she was sitting in the dentist's waiting-room and Rose had wanted to distract her. So was this just one of those fairy tales, because that was what they were? Was she trying to close her eyes to the painful truth about someone she'd loved and looked up to who had let herself down so badly?

Addy didn't think so. It all fitted too well together, and as her fears hardened into a certainty she saw how she herself had been used – drawn into the plot without knowing it. How she'd been acting out a script, a drama written by another's hand in which her own part had been clearly laid out, and if that was so, then she had to look at everything that had happened to her since the door to Rose's house had burst open. *Everything.*

The realization brought her to a halt, and as she stood there, staring at the ground in front of her, hardly able to take in all the implications of this new discovery, she remembered some-thing she had taken note of earlier in her walk. She'd been wandering about, not following any particular route, choosing paths at random, but stopping now and then to get her bear-ings, and it was then she had spotted a man walking behind her some fifty paces back, apparently following the same haphazard route she was taking. She'd thought nothing about it at the time, but now she wondered.

Could he be a cop Malek had put on her tail, someone to keep an eye on her and see that she was safe? Addy doubted it. He would have told her if he was going to do something like that, she was certain.

But there was another explanation, and it so happened it fitted all too well into the puzzle she'd been piecing together. Addy turned to look at the man. He had stopped beside a bench and appeared to be watching her. If she hesitated at all it was only for a second – her mind was made up – and she began at once to retrace her steps, walking rapidly towards him, muttering as she went.

'Enough of this bullshit.'

Hideki Kimura.

She had known it was him the moment she looked into his eyes and remembered the same dark orbs that had stared into hers from behind the black mask. But watching him walk away now into the gathering dusk she still had no idea what was going on behind them.

They had spoken together, if you could call it that, but since Addy had done all the talking and only got an occasional 'ah' or 'oh' in return – just grunts really – and with no change of expression on his face, it had hardly been what you would call a conversation, let alone an exchange of views. Only once had he actually said something that she caught. It was right after she had introduced herself, when she had stood in front of him and said bluntly, 'Mr Kimura, we need to talk,' and he had replied, but with only two words.

'Deep regret.' They were spoken in a guttural voice and accompanied by a low bow.

For what? Addy had wondered. For having knocked her to

her knees, practically pulled her hair out by the roots and then dragged her up the stairs? It had taken all her self-control not to tell him exactly what she thought of such a piss-poor apology. But she'd kept a hold on her temper. OK, so he was a man of few words, and even fewer of those were in English as far as she could tell. But just how much had he taken in of what she was saying? That was the important thing. Addy had no idea.

Eventually, when she could think of nothing more to say – when she had exhausted every possible means of explaining herself to him – he had risen to his feet and bowed once more. A last grunt and he was on his way, heading off into the gathering dusk, leaving her none the wiser.

Watching him go, Addy had fumed in frustration. What a moment to be left wondering whether she'd wasted her breath. She could only pray he had understood her.

Now there was nothing left she could do but return to Rose's house and as she walked back, she went over everything she had said to him, wondering if any part of it had stuck. It was then that another thought occurred to her, one she hadn't considered before. Like most of her other thoughts, it had to do with Rose and why she had behaved as she did. But this time Addy was on a different tack – now she found herself wondering in quite a detached way what her aunt might have done after she learned the truth about the man who'd deceived her. How would she have reacted?

She had reached the entrance to the mews and stopped there for a minute. The lights were on in all the houses except Rose's and the one opposite, Sarah and Ben's. She considered the teasing question she had put to herself, turning various possibilities over in her mind, quite cool now, quite ready to believe almost anything.

What if Rose had . . . yes, *what if*?

Addy stood rooted to the spot, her eyes fixed on the cobbled lane in front of her, not seeing it though, not registering the sight of the trodden snow that no longer showed white except in patches because a quite different picture filled her mind: an oh-so-familiar image.

Fuck it, she was *right*! She just *knew* it. And if it was true, then everything else came together.

There was no need to delay any longer. She hurried on. All she needed to do when she got to the house was turn off the heating and collect what she wanted from the bedroom upstairs, which included Rose's MacBook along with an old shoulder bag belonging to her aunt that she thought might come in handy. Oh, and attend to one other small piece of business that would take no time at all – just a minute or two – but one that brought a bitter smile to her lips (though it might just as easily have drawn tears . . . oh, Rose!).

Now it was just a question of letting events take their course, she told herself as she switched out the last light in the sitting room and then locked the front door behind her. While she was talking to Kimura, she had formulated a plan, a crazy idea that had kind of crept up on her without her realizing it until she found it had its teeth in her and she couldn't shake free of it. She had seen where this might be going and how it might end, and, for better or worse, all the pieces were in play.

According to the programme, which she'd checked on her phone, the performance at the Globe didn't start until eight, which gave her plenty of time to return to Molly's and take a shower and change. She might even have some supper before she went out, a suggestion Molly was sure to make when she heard what Addy's plans were for the evening.

But before that, there was one last thing she had to do, and since she was within easy walking distance of Harrods (and remembered Rose telling her you could buy anything you wanted there), she walked the short distance down to the department store, where the great shop windows with their Christmas displays glittered like jewels in the darkness, and went inside to buy the one last thing she knew she would need.

TWENTY-SEVEN

The money was something to marvel at, and Charon let his mind play with the pleasing image as he walked without haste down the Strand. He was actually *picturing* it, not as a pile of banknotes – though if you *were* to stack the dollar bills up one on top of the other, they would reach a truly impressive height – but rather as the impregnable wall that he planned to build around himself. There would be no breaching it. With a billion dollars you could do almost anything: buy a castle, buy an island, and with the help of plastic surgeons buy a life so divorced from the one that preceded it that no amount of investigative work would ever succeed in connecting the two persons, the before and after. It was a dream he had had for some time – the perfect escape.

The idea had its seeds in a job he had undertaken some time ago in Singapore – a simple extraction that he'd attempted to turn to his own advantage, but which had gone seriously wrong, leaving any number of vengeful pursuers on his trail, one of them a man he regarded as particularly dangerous. Hideki Kimura was not an enemy to be taken lightly and Charon had no wish to spend a lifetime looking over his shoulder. Nor was he blind to the lesson he'd been taught. The error he had made in Singapore was a timely reminder. He wasn't getting any younger, and while his speed and strength were still as they had always been and his judgement as razor-sharp, he wanted to quit the life while his powers were still intact. Not for him the role of the ailing wildebeest, a prey to hunters who were quicker and deadlier than he. A civilized retirement beckoned.

At present he was toying with two possibilities (though he had others in reserve). A chateau on the Loire had its attractions, as did a villa in the Veneto. (Why not both?) The furnishing of either would be a pleasant task. He had the money now – or soon would have – to buy the kind of paintings and ornaments he wanted to see decorating his homes. But those apart, there would be no vulgar display of wealth. His taste ran to austere beauty and he would indulge it to the full. In fact, when he thought about it, there was almost no limit to his prospects and he could already see that his first problem would be to decide among so many enticing futures.

He turned off the Strand and strolled down the short cul-de-sac to his destination. He no longer walked with a limp and the grey hair he had sported for a day or two was reduced now to a faint shading at the temples that lent him an air of distinction, or so he thought. Otherwise he was himself and would unquestionably have been recognized by those now busily scouring the great metropolis for him had they thought to include the Savoy Hotel in their searches. But Charon knew they would not. It simply wouldn't occur to them, and although he scanned the lobby out of habit as he entered the hotel he knew the precaution was needless.

He had reserved a table in the restaurant but he paused in the bar with its comfortable armchairs to drink a *blanc cassis* and to study the catalogue he had picked up at a Bond Street art gallery earlier in the evening. They were exhibiting a small collection of Giacometti sculptures that were up for sale and since the spare, anguished figures were precisely the sort of objects that appealed to him, Charon had spent some time admiring them and enquiring as to their price, which no longer seemed exorbitant to him. Yes, why not a Giacometti or two? As he studied the catalogue he sensed another's eyes on him and glancing up he saw there was a woman sitting at a table across the room who looked away quickly, but then looked back, and as their eyes met for a moment she smiled and dropped her gaze. She was with a man who was talking without interruption, leaning forward and gesticulating in a way that suggested he was trying without success to engage her attention. She glanced up again, and this time it was Charon who smiled and shrugged. *If only . . . another time perhaps?*

But as he rose to leave he felt a pang of regret, not for the woman across the bar, attractive though she was, but for another, recently lost, for whom he had felt as much as he would ever be capable of feeling and who he had hoped might share his gilded exile; for a while at least. But it was not to be, she had put him in an impossible position, and while there would surely be no shortage of volunteers to fill the vacancy – there was already one waiting in the wings should he so choose – he couldn't entirely blind himself to the suspicion that like the base Indian, he had thrown away a pearl. But such was life.

And since he'd never been one to dwell on the past, he had already forgotten his momentary surrender to sentiment as he entered the restaurant and was shown to his table which, at his request, was one of those by a window overlooking the Thames. He planned to enjoy an unhurried dinner while he watched the lights of the river craft moving up and down the great waterway and relive the steps of the elaborate game he had played so successfully, which even now was drawing to a close.

The last act of the drama was about to unfold, and though he wished it weren't so, there was one loose end to be tied up. His disappearance had to be complete. He must leave no tracks behind him. There would only be his legend for others to marvel at. *Whatever became of Charon?* they would ask themselves. Let them wonder.

So it had to be done, but as he sat there drinking his wine and readying himself for what was to follow, he made a silent vow. It would be quick and painless, that much he could promise, and if it could be achieved by surprise as well, so much the better.

It was Christmas, after all.

TWENTY-EIGHT

I t was cold by the river. The earlier winds had dropped to a gentle breeze, but the air was icy and Addy kept her gloved hands buried in her coat pockets as she gazed across the dark water at the lights on the opposite bank. The performance wasn't due to begin for another ten minutes and there was no reason why she couldn't have waited in the theatre behind her where it was warm. But a prey to uncertainty now, she had chosen to remain outside and shiver in the cold while she tried to fight the rising tide of doubt that threatened to engulf her.

Was she crazy? Did she really think that she could pull this off?

Or was it something more humiliating that was troubling her – was she simply losing her nerve?

All she knew for certain was she was scared, and it wasn't just a case of an overheated imagination (though she had one of those too). If she'd got this right – if she wasn't so far gone in paranoia that they'd be sending out search parties soon – she was on the point of walking into something so dangerous she'd be lucky if she came out of it alive, which seemed a good reason, if one was needed, for calling the whole thing off.

The plan she had begun figuring out while she was talking to Kimura, the scheme that seemed flawless and foolproof two hours ago, was starting to feel like one of those yarns she and Rose used to dream up for their own amusement and to while away the hours; fictions that might have looked at home in a book of fairy tales, but nowhere else.

The doubts had been gnawing away at her almost from the time she'd got back to Molly's and her hostess' reaction when she'd heard Addy's plans for the evening had done nothing to reassure her.

'What a wonderful idea!' Molly had been gushing. 'How good of Peter to suggest it. And how like him.'

She had been garbed as though for a party in a slinky black dress cut low in front that went well with her golden hair which she'd left hanging loose on her shoulders.

'I was going to suggest that we went out to dinner rather than stay cooped up here feeling miserable. But this is a much better idea. Do give Peter my love and say we really ought to get together. I was thinking we might have him round after Christmas if he's not too busy.'

She'd been giving it her best, wanting to show how happy she was at the news, but Addy wasn't convinced. Her hostess had seemed on edge, plucking nervously at her pendant and running her fingers up and down the thin gold chain it hung from. She'd been on the phone in the sitting room when Addy got back and when she came out into the hall to greet her Addy could tell she was upset.

'That was my former sister-in-law I was talking to.' Molly had thought it necessary to offer an explanation for her manner. 'She always rings up at this time of year full of maudlin reminiscences. I sometimes think Christmas brings out the worst in people.'

Molly's late husband was a subject seldom referred to, Addy remembered Rose telling her. Some years older than her, he had died in a skiing accident in the Alps and his widow had had to console herself with a handsome inheritance along with the title. If Molly was bothered by the loss, she'd never shown it before, and Addy was surprised to see how jumpy she was that evening, fumbling with the frying pan when they went down to the kitchen for supper – she had made them an omelette – stopping in the middle of what she was doing to stare into space, and when they finally sat down to eat, picking at her food.

Was her dead ex really such a burden on her conscience, or was there another reason for her distracted manner? By now Addy had come to think of her hostess as being made of . . . how would the Brits put it . . . sterner stuff?

'I'd offer to take you up to the theatre, dear. But I've promised to look in on some friends across the square. They've asked me in for a drink.'

'No problem,' Addy had assured her. 'I'll use Uber. But I expect I'll be late getting back. Peter's going to show me the theatre, the Globe that is, after the performance is over.'

'Is he really?' Molly's face had lit up. 'How very kind of him!'

'That's what I thought.'

'I can't wait to hear what it is that he's going to tell you.'

'Me neither.'

Addy had spoken the line with feeling. But now she wondered. Was she really that eager to find out?

The pub was crowded. Although there was a broad terrace in front of it furnished with chairs and tables, it was far too cold to sit outside and Addy had been lucky to find space at the end of a bench in one corner where she could sit wedged against the wall while she nursed the glass of wine she'd bought, untouched apart from a sip or two, and waited for the call she was expecting.

At least she'd had the play as a distraction – something to take her mind off the gathering sense of doom that was gradually settling over her like a cloud in a Wile E. Coyote cartoon – but watching it had been the weirdest experience. Not surprisingly, her mind had wandered and even as the actors were doing their thing, speaking their lines, some of them familiar – Addy and her group had spent a term at drama school doing Shakespeare plays, performing one or two and reading through several – there were other voices in her head as she remembered the events of the past few days, things that had been said to her that now seemed to carry a different meaning. Maybe the setting had had something to do with it. The theatre where the play was performed, part of the Globe complex, was small and intimate and the only stage lighting was provided by candles, an attempt to lend a historical atmosphere to the occasion Addy supposed. The play she was watching was a comedy, but seeing the actors go about their business she had found herself imagining other times and other plays by the same magical hand, of the doomed and driven characters who had strutted their way to dusty death across the centuries while audiences sat spellbound. And thinking these thoughts, Addy knew she couldn't kid herself. Like it or not, she had stumbled into a drama no less bloody and tragic than any played out on the boards, and who could say how it would end?

And so she had sat there in the pub with her phone resting on Rose's shoulder bag, which she'd placed on her lap, until finally it rang and she picked it up.

'Peter?'

'Addy! Did you find your way to the Anchor?' The soft Irish tones sounded sweetly in her ear.

'I'm here now.'

'Sorry to keep you waiting, my dear, but I'm glad to say everyone's gone home and we'll have the theatre to ourselves. Just go round to the stage door. You'll find it open.'

'Thanks again for doing this, Peter. I'll see you in a few minutes.'

'I can't wait. By the way, did you enjoy the play?'

'Loved it,' Addy said. 'And I thought you were great.'

Which was true as far as it went. Peter Flynn had played Malvolio and it was clear to Addy that he had the role down cold. She felt he'd probably acted it many times and if he'd made a little too much of the comic passages, overdoing the facial expressions for one thing, it was only to be expected from a seasoned thesp. She'd seen older actors, sure of their place in the hearts of theatregoers, do the same thing on New York stages. But he knew what the part called for and after making himself look ridiculous in the cross-gartered scene, he had still managed to win the audience's sympathy at the end for the cruel trick played on him. Any other evening she would have watched fascinated, taking it all in and learning in the process. But seeing the character tormented by the others made her all too conscious of the fraud that had been practised on her and his closing vow to be revenged on all of them had struck a chord as deep as any in her.

Just as she'd been assured, the pub where she'd waited for his call was only a few minutes' walk from the theatre, but now that the meeting she'd been readying herself for all evening was about to take place, Addy found she was in no hurry to get there. Walking slowly along the path that ran beside the river, she anxiously scanned the faces of other late-night strollers. She wished she had Dave Malek with her, though the thought was meaningless. This was something she could only do on her own. It was personal, a blood debt. It was for Rose, who had saved her life by throwing herself on to that psycho's knife. It was time to settle their account. And quite separate from that, underneath all her doubts and hesitations, her anger remained untouched. Like a slow-moving stream of lava it continued to burn white-hot and would only be quenched by the cold hand of justice: the ice-cold hand. Addy shivered at the thought.

Ahead of her now she saw the unmistakable circular shape of the Globe and she thought about acting then, what it was, the whole business of suspending reality and drawing your audience into the drama you were playing; of bringing them out of their private worlds for an hour or two, and if you were good, or better, really great, holding them in the palm of your hand.

But even as she turned into the alley that led to the stage door, she felt fear take hold of her again and she would have stopped then and turned back if the thought of failure hadn't tasted so bitter. Like a drowning victim clutching at a spar floating by, she reminded herself that, as the bard himself had put it, there was a tide in the affairs of men (and of dumb-ass girls too who ought to know better, who ought to have their heads examined for signs of incipient lunacy) that taken at the flood led on to something, and anyway it was too late to turn back now. She had reached the gate he had told her about. It was there next to a bigger set of wrought-iron gates used by vehicles. They were securely locked, but when she pushed on the smaller one, it swung open and she went into the courtyard beyond and then walked across the cobbled space to the stage door. Like the gate, it was unlocked, and after a moment's hesitation she opened it and went in.

The die was cast.

Addy stood shivering, and not just from the cold. Stage fright was never like this. She could feel her heart fluttering inside her chest like a trapped bird as she stood at the edge of the wooden platform gazing up at the sky. Like the man had said, the Globe was open to the elements and the stars above glittered like splinters of ice in the moonless night.

In spite of the darkness backstage, she had managed to find her way through the cramped dressing-room space – called the 'tiring room' in Shakespeare's time according to a leaflet Addy had picked up in the lobby earlier – without help, drawn by the only source of light she could see, which had led her through an arched doorway out on to the stage that she found was illuminated by a single spot fixed to the rafters above. The beam was directed at an area near the back of the stage where two straight-backed chairs stood half turned towards each other.

After pausing to take in the sight she had carried on walking upstage until she reached the edge of the platform, which was raised several feet above the bare cement flooring below (where the so-called 'groundlings' had stood in Shakespeare's day – another nugget gleaned from the leaflet) and stood peering out into an auditorium that was plunged in darkness.

'Hullo there!' she called out.

The silence that greeted her words was scarier than any reply would have been, and she turned round and called out a second time.

'Anyone at home?'

This time she heard a faint noise, movement of some kind. It came from backstage, but not on her level; it was from above where she could see the faint outlines of two balconies against the dark backdrop.

'Addy! I've been so looking forward to this moment.'

Looking up, she saw that the figure of a man had appeared at one of the balustrades. Still only a faint silhouette, he stood outside the circle of light cast by the spot. But after a second he moved forward into the outer edge of the beam and Addy saw his face.

'Hey there, Uncle Matt.' She waved a hand in greeting. 'Look at you.'

TWENTY-NINE

I t was too bad he was standing up on the balcony. Addy had hoped at least to see the expression on his face when he heard her speak his name. But she had to wait until he came down and by the time he appeared in the wide doorway that was positioned between the two arched entrances at the rear of the stage her heart was beating so wildly it was all she could do just to stand there with a stupid grin on her face. It was a couple of years since she'd last seen him in the flesh but she hadn't forgotten the easy grace with which he moved as he strolled upstage to where the two chairs were placed; there was the same casual elegance she remembered, the same sense of a man at ease in his own skin. Watching him as he approached though, she wondered why she had never been afraid of him before. How had she come to miss the menace that seemed a part of him?

'Did you know it would be me?' If he was surprised, he didn't show it. Rather he seemed amused. 'Did Rose tell you?'

'No way – I just guessed.'

'Guessed?'

'It had to be you, Uncle Matt. Rose wouldn't have done what she did for anyone else. Once I realized that, the rest made sense.'

'What she *did*?' He frowned. 'What do you mean exactly?'

'Look, you probably don't know it, but the police talked to a guy called Bela Horvath after Rose was killed. His company was supposed to be protecting her. They told me what he said. It seems he came clean about you and that memory stick.'

'Bela who?'

'Oh, come on, Uncle Matt.' Addy put her head on one side. Playing the role she'd chosen was even tougher than she'd thought. It was a battle just to keep her breathing in check. The fluttering bird in her chest wouldn't stay still. 'You don't have to pretend with me. I know you and Rose were in it together. I didn't come here to accuse you. So you stole some money from a bunch of Russian crooks. That's cool in my book. I just want to know how Rose ended up dead, that's all. What went wrong?'

He gave her a long look. Though she couldn't see his eyes from where she was standing, she remembered them: they were hazel and flecked with gold.

'Are you serious, Addy?' He might have been asking himself the same question. 'Do you mean to say you're not even shocked? I don't know what Rose would say if she could hear you now.'

'Maybe not much.' Addy shrugged. 'She was great to me when I was little. But we've kind of drifted apart since then. The last time I saw her was six months ago, and then only for a couple of days in New York. I think she preferred it when I was a kid and dependent on her. She helped for a while with my fees at drama school, but that was it. To tell the truth we'd pretty much lost touch, so I was really surprised to get that letter. It was the last thing I expected. But hey – a free trip to London! I couldn't turn that down.'

He shook his head. 'Do you know it pains me to hear you talking this way?' While she was speaking he had seated himself on one of the chairs, shrugging off the city coat he was wearing and draping it over the back along with a white silk scarf that hung from his neck. 'Somehow I thought you two would always stay close.'

He didn't mean it. They were just words. She could feel the weight of his gaze on her: probing, weighing; wondering what to make of her.

'Well, that's life, I guess.' She made a gesture with her hands. 'All the same, I'd like to know why things turned out the way they did. I feel I owe it to Rose. Past favours and all that.'

'Well, if it's so important to you . . .'

He wasn't buying what she was selling – not yet. But she'd piqued his curiosity: he'd want to know now how much she knew. She was counting on that.

'The full story, you said. Then why not come over and join me here?' He patted the empty chair beside him.

'If it's all the same to you, Uncle Matt, I'd prefer to keep moving. I'm just too cold to sit still.'

She began to pace back and forth on the stage in front of him, rubbing her hands together.

'Where shall I begin then?' He settled back in his chair, legs crossed. She remembered now – he'd always had the gift of seeming to be at home wherever he was.

'How about that letter I got from Rose inviting me over for Christmas? Except it wasn't from Rose, was it?'

'Good guess. It was by another hand.'

'Not Bela Horvath's, by any chance?'

'So you figured that out too?' He looked at her admiringly. She could see he was starting to enjoy himself, but she couldn't relax, not for a moment. He'd be listening for any wrong note.

'It wasn't hard. He had to be part of it. I couldn't understand why he took so much trouble to locate Rose after she disappeared, getting Ryker on to that plane just so he could keep tabs on me in London. She was only another client, after all. There had to be more to it than that. Then I learned from what Horvath told the cops that you two knew each other, you'd both worked for the CIA. Did you tell her Horvath was working for a security firm now and she should go to him if she needed help?'

He gave the faintest of nods.

'Then Rose must have guessed. Maybe at some point she realized she'd been suckered and that the two of you were in it together – maybe Horvath was just too helpful – and she knew she had to escape from you both. What happened, Uncle Matt? What went wrong between you and her?'

'I only wish I knew.' He sighed heavily. 'It's something I don't understand myself. You're right – I was looking for her. But it was only to discover what the trouble was. If I had to make a guess, I'd say it was the fact that we'd been separated for so long. I think she lost her nerve. You must have guessed by now that that plane crash I died in wasn't quite what it seemed.' He pursed his lips. 'Without going into details, I can tell you that the work I'd been doing for the CIA took me into some dark places and I'd made some dangerous enemies. I had no choice. I had to disappear.'

'That plane crash, yeah . . .' Addy nodded wisely. 'I was wondering about that.'

'Rose knew I had to lie low. It can't have been easy for her to play the grieving widow, but she managed it somehow, for a while at least. What I didn't realize was how scared she must have been, how lonely. It was difficult for us to keep in touch. I was afraid she was being watched, that her calls were being traced. We went for weeks without any contact between us.' He bit his lip. 'No matter what you think of me, Addy, I can't tell you how distressed I was to hear of her death. I can't begin to describe the pain it has caused me. And the worst of it is it should never have happened. I blame myself. I should never have put her in that position.'

'That's OK, Uncle Matt. I understand.' Addy did her best to sound consoling. 'I can't believe you meant her any harm. So after the crash you had to disappear. And I guess it was then you got hold of the memory stick? Being dead must have been an advantage. You were the one person the Russians would never have suspected.'

'Right again.' He chuckled. 'I'm really impressed, Addy. You've thought it all through.'

'And you left the stick with Rose – right? Because you had to keep your head down, stay out of sight. What was she supposed to do with it?'

'Place it in a safe deposit box in a bank in Zurich.' He shrugged. 'It's true I had a partner at the time, but I didn't trust him for a moment, so it seemed the most sensible course to take. I meant to leave it there until things calmed down, until the trail had gone cold.'

'This partner of yours – was he the guy who stabbed her?'

'I fear so. He was a Russian called Klepkin, an agent gone rogue, a degenerate, an alcoholic. I needed his help to get hold of the memory stick. But I can never forgive myself for what happened afterwards. He was supposed to watch you in the hope that you would lead us to Rose. I knew if I could just talk to her, I would put things right between us. But I never got the chance. He's dead by the way – Klepkin, that is. He took his own life this morning. I think he knew he'd reached the end of the line.'

'And if he couldn't locate Rose, you had Molly for backup.' Addy threw him her curve ball and saw him blink. 'Isn't that so?'

'Now how on earth did you guess that?' She'd surprised him. 'I had no idea you were so smart, neither did Rose: so smart *and* so hard. To tell you the truth, I'm a little shocked listening to you, Addy. How did you get this way?'

'I don't know.' She shrugged. 'Maybe I just grew up. About Molly, though . . . all that crap about Philip Moreau and how he and Rose met in Paris and, gee, wouldn't you know it – he looked a lot like that guy, whoever he was, whose photo Bela Horvath gave to the cops, the one who was supposed to be Charon. But you're Charon, aren't you?'

She waited for his reply, eyebrows raised, but he offered no response, simply smiled.

'Anyway, what I wanted to say was it was all a bit too staged, Uncle Matt, like a bad movie plot. And incidentally, your Irish accent isn't bad, but it could do with a little work. I thought you should know.'

'You leave me speechless.' His chuckle was unfeigned. 'I never knew you had it in you. And thank you for the advice. I'll keep it in mind for future reference. As for Molly, you're right – she was in it from the start. I needed her to keep an eye on Rose.'

'And to collect me when I arrived in London, so she could watch me as well. I might as well tell you, I never liked her but she was Rose's friend, and I took her as such, and I guess Rose did too. We were both fooled. She's quite an operator.'

'The trouble was I was starting to have my doubts about your aunt, Addy.' He sighed. 'I thought we understood each other. I'd told her I had to disappear, and that the condition would be permanent. I needed a new life, a new identity. I had to cut my ties with the past, though not with her, of course.' He held up his hand like a cop. The very notion! 'Once I was settled we'd be together again. I made that clear. And when I explained to her about the memory stick and how I planned to get hold of it, she seemed to accept the idea.'

'So what went wrong?'

'To be blunt, Rose was happy enough with the idea of the money, but . . . how shall I put it? Some of the side effects proved hard for her to swallow.'

Like the guy whose body was in the plane that crashed – the man Rose had had to identify as him – and the other one in Cyprus, the banker, who was sliced up and left floating in the water. *Fucking side effects.*

Addy had to keep a check on her tongue. She'd been doing OK up till then, carrying him along with her, playing the part of a cold-hearted little bitch, which might just have been to his taste. But she had to be careful. It could be that he didn't believe a word she was saying: maybe he was just amusing himself, filling in the time until he was ready to wind things up.

While she was speaking he had cocked his head to one side and now he was looking at her in a different way – more intently. His eyes were heavy-lidded and it was then she realized what those yellowish tints in the iris, those flecks of gold, made her think of: they were the eyes of a predator, some big cat. Killer's eyes. As long as he stayed entertained she was safe, but the moment she lost her audience . . .

'Thanks, Uncle Matt. I think I've got it now.' She hurried on. 'I wanted to hear the truth about Rose and I guess you've pretty well told me all there is to know. She was on her own when you went under cover and she lost her nerve. And she may have thought the Russians were after her as well. That could help to explain her behaviour.'

He said nothing. He was studying her in earnest now, trying to probe beneath the surface, to discover what she was up to.

'And I've got to hand it to you. A billion dollars! What a coup! I just wish Rose had been alive to share it with you. But there it is. Fate moves as fate will. That's a quote from somewhere.' She grinned. 'You liked quotes, I remember. You always had a whole bunch of them ready at hand.'

'It's a weakness of mine, I confess.'

He stirred, stretching. It looked like he was about to rise

from his chair. Was he getting bored? Losing interest? Somehow she had to hold his attention.

'Now don't get mad, Uncle Matt, but I've a proposition to put to you.'

He showed a flicker of interest.

'It's only a suggestion, but I think it'll appeal to you.'

'Tell me then. What do you have in mind?'

'A deal.'

'A *what*—?' His eyebrows shot up. She'd managed to startle him.

'I want a cut, Uncle Matt, just a small one. What did that banker ask the Russians for – ten million bucks? I'd be happy with that. And before you blow your top, let me explain. It'll be to your advantage.'

She'd done it – snagged his interest. This was something he had to hear. She could see it in his face.

'I give you ten million dollars, but you'd be doing me a favour?' He seemed tickled by the idea. 'I must be slow. Explain that if you would, Addy. We still have a little time.'

What the fuck did that mean – a little time? As if she needed to ask. She could see the answer in his eyes: his killer's eyes. Frantically she scanned the dark backdrop behind him. She was starting to lose hope.

'If you give me a cut, then I'm involved, don't you see?' Desperation drove her on. 'I'd be a co-conspirator – isn't that what the law calls it? I'd never rat on you because I'd be ratting on myself. You wouldn't have to worry. You'd be safe.'

'Ingenious!' He slapped his knee. 'I'd never have thought of that. Ten million dollars! But I'm afraid I'll have to disappoint you, Addy. I'm not worried, you see. I know you won't rat on me. It's written in the stars.'

The way he said it – Jesus! It felt like a hole had opened in the pit of her stomach. Addy shut her eyes. But when she opened them again she just stood there, stunned by what she saw – disbelieving.

'Is something the matter?' He managed to sound concerned.

'No . . . no, just the opposite . . .' She stumbled over the words. Her head was spinning. 'I've been saving the best news till last. I wanted to surprise you. It's that memory stick. I've got it with me.'

'You *found* it?'

'You bet.' Addy managed a grin.

'Where exactly?'

'Just where Rose hid it. Isn't that why you set up this meet? You wanted to make sure all her belongings were safe, that the cops weren't holding on to them. It was the next thing you were going to ask me. They've been searching the house and going through her clothes, but they finally decided it must still be with that bank in Zurich. I wasn't so sure. What if Rose never put it there? What if she was carrying it around with her? In that case, chances were she'd put it some place where no one would think of looking. Maybe some place where you'd *told* her to put it. So I checked – and bingo!'

Addy put her hand in her pocket.

'Here, Uncle Matt – catch!'

She tossed the small object across the stage to him. Rising to his feet, he followed its path through the air and then stuck up a hand and grabbed it.

'Is this a memory stick I see before me? Come, let me clutch thee.' He shook his head in awe. 'You really are a most remarkable young woman, Addy. What a pity we never got to know each other.'

'And now we never will, huh?' Addy smiled back at him. It was easy – she'd got over her shock. It was no trouble at all.

'However, there is one small problem.' He was examining the stick closely, holding it up to the light.

'Is it the right one?' Addy nodded. 'I thought of that. I knew you'd want to check, so I brought along a MacBook. It's in that shoulder bag hanging on the chair.'

Keeping his eyes on her he fished the small computer out of the leather holdall.

'Rose's?' he asked as he opened the lid.

Addy nodded.

'How appropriate.' He pressed a button. 'It'll take a minute to boot up. Is there anything else you'd like to discuss while we wait?'

Like her last will and testament? She had heard the cold note in his voice.

'No, but there's a story I want to tell you. It's about Rose and me and a late-night movie we used to watch together. We must have seen it three or four times. It was about these gangsters in Boston and a plan they had for robbing banks, which was pretty smart, in fact they'd pulled the same stunt a couple of times and it worked like a dream.'

'Fascinating.' He slipped the USB into its port, glanced at the screen, and then looked up at her again. 'Is there a point to this story?'

'It's coming. Be patient. What they did was go early in the morning to the house where the bank manager lived – the one they were going to rob that day – and hold his family hostage. Then while one of them stayed behind to keep an eye on mom and the kids, the others would take the manager to the bank and get him to clean out the vault for them. So now they're on their third bank and the leader of the gang, who's masked like the rest of them, goes into the house where the manager lives expecting to find the family in the kitchen having breakfast, only they're not there. Instead he comes face to face with a cop who's pointing a shotgun at him. It's what the cop says, that was what Rose and I loved. We'd crack up every time we heard it.'

'And what was that, Addy?' He smothered a yawn. 'What did he say?'

'Look at your screen, Uncle Matt.'

He dropped his eyes, and Addy watched while he took in the words that she knew he'd find printed there.

APRIL FOOL MOTHERFUCKER

'Is this a joke?' He looked up.

'What do you think?'

'Oh, Addy . . . and I was going to be so gentle with you.' He laid the computer carefully down on a chair.

'I'll bet. But before you get started, Uncle Matt, I've got a couple of things I want you to hear. Rose didn't lose her nerve. She'd got your number all right, but she couldn't bring herself to do what she knew she had to because she loved you. Loved you and hated you and it tore her apart. Those months after you "died", she was in agony. I know. I saw it. But in the end she did what she had to. It must have hurt like hell, but she knew the only way to get rid of you was to set you up, you murdering sonofabitch, to send you the way you'd sent those others. She tried by telling the Russians about you, but it didn't work out, and she knew what to expect after that. All she could do was run for her life, but you had that covered too thanks to your pal Bela Horvath – the late Bela Horvath who wasn't such a pal after all, it seems. I don't know if there's a special hell for people like you, Uncle Matt, but I guess you'll find out soon enough.'

'Touching. I'll save it for my memoirs.'

He took the white silk scarf off the back of the chair and began to wind it slowly around his hands, first one, then the other, until he had a cord stretched tight between them.

'And now it's my turn, is it?' Addy laughed. 'Well, I'm sorry to disappoint you, buster, but it ain't gonna happen. Not tonight, Josephine. Take a look behind you. I brought a friend.'

He looked round then and spotted the figure that had appeared silently in the dark doorway behind him. As Kimura stepped forward into the light, Addy saw he was carrying something that glittered, and when she realized what it was her heart turned a somersault.

'Jesus!'

It was a sword. A freaking *sword*!

Uncle Matt had seen it too, and in the silence that had fallen, she caught his shocked whisper.

'Oh, shit!'

And that should have been that – *sayonara*, Uncle Matt. Hideki Kimura was going to do the business on him, slice him up and leave the bastard to bleed to death just like that poor guy in Cyprus; just like Rose. And scared though she was, Addy was determined to stay and watch. She was the one who had set this up. She couldn't chicken out now. But she'd assumed Kimura would simply plug him or something. If she'd known about the sword!

And then she saw the other one, the *other* sword. She hadn't noticed it hanging from Kimura's shoulder until he unhitched it and tossed it across the stage to Uncle Matt, who had moved away and was standing poised on his toes, wondering whether he could make it to one of the exits before his enemy nailed him – that was what it looked like – but who had caught the second thing thrown to him that evening, and once he had it in his hands, once he'd slipped the blade from its sheath, had readied himself for action.

Addy couldn't believe her eyes. What kind of crazy Japanese shit was this – like give the other guy a chance? Her knight in shining armour must have a screw loose. What made it even worse was the look on Uncle Matt's face as they squared up to one another. He was happy now that he had a weapon in his hands. He believed he could take the other guy. It was written all over him – the self-belief, the arrogance. He was actually smiling, and he even had the presence of mind to glance her way. It was just a look, nothing more, but it told her more clearly than any words what lay in store for her once this was over.

And from the start it began to look like he was right. As they circled one another, Uncle Matt seemed the quicker of the two, lighter on his feet and making quick feints with his sword, which Kimura would respond to with defensive blocks that never quite made contact with the other's sword, because Uncle Matt would check his stroke. It was like he was just feeling out his opponent, testing his reflexes.

Kimura on the other hand was into some weird ritual – at least that was what it looked like – the kind of thing that Addy remembered seeing in old samurai movies, twirling his sword around in his hands, pointing it first this way, then that, and moving in a stylized way, too, until it began to seem more like he was performing a dance rather than a fight for his life (and hers, incidentally).

Neither man said anything, both of them intent on the moment, only their breath, which Addy could see issuing from their mouths in frosty puffs, giving some indication of the intensity of the duel they were locked in. Uncle Matt had changed his tactics. Previously, like Kimura, he had been holding his sword with two hands, making his sudden feints and each time drawing a reaction from his enemy, though their weapons didn't touch. Now he switched to a one-handed approach and, looking more like a classical duellist standing sideways on, he began a series of sudden lunges with the point of his weapon, his long reach seeming to give him an advantage over the shorter man. The strategy had forced Kimura into making some last-minute parries and now the silence of the empty theatre was broken by the ring of steel on steel, and it was Uncle Matt who was advancing, pressing his opponent back.

It was during one of these repeated attacks that disaster all but overcame Addy's guy. As Uncle Matt lunged forward once more and Kimura brought his sword down to parry the thrust, his back foot slipped on what might have been a wet patch on the boards. The error was slight, but enough to cause him to drop his sword a fraction, allowing the point of his opponent's weapon to pierce his guard and nick his side. Or so it seemed to Addy, who could see the tear in Kimura's padded jacket. But the wound, if it was a wound, didn't seem to slow him – he had quickly regained his balance – and there was no sign of blood, though that might have been down to the jacket's dark material.

Whatever the result, the sight seemed to encourage Uncle Matt, who pressed his attack and having driven Kimura back with a series of thrusts, he suddenly changed tactics again and, grasping the hilt of his sword with both hands he aimed what looked to an appalled Addy like the death blow, slicing his blade across and down at his opponent's unprotected body.

Except Kimura wasn't there.

How he was able to react so quickly Addy never knew, but all of a sudden he was into a pirouette, spinning around like a ballet dancer on his points, and not retreating this time, stepping inside the descending blade, his own sword flashing in the light, and for a moment the two of them were locked together, bodies fused, before they broke apart and Addy saw one of them stumble and then fall flat on the boards while a round object came spinning through the air towards her, spraying blood and landing not two steps away from where she stood.

It was too much, more than she could deal with, and she felt her knees start to buckle. A few seconds more and she'd be stretched out on the boards herself, right alongside the blood-streaked head. Yet somehow she fought off the feeling of dizziness. Somehow she forced herself to look down at the lurid face.

The eyes were bad enough – they were empty and staring. But it was the mouth, stretched wide in a silent scream, that held her stricken gaze. Weird as it seemed, he might just have been grinning at her, and without thinking – barely aware of what she was saying – she repeated the words with which she had greeted him earlier.

'Hey there, Uncle Matt! Look at you.'

THIRTY

With the hood of her padded jacket pulled up against the bitter cold, Addy stood shivering in the deserted street, waiting for her Uber ride.

She was trying to get a grip of herself. Like a junkie coming down from a high, the experience of the past hour had left her in pieces, hardly able to function, while a succession of images shot through her mind, one after the other, like snapshots from a carnival peep show.

Worst of all was the picture of Uncle Matt's face grimacing up at her from the floor like some demented gargoyle. She couldn't deny she'd wanted to see him dead – couldn't and wouldn't – but reality had a way of bringing things home to you and she wondered how long it would take to erase that particular memory from her mind. (Try never.) But if that was the price she had to pay for those last shocking seconds when his head had parted company from his body, so be it. Although the good book might look at it another way – *Vengeance is mine* the Lord was supposed to have said – Addy could see why He might have wanted to keep that particular satisfaction for Himself.

It sure beat turning the other cheek.

What followed, though, had left its own bittersweet mark, even if it was less harrowing than the drama she had just witnessed. Unable to move from the spot where she stood, she had watched as Kimura went about the business of setting things to rights – she could think of no other words to describe the way he had calmly brought order to the bloody spectacle. First, thinking perhaps to protect her from the worst of the scene, he had taken Uncle Matt's coat from the chair where it hung and covered his headless body. Next he had collected Rose's MacBook, with the memory stick still fixed into it, from the floor where it had fallen – though Addy hadn't seen it happen, she realized Uncle Matt must have dropped it

– and placed it in the shoulder bag, which he took from the chair where Addy had left it hanging. He had carried the bag across the stage to where she was standing and solemnly handed it to her. Coming to herself with a start – she'd been watching it all in a half-drugged state – she noticed that the tear in his jacket was showing a darker stain around it.

'You're hurt.'

Instinctively she'd reached out a hand to him, but he had checked her gesture, taking hold of her wrist in a light grasp and pushing it away. He had looked at her then for a long moment, so long in fact that Addy felt they had been struck that way, the pair of them, petrified, turned to stone, his dark unblinking eyes fixed on hers just as hers were nailed to his. It was as if he were searching for something in her face, she thought, and then, as if he had found what he was looking for, he lifted his hand and laid it gently against her cheek.

'Brave girl, you go.'

It was an order she was only too ready to obey, and when she saw he had nothing more to say to her – they would be his only words – she had walked on uncertain legs across the stage, avoiding the spot where Uncle Matt's life blood lay spread in a wide puddle, to the same arched doorway she had come through. There she paused to turn and look back one more time. He was watching her, and when she lifted a hand in farewell he had replied with the same gesture.

It was the last glimpse she would have of him, she was certain of that, and when she walked off-stage a moment later it was into darkness, and she was lost to his sight as well.

All she felt now was exhaustion. She was drained, more tired than she'd ever been in her life; it was the relief of tension, the simple fact that against all the odds she'd somehow escaped unharmed from what she knew was a piece of hare-brained recklessness, one that was all of her own making. Riding back to Molly's she tried to go over it in her mind, everything that had happened, all that had been said in the nerve-racked minutes she had spent facing a man she knew was a killer, but the effort was too great and before long she dozed off, only waking when the car drew to a halt at Carlyle Square.

All she wanted now was to crash. Dealing with Molly Kingsmill would have to wait till tomorrow. But she knew she couldn't bring herself to spend another night under the same roof as the woman and she asked the driver to wait for her. She would only be a few minutes.

What she had planned to do was slip into the house quietly, retrieve her stuff from the bedroom upstairs and then make tracks for Rose's house where she meant to remain. But when she opened the front door, it was to find Molly standing in the hallway. She must have been watching through the darkened windows of the sitting room and seen the car arrive.

'Expecting someone else?' Addy asked. Molly's mouth opened and shut, but no sound came out. It made Addy think of a goldfish in a tank. 'Are you feeling OK? You look a little pale.'

'Addy?' She finally got a word out. 'I'm sorry . . . what?'

'Gotta dash.' Addy kept on going and sailed past her to the stairs. 'Be down in a minute.'

'No, wait . . .' Molly called after her, but to no effect.

It was the work of a minute to dump all her stuff in her bag, not forgetting Grumble, who had made the trip back from Rose's house with her earlier that evening and was looking a little the worse for wear what with the slit in his stomach that was yet to be repaired. Rose had hidden the memory stick in the one place no one would have thought to look, or so Addy had reasoned before performing her small act of surgery earlier. But she was sure now that it must have been Uncle Matt's idea in the first place. He had wanted to get rid of her before collecting the bear, which he knew would be among her things, either at Rose's house or Molly's.

'Don't worry, old fellow,' she murmured as she slipped the bear into her bag. 'I'll soon have you looking yourself again.'

When she went downstairs again it was to find that Molly hadn't moved. She was standing in the hall under the chandelier with its spray of jewel-like pendants, hands on hips.

'Just where do you think you're going?' The change of tone was a sign she'd collected herself.

'What does it look like?' Addy stopped. Their eyes met. 'Normally I'd thank you for having me, but in the circumstances that hardly seems appropriate.'

'What on earth are you talking about?' Molly glared.

'Peter Flynn sends his regards. No, I lie. Actually he's never heard of you.' Addy saw her hostess catch her breath. 'I meant Uncle Matt. He's the one who said to say hello.' Addy paused, relishing the moment. 'If you could see the look on your face . . .'

'This is a ridiculous conversation.' Molly was treading water, trying to stay afloat. 'Uncle Matt! Are you out of your mind? Can't we at least go into the sitting room and talk like civilized human beings?'

''Fraid not, I'm in a rush. Before I go, though, there's something I want to ask you.' Addy held her gaze. 'When I left the house tonight, did you wonder if you'd ever see me again?'

'How can I answer a stupid question like that?' Molly's face had gone pale.

'I'm just curious.' Addy shrugged. 'But I can't stay to talk about it. The truth is I'm bushed. We can discuss it another time.'

She started towards the door, but the other woman moved to block her.

'You're not going anywhere.' This was Molly the way she had been with the cops that first evening, Addy remembered. This was Molly taking no shit.

Addy's eye fell on a porcelain stand placed on the floor next to her. In addition to a pair of umbrellas it held a walking stick with a brass knob and she plucked the object out.

'Oh, this is going to be fun,' she said. 'I've been longing to take a swing at you.'

'Have you gone quite mad?'

'Cut the crap, Molly. Game over.' They were facing each other like a couple of cats, Addy thought, on the point of mixing it, hair on end, claws out. 'Didn't I just say I'd been talking to Uncle Matt? You might be interested to know we had a really good chat, covered a lot of ground. I got the whole story. And don't think your name didn't come up. But then sad to say things went haywire and Uncle Matt kind of lost his head. You won't see him again.'

She let it sink in. Molly's face was ashen.

'You're quite the piece of work, aren't you?' Now that she was into it, Addy found her blood was up. 'Do you know what first put me on to you? It was that calendar you've got hanging in the kitchen. I noticed it when I was talking on the phone, but it didn't strike me then the way it should have. Later I remembered though – there was one day in the month of December that had a cross marked on it, just one, and it was the day I arrived, the day you turned up at Rose's house saying you were looking for her and what the hell was I doing there? But you knew I was coming, didn't you? Later, too, I couldn't figure out how that Russian creep just happened to be outside Rose's house when I went there with Mike Ryker. All I could think was he must have followed us from that pub where we met. But nobody knew I was going to meet Mike there, so I couldn't understand it. And then I remembered. You did. I should have got on to that sooner, but I was a little shaken up what with Rose being dead, and you being oh-so helpful. Still, I'd managed to figure out your part by the time I talked to Uncle Matt. He just added a few touches. And now there's only one thing I'm curious about. Perhaps you'd enlighten me. Were you fucking him too?'

'God! Must you be so coarse?' Molly looked away.

'Coarse!' Addy flared. 'I'll show you coarse. Rose's funeral is coming up in a few days and I'm telling you now if you show, I'll spit in your face. And that holds for any other venue. You cross my path in New York, you get the treatment, my word on it, and if people want to know why, I'll tell them, down to the last detail. How you made a friend of a woman whose shoes you weren't fit to lick and then betrayed her. How she ended up dying in the snow while you waited around for your pay-off. Yes, the fucking money – that was all it was about. Christ! What sort of person are you?'

Addy thrust her face up close to the other woman's.

'And when I'm done with that, when I've given them the

whole story, I'll tell them what you are, Lady Kingsmill, and that's a piece of shit. Now get the fuck out of my way.'

She swung the brass handle of the stick over her head as hard as she could, shattering the chandelier, and as Molly cowered, hiding her face from the flying shards, Addy pushed past her to the door and there was no one to stop her.

THIRTY-ONE

T he pain had lessened somewhat, but the wound kept bleeding and Kimura realized it must be deeper than he thought. He had started with the idea of cleaning up the site of his duel with Charon, of leaving the police with no clear idea of what had happened other than that one or more people had broken into the theatre and blood had been spilled. The stain on the stage could not be wiped clean.

But he had toyed with the idea of removing the body, which was no longer bleeding, of dragging it through the backstage area out into the courtyard and then, if he could find the strength and providing there were no witnesses around at that late hour, dropping it into the river.

But as soon as he tried to shift the corpse he realized that the task would be beyond him in his weakened state. He would have to simply leave things as they were and quit the scene. The police would be left with a puzzle it would take them a while to fathom, and since he saw no reason to aid them in their task he had picked up the severed head by the hair from the spot where it lay and, with the two swords hitched over his shoulder, set off.

Given what he was carrying he could hardly travel back to where he was staying by taxi, and in any case, he knew that the police would soon be questioning cab drivers who had picked up late-night fares in the vicinity of the theatre. He would have to return on foot. But he had no sooner started on his journey when he discovered that the effort might be beyond him.

Barely halfway along the footbridge he had used earlier to cross the Thames on his way to the theatre, he had to pause to rest and, finding the long pedestrian way virtually deserted, he dropped both the head and the two swords into the river. The swords would sink while the head would be borne away downstream and quite likely never be found.

When he had crossed the bridge earlier, he had come from the direction of the Houses of Parliament – familiar to him from photographs he had seen – and he set out to retrace his tracks, moving more slowly now and feeling the pain in his side growing sharper all the time. His jacket and the shirt and sweater he wore beneath it were all soaked in blood. Although he could see the glowing eye of Big Ben drawing closer, he had not yet reached the end of the long stretch of road flanking the river when he knew for a certainty that he would not have the strength to complete his journey.

Yet he soldiered on, finally reaching Westminster and then skirting the square in front of it with faltering steps, following the route he was familiar with. Beyond was a park that he remembered pausing in earlier to check the map he had with him. Discovering that its wide gate was unbarred despite the late hour, he went in and found it all but deserted, the few people he met all hurrying towards their destinations, hands buried in coat pockets and hoods pulled up over their heads against the bitter cold. The path they were on was largely free of snow, but the grass on either side of it was still mantled in white and when Kimura ventured on to it, he found he was treading on an icy crust.

Taking care not to slip – he was losing blood fast and a fall would only weaken him further – he made his slow way to a small copse of trees, and finding one with a broad trunk to lean against he cleared what snow remained at its base and then lowered himself painfully on to the cold ground. In truth he could go no further. The snow-topped mountain they had pictured together, its lower slopes carpeted with pine trees, remained what it had always been: just a dream. He had done what he meant to do and now he was at peace.

From his pocket he took a box of matches, which he had bought in order to light a pair of candles that he had added to the sparse decor of his room so that he could eat his evening meal by candlelight. It was something Suzume had suggested they do during their time together and he recalled with a pain so mixed with pleasure it was all but impossible to separate the two, the play of light and shadow on her young face as she bent over their small table to serve him.

Taking the snapshot of her he always carried, he lit a match and held it close to the photograph, drinking in her features for the last time, hoping that by fixing the image of his loved one in his mind, by welding it to his memory, he would somehow carry it over with him into death, where by some miracle they might be reunited. When the match flickered out, he lit another . . . and another . . .

'Night, and while I wait for you . . .' He began to whisper the words she had murmured so often in his ear.

'. . . cold wind . . . cold wind . . .'

How did it end? His mind was failing.

'. . . cold wind turns into rain.'

The lighted match he was holding had burned down to his fingers, but he felt no pain.

He no longer felt anything.

THIRTY-TWO

'So you made it?' Pushing his forelock back, DS Dave Malek glanced up from the table where he'd been checking his phone. The sunlight was so bright he had to shade his eyes. 'I was starting to wonder if you'd come.'

'You said it was important.' Addy scowled.

The text he'd sent her had used that word together with 'developments'.

Important developments – meet me at pub called Anchor, Southwark Bridge, noon.

The message had sent a chill through her. She had not heard from him for two days, and although part of her had missed his calls, she'd been tempted to hope that her name had not come up again in the ongoing investigation. But the Anchor was the pub where she'd sat waiting for Peter Flynn's call, just a few steps downriver from the Globe Theatre. What was Malek doing there? What did the police know?

According to a news programme she had watched the night before, there was no explanation as yet for the headless body of a man discovered in the theatre on Christmas Eve. But the police were thought to be actively pursuing 'several leads', the newscaster said, and one theory was that the crime was linked in some deranged way to William Shakespeare. Was the killer sending a coded message, he had asked – and if so, to whom?

Addy wasn't taken in. For all she knew it was just a story cooked up by the cops, a way of lulling her into a false sense of security, letting her think she was in the clear before they pounced. The only thing she could do was try to brazen it out. She sent a reply back – *see you there* – and then spent a sleepless night tossing and turning and wondering how in Hades she was going to talk her way out of this.

And it wasn't as though she didn't have other things to worry about. There was Rose's funeral for one thing, which

she would have to handle herself now that Molly was out
of the picture, and decisions that would need to be made
regarding the house and its contents. Addy didn't even know
if Rose owned or rented it, but she would have to find out,
and talk to her lawyer too, because there'd be a will and it
was likely she'd be Rose's beneficiary, or one of them,
she might even be her executor, and these were all matters she
would have to deal with in an adult way. And as if that weren't
enough, there was something even more important weighing
on her mind, a decision she would have to take, and as she
made her way over to the South Bank where Malek was waiting
for her she told herself it couldn't be postponed any longer.
One way or another, the issue had to be resolved.

She had thought of using Uber to get where she was going,
but changed her mind in favour of taking the Underground,
mainly because she was in no great hurry to confront whatever
awaited her at the Anchor. Although Malek had been friendly
enough up till now, she had no illusions: he was a cop first
and foremost and would not take kindly to the thought that
he'd been misled by her at any stage. So far she had been
straight with him, but the situation had changed radically since
their last meeting and she was going to be faced with some
tough decisions.

A study of the Tube map in Knightsbridge station had
shown her there were basically two ways of getting to
Southwark. One took her over the footbridge from Embankment
and then along the South Bank. It was the shortest way, but
it also went right past the Globe where there were likely to
be cops still hanging about, or so Addy reasoned, and
although she had no cause to think that she was under suspicion she felt it might be wiser to steer clear of the area for
now. The other way, which was slightly longer, would take
her to a station called Monument from where she could walk
across Southwark Bridge to the Anchor, and it was this route
she had opted for.

Crossing the bridge, she had paused to look down at the
river. She had read somewhere that the water moved both ways
in the Thames – upstream when the tide was coming in – but
at that moment it was flowing strongly downstream and with

the winter sun shining brightly overhead, it had a sparkle she hadn't seen before.

At the end of the bridge there were steps going down to the riverside walkway where the Anchor was situated. In spite of the sun the air was still frigid, but there were a few hardy souls sitting at the tables placed on the terrace outside and she saw that Malek was one of them. He was checking his phone and didn't notice her arrival until she was standing by the table in front of him, at which point he had looked up.

'So you made it? Sit down, won't you?' He gestured at a chair beside him. 'I've got a lot to tell you. Do you want something to drink? Coffee maybe?' He had a paper mug on the table in front of him.

She shook her head. 'What's so important?' She didn't need her fur stroked. If she was in trouble, she wanted to know it. But she accepted his invitation to sit.

'Well, I take it you've heard about the headless body they found in the Globe?' He gestured in the direction of the theatre.

Addy nodded. 'It was in the news on TV. They said he hadn't been identified. What about it?'

'I'll tell you in a moment. But first, there's been another body as well that's turned up with no explanation.'

'You're kidding!' Addy's eyebrows went up. 'Where was that?'

'In St James's Park. He was found sitting propped up against a tree. The story was in the papers.'

Addy shrugged. She hadn't seen any papers. 'Who was he?'

'A Japanese gentleman by the name of Hideki Kimura. Ring a bell?'

Addy was silent.

He cocked his head to look at her.

'What?'

'Nothing . . .' She sat blinking. 'It's just . . . are you sure it's him?'

'I told you we sent a request to the Tokyo police for a photograph of Kimura and they wired one back. It's him all right. He'd been injured, wounded – he had a deep cut in his side. It seems he just bled to death.'

Addy said nothing. He studied her face again.

'What is it, Addy? What's the matter?'

She shook her head. 'You say he just bled to death?'

'Apparently. But it needn't have happened.'

'How do you mean?'

'The wound wasn't fatal, the medics said. If he'd gone to a hospital it could have been treated. Instead he just let himself die . . .'

Addy was lost for words.

'They found a photograph in his hand. It was of a young Japanese girl and he had a spent match in his fingers.'

'A match?'

'He'd been striking them – there were dead matches on the ground beside him. Perhaps he wanted to look at her face.'

But it was Addy's face *he* was watching. He wanted to see her reaction. She put a hand to her head. She wasn't prepared for this, not even close. She remembered the look in his eyes as they stood face-to-face with the bloody head at their feet; what he had said to her.

'So what's it got to do with this other business?' She had needed time to compose herself. 'I mean the guy with no head?'

'That's a good question.' Malek looked thoughtful. 'At first it seemed we wouldn't be able to identify him.'

'Without a head, you mean?' She was trying to sound interested.

'And even when it showed up that didn't help.'

'I beg your pardon.' Addy blinked. 'What do you mean – showed up?'

'It washed ashore on a mud bank down Bermondsey way, but nobody spotted it at first, and when they finally did, it turned out the rats had been at it.'

'Ugh! Thanks for that detail.' She winced.

'The face wasn't recognizable, or so the detectives handling the case told us. But although there was nothing on the body in the way of papers to identify the man and his fingerprints weren't on record here, when Scotland Yard sent them to Interpol they got a hit. They were prints that the police in Stockholm and Ankara both had on file and were connected to a couple of unresolved homicide cases. They couldn't give us a name to go with the prints, but the murders involved were political and in both cases the police thought they might have been ordered by some intelligence agency.'

Addy grunted. 'So what you're saying is it could be . . . what was the guy's name?'

'Charon.' He nodded. 'That would be my guess.'

'And you think Kimura caught up with him?'

Malek shrugged. He was still watching her face for any change in her expression – too closely for Addy's taste.

'And what – cut his *head* off?'

'It sounds unlikely, I agree.' He nodded. 'But word went out to all stations to ask around and would you believe it, a dealer in old weapons – swords and so on – with a shop off the Portobello Road reported he had sold a couple to a Japanese gentleman only a few days ago.'

'Swords, you mean?'

'That's right, the Japanese type. You may have seen some of those old samurai movies.' He waited for Addy's nod of assent. 'That kind. There was no sword found by Kimura's body, but if he walked there from the Globe he could have dropped it in the river. Anyway, since it was my day off, I thought I'd come down here and talk to the boys working the case, tell them what we'd learned about Kimura from Bela Horvath.'

'Which explains your presence?' But she didn't believe it. There was something else going on here, something she couldn't put her finger on.

He scratched his head.

'What really puzzles me though is how they happened to meet at that theatre of all places. Any ideas?'

'Who?' Addy pointed at herself. 'Me?'

'And how they got in? The gate to the courtyard outside the stage door has a coded lock. Normally you'd need a card to open it. I suggested to the detectives working there that if the dead bloke really is Charon, he might have been taught some tricks by the CIA, like how to open a lock like that. The only problem with that is it suggests he was the one who set up the meeting.'

'With Kimura of all people? I see what you mean . . .'

'Doesn't sound very likely, does it?'

He paused as though he actually wanted to hear her opinion, but Addy wasn't fooled. He was playing with her, just waiting to spring the trap he had set.

'Then with who?' She dared him to come out and say it: that it was her. But his reply came as a surprise.

'Oh, that's anyone's guess.' He waved the question aside. 'The world he lived in, those people, some other old enemy of his – could be almost anyone. We'll keep working the case. Maybe we'll come up with a name.'

Smothering a yawn, he stretched. It seemed he wanted to toy with her a little longer.

'So how was Christmas?' he asked.

'Christmas was fine.'

Actually Christmas had been cancelled. There'd been no turkey, no crackers, no paper hats. Addy had spent most of the day in bed catching up on sleep, and when she wasn't doing that, just pottering around the house, thinking about Rose, thinking about other things. She'd done a lot of thinking.

'How's Molly holding up?'

'Why do you ask?' She eyed him with suspicion.

'No reason.'

'Molly's out of the picture.' She might as well tell him.

'You know, I wondered about her.' He tugged at an earlobe. 'That first evening at your aunt's house, when she had a go at us. I thought it was an act. I thought she was putting it on.'

He'd spotted that. Addy had to admit he'd been quick there, quicker than she had been.

'I was wondering – has she got anything to do with all this?' He sent her a questioning glance. 'Could she be mixed up in it in some way? What do you think?'

Addy was ready this time. 'My dear man, are you quite insane?' She gave him her version of Molly's fruity voice and saw him chuckle.

'It's a pity that headless bloke's face was all chewed up.' He mused. 'We could have asked her if he was Philip Moreau.'

'Why not show it to her anyway? Give her something to think about.'

'Addy . . . Addy . . .' He shook his head. 'Remind me never to get on your wrong side.'

'Why? Do I scare you?' she challenged him.

'And how!'

But he didn't mean it. He was giving her that look again, trying to read her expression, trying to probe beneath the surface.

'OK, out with it.' She'd had enough. She was sick of being played with. 'If you've got something to say, say it.' And when he didn't reply at once: 'Do you think I've been lying to you?'

He looked startled. He'd even managed to blink.

'No, I think what you told us was the truth.' But then, as though he'd had second thoughts, he cocked his head on one side to peer at her. 'But since you brought it up, I just wonder if you told us everything.'

Was he serious? For a second she thought so . . . thought, oh shit! Then she saw him grin.

The sonofabitch was teasing her.

'What can I say?' She spread her hands. 'If you're going to arrest me, do it.' She offered him her wrists. 'Bring out the cuffs. It's a fair cop, guv. Isn't that what they say?'

He started laughing.

'It's a fair cop . . .' He shook with laughter. 'I'm not going to arrest you, Addy.'

'Then why did you get me here? Come on, let's have it – the truth.'

He took his time replying, catching her eye and then holding it. Finally he shrugged.

'I thought we might do something together.'

Her double-take could have won the mime-of-the-year award if it hadn't been totally genuine.

'You mean that's what all this is about?' She couldn't believe it. 'You're just hitting on me?'

He weighed the question, grinning.

'I was thinking more along the lines of a pizza.'

Like hell he was. Addy had seen a look in his eye she thought she recognized. He had something entirely different in mind – and about time too! A shiver of anticipation went through her, more like a tingle really.

'A pizza, huh?'

OK, let him have his little joke. But first things first.

'Wait here,' she said. 'Don't go anywhere. There's something I have to do. I won't be long.'

She got up to leave, then stopped and looked back.

'Aren't you going to ask where I'm going?'

He shook his head.

'I wouldn't want to spoil the picture I have of you.'

'What picture?' She scowled. 'What are you talking about? How do you see me?'

'As a woman of mystery, of course.' He spread his hands. 'What else?'

Addy couldn't hide her smile as she went off. And to think only a few days ago she'd been a girl: a brave girl, mind, but still just a girl.

Now she was a woman of mystery.

It felt like a step up.

Leaning on the railing, Addy looked down at the sunlit river. It was running as strongly as before. The tide must still be out. She had walked some distance downstream, out of Dave Malek's sight, though that wasn't the reason. She simply wanted to be on her own and to think, and when she'd finally stopped it was at a spot where there was a bench where people could sit and look out over the river (in warmer weather, anyway). Just now, in the crisp, biting air, there were no takers and Addy had positioned herself between the bench and the wall flanking the river.

She put her hand in her jacket pocket and took out the memory stick. It was the real one, the stick she had found inside Grumble and *not* brought along to her rendezvous with Uncle Matt. If things had gone south at the Globe, the one thing the bastard wasn't going to get his hands on was the money. She had made sure of that. It was the other stick she had taken with her – a twin of the real one – which she had bought in Harrods.

What to do with the proper one now, though? That was the question she had to decide. Give it back to the Russians? No way. They wouldn't thank her for it, those crooks. They might even decide she knew too much and she'd wind up as another fucking side effect.

According to Uncle Matt, Rose had gone along with the idea of stealing the money; it was the killing she couldn't stomach. But he could as easily have been lying and would have done so without compunction. Addy preferred to think he'd told Rose the stick held something of value other than money, something important to their country perhaps. She must have known that he'd worked for the CIA and maybe thought he still did. Maybe she'd only discovered the truth about him later – after the plane crash he was supposed to have died in – and had played the stick on her MacBook and found out what was really on it. It was more comforting to think of her that way, but it was also wishful thinking, and the truth was, when it came to money, you couldn't be sure how people would behave. Addy knew it wasn't beyond the bounds of possibility that when Rose planned to join her in New York – she'd booked her flight after all – she was going to tell her they were rich. All they had to do was lie low for a while and wait for the right moment to cash in. Or maybe she had realized that the Russians would always be on her trail once they had figured things out and just wanted to say goodbye to Addy before she tried disappearing herself.

But what to do with the stick?

Maybe she should just keep it, Addy thought, put it somewhere safe and give herself time to decide what to do with it. The idea was enticing, but that was the problem: it was too seductive. It was a way of hanging on to the stick for now while telling herself she would just put it away and make sure it didn't fall into the wrong hands. But she knew she was kidding. It wouldn't work that way. The longer she had it in her possession, the more it would eat away at her – the thought of the money. It was like that ring in the book that she and Rose had read together when she was a child, the Tolkien epic. It would wind up devouring her.

So in the end it came down to what you really wanted in life, and if it was money then the solution to her dilemma was clear enough. She should just keep it, put it away for a year or two and then take her time figuring out the best way

to extract the loot from it. Or sell it to someone else maybe
– that was an idea – some big-time billionaire who would
know how to deal with the problem in such a way that the
Russians wouldn't be tipped off, while paying her a nice fat
finder's fee.

And then she could join them, the ones who lived in that
other world far above the struggling mass of humanity, who
were going to get fried anyway if global warming turned out
to be true, or maybe drowned when the oceans rose. The
ones who stayed safe in their palatial homes (their four or
five palatial homes), untouched by the pain and misery that
seemed the lot of a good percentage of the planet's population. The ones who wouldn't know a day's hunger or a
sleepless night spent figuring out how to pay the rent, who
would just sail on regardless.

Yes, she could be one of them – and why not? It was a
tempting thought.

Addy thrust her hand out over the fast-flowing river – *quick,
before you change your mind* – and dropped the stick into the
muddy water just a few feet below. It vanished in a moment.

'Oh, Rose . . .'

It was all she could think of to say.

She was in no hurry walking back. Though free of the
burden she had just shed, there was still a lot she had to
think about, and they were not questions that could be settled
in a moment. More had happened to her in the past few days
than in the rest of her life put together, and it was hard to
believe she was still the same person who had trudged through
the snow only a week ago toting her bags and searching for
Rose's address. Yet she was the same girl, just a thousand
years older.

She had learned things about Rose she never would
have thought possible, and if she had put her on a pedestal
before, she had only herself to blame. The person she had
loved above all else was the same woman who had fallen for
a man devoid of any moral sense and, for better or worse,
Rose had cast her lot in with him almost to the bitter end. If
there was anything to learn from it, it was that love made its

own rules, and the same was true of Hideki Kimura who had risked all for love and, when love was gone, had let himself bleed to death rather than let his life go on. And if it came to that, she could apply the same lesson to herself because in spite of all she knew about her now, she loved Rose as much as ever and always would.

Yes, and there were other darker things she had learned and they were about herself. She had watched a man die in savage circumstances and no matter how great her shock at the time, so far from experiencing any regret at the part she had played in Uncle Matt's death, she felt only a fierce satisfaction. It was no more than the bastard had deserved. But what that said about her was something she hadn't yet come to terms with and would have to one day.

What Addy felt as she made her slow way back up the river was that somewhere inside her was a great lump of experience which, like a rock brought back from the moon or some asteroid, she would have to examine grain by grain until all its secrets were revealed. She would have to carry them through her life – her dark secrets – along with a sense of loss and bereavement that would always be a part of her now: a part that might also serve to turn her into the kind of actor she hoped to be one day. Though nothing was certain, she could see herself one day in a darkened theatre holding an audience rapt. Yes, in the palm of her hand, and they would be following every word that came from her mouth, every gesture she made, all held captive in the moment, all wondering where this knowledge she seemed to possess, this understanding of the human heart and of the pain that love could bring in its wake had its source. From what depths had it been drawn; where had she learned it?

And they would never know.

But all that lay way in the future, years ahead, and meantime there was life to be lived.

The Anchor was just ahead of her now and she saw he was still there, sitting where she left him, and she paused for a moment to watch as he scanned his phone, pushing his forelock back in an unconscious gesture.

Cute. Definitely cute.

As she stepped on to the terrace and came over to the table, he looked up with a smile.

Addy cocked an eye at him.

'So how about this pizza?'